Ab(

Margaret Moore was born in the East End ⌐   ⌐
during the war years. Leaving school at the age of 15 with
no qualifications she took further education to achieve the
skills of a secretary during this career spanning 37 years,
she worked as a legal secretary in London, Essex and
Suffolk, retiring in 2006. She began her writing career
with a children's book. She lives in Suffolk with husband
Norman. They have two sons, two grandsons and two
great grandchildren.

For my brother, John Low, and my brother-in-law,
John Moore.
Both would have been familiar with the characters in
this book.

Margaret Moore

A STREET OF SECRETS

AUSTIN MACAULEY
PUBLISHERS LTD.

A CIP catalogue record for this title is available from the British Library.

ISBN 9781787102002 (Paperback)
ISBN 9781787102019 (E-Book)
www.austinmacauley.com

First Published (2017)
Austin Macauley Publishers Ltd.
25 Canada Square
Canary Wharf
London
E14 5LQ

Chapter 1

Stan was sitting in his small dark kitchen, mulling over papers he'd received from the bank. The accounts laid out before him brought a smile to his face. He had moved into this property on Angel Street ten years ago after finally leaving the home he had spent most of his life in. So far he had managed to remain out of the rumour machine which took no prisoners. There were always people around in these streets like Liz, who meant well but who gnawed away at any suggestion of scandal or a good story to be told but he hadn't given any hint to his neighbours that his past, which he had taken great care to conceal, would supply them with endless questions should his circumstances change.

This unassuming and small man lived alone, except for his cat, and had found a job in one of the local factories where he mixed in well with the other workers, although some were curious about him because it was obvious he was well educated; but they accepted everyone at face value. If he was prepared to graft like the rest of them, that was good enough. No questions would be asked.

He was due on the afternoon shift and so he gathered up the papers in front of him and carefully placed them in the large tin box at his feet, which held documents and papers for safe keeping. Once the key had been turned in the lock he knew his secrets were safe from any prying eyes. The only reason its contents would be spilled out would be the event of his death.

Bending down and grasping the box, he lifted it up and made his way up the stairs to place it in the bottom of the wardrobe. There was some personal satisfaction in knowing that his affairs were in order.

The box contained not only account papers but beautiful handmade cards from his past. Also, the old photographs always brought a smile to his face no matter how often he looked at them.

Closing the door of the wardrobe, he made his way down the dark stairs and into the kitchen to get ready for work. He checked the tyres on his old bike and they were well pumped up. It would be a smooth ride to the factory.

Further along the street, the day was being played out in its usual routine. There were conversations and stories being endlessly mulled over. Most people in this street were like open books.

Ethel and Bill still lived in the downstairs rooms of the house they had shared for the past fifteen years, with Cyril and Annie upstairs, who were decent people. Bill was a man who enjoyed a pint or two down The Bell, was always ready with an opinion about the latest football results and continually moaned that he still hadn't won the Pools, all £75,000 of it, even though he did them every week. Their landlord was a good bloke, although they had never actually clapped eyes on him. Most people paid their rent to the landlord's agent, Fred Talbot. He came round every Friday with his little payment book, marking each tenant's rent in it. He was a good bloke as well, because if anyone was on the drag with their rent any time, he had permission from the landlord to accept whatever they could come up with by way of rent for that week. Everyone felt lucky to have such a reasonable landlord, whoever he was, because there were some terrible tales about when people missed payments. Only last week they had heard that a whole load of tenants over in South London had been evicted because they had fallen behind with their rent. Families with young children were among them and winter was only a few weeks away.

Their street in Leytonstone, the East End of London, had miraculously not been bombed even though they were not that far from the docks, which had been targeted. Only a street away the remains of a terrace of Victorian houses continued to crumble and collapse into a silhouette of heartbreaking memories for them. They had known the people who were killed during that raid.

Ethel glanced at the clock on the shelf above the fireplace. The constant tick of that clock seemed like a heartbeat that refused to stop. The windows of the front room had been blown out during a bombing raid and the chimney stack had suffered a bit of damage, causing a lot of soot to come into the pristine kitchen, but nothing had stopped that clock from ticking away, not even a war. Now that was all over, this little icon of stability was what set each day in motion because there were everyday things to be done at certain times which gave order to even the most mundane chores.

Bill eased himself off the kitchen chair.

"I've gotta go, luv. That new foreman they landed us with keeps one eye on the clock and the other one in the back of 'is 'ead. We're all sure 'e'd spot it if one of us so much as stopped work fer a minute, if only ter fart."

"Don't be so coarse, Bill. There's no need fer that."

Picking up his cup, he gulped the last of the tea and left.

Ethel was still mulling various things over that were on her mind while washing up when there was a knock on the front door. Bill had firmly shut it when he left. Ethel always had it ajar. Everyone knew that one knock was for them and two knocks were for Cyril and Annie. Picking up the tea towel from the draining board, she went along the passage, drying her hands, and could see through the panel of frosted glass that it was Liz, who had the annoying habit of trying to peer through the pattern etched on the panel.

Once the door was open, Liz couldn't wait to be asked in. She hurried passed Ethel and headed straight for the little kitchen, the slippers she had on making no noise, as if she was walking on air.

Ethel was still standing at the door with her back against the wall.

"Don't mind me, Liz. I take it yer've got something yer want ter tell me about."

With that said, she closed the door.

It was only a few paces to reach the kitchen and Liz was already sitting at the table. With her hair tightly stretched around an orderly army of metal clips, her turban barely held them in place. Her floral frock pinafore was wound tightly around her ample body and the sleeves of her jumper were pushed up her muscular arms. She looked ready to burst.

Before Ethel could even suggest putting the kettle on, Liz pulled the kitchen chair closer to the table as though she was about to address a committee meeting.

This, thought Ethel, was going to be worth hearing.

"Right," said Liz. "What I'm going ter tell yer is fer your ears only. I promised I wouldn't talk about it but me and you 'ave an understanding, don't we and so I thought yer'd wanna know."

She leaned on the table.

"It's coupons what Vi 'as got. Not flu."

Drawing in a long breath, Ethel folded her arms across her chest.

"What's coupons? Is she suffering from coupons? I've never 'eard of that one. That is a new one on me."

With a resigned feeling that she could not short cut this news, she pulled a chair out from the table and sat down.

Liz licked her lips as though she was about to savour every word she uttered.

Well, 'er daughter Janet's 'usband 'as, so they say, been getting clothing coupons from boss-eyed Ben, yer know 'im. When 'e speaks ter me I 'ave ter make up me mind which eye ter look at."

She had a little chuckle.

"Anyway, Vi said someone 'ad told the police that Janet's 'usband could get yer extra clothes coupons any time. She is frightened ter death that the police will come round ter 'er place about it because, being family, they will think she is involved as well."

She changed position on her chair.

"Yer see why she is in a state. Janet invented the flu story ter stop people asking questions. She thought nobody wants ter catch flu and so they'd stay away."

Liz took a deep breath and pursed her lips.

Before Liz could say any more, Ethel raised her hand.

"Stop there."

Liz was taken by surprise at this. She had thought she was in for a good session of passing on this snippet of vital information. With her back stiffened, Ethel had decided in her own mind that she didn't want to hear any more. Here she was, sitting in the comfort of the peaceful haven her kitchen had become, only for it to be invaded by what Liz obviously considered essential information which nobody else had been given.

"I don't think it's anything ter do with us whether Janet's 'usband is involved with black market coupons. What I do think and, more ter the point is, 'ow ter get Vi ter calm down before she gives 'erself a heart attack."

Liz looked crestfallen. She had always been the street's main source of exactly what everyone was up to, no matter how trivial it may seem. She couldn't understand why Ethel didn't want to know more.

Raising herself slowly from the chair, pressing her ample hands onto the table, she silently went towards the door. Turning to face Ethel she said, "Well, I don't think it's nice if one of us is in trouble and we're going ter ignore 'er. What's 'appened ter yer?"

Going the few steps it took to reach the front door, she paused and silently pulled on the lock.

"I'll leave yer ter think about it."

The sun streamed in as the door pushed back, revealing the pavement outside. Ethel watched her as she made her way along the street to her own home just a few doors away. She sighed and realized it was nearly two o'clock. She had to get to the butcher's.

Grabbing her bag she quickly picked up the key and, closing the front door, turned it in the lock, something she didn't usually do in this street because there was never any need. No one was going to knock on her door this afternoon. She was not expecting any visitors.

As she walked along the familiar street she was thinking about poor Vi and the state she was probably in. She was a nervous person anyway.

She reached the end of the street and could see the butcher's from the corner. Luckily, there wasn't the familiar queue trailing along the pavement.

She stepped forward off the pavement without thinking. The bike wheel rammed into her leg as she heard the shrill ringing of its bell. As she toppled over, her elbow hit the tarmac with a thud as her body crumpled onto the road. She automatically brought her hand up to shield her face which, seconds later, came to rest just beyond the edge of the pavement. She looked up.

Sprawled on the road, she saw her neighbour, Stan, who didn't appear to be moving. He was lying on his back with one of his legs bent and blood was seeping through his trousers. His head was tilted to one side and Ethel could see a trickle of blood coming from his ear. He wasn't a big man and the way he was lying, he seemed almost like a sleeping child.

She sat up. Immediately a small group of people appeared. Most of them she knew and was thankful for the attention she was getting. A chair was brought out from somewhere and, with a little help from Joan from the greengrocer's over the way, she managed very carefully to heave herself onto it, thankful she hadn't remained on the ground as, even in this situation, she felt embarrassed about it all. Madge from two doors along arrived with a cup of water and some smelling salts, although they weren't needed.

Jim the butcher had rushed over to where Stan was lying. He still hadn't moved. His bike was a twisted wreck which had ended up some yards away.

The whole street seemed to have come alive. As far as you could see, front doors were open and sash windows were being pushed up, with faces appearing to see what was going on. As there was always a kettle on somewhere in this street; it was only a few minutes before a cup of tea arrived, brought out by 'Churchy', a neighbour who was a regular

13

churchgoer by the name of Edith, although nobody used her name. Bill always called her the bible thumper.

With a crowd gathering around the unconscious Stan, Ethel was pleased attention was drifting his way. She raised her hand to accept the cup of tea when suddenly an agonizing pain shot up to her shoulder. With a wince and a moan, she dropped her hand onto her lap.

"What is it, dear?" Churchy could see she was in pain and quickly put the cup down beside the chair. "I think yer need ter go ter 'ospital about that."

At that moment, the shrill sound of an ambulance bell was getting closer. The landlord at The Bell had seen the accident and called the ambulance service. He was the only one with a phone in the street.

The crowd stood back from where Stan was lying, still in the same position.

"Oh, my Gord, what's going on 'ere?"

The familiar voice of Liz could be heard above all the other noise. She was always a bit of a fog horn. She had been in her garden putting the washing on the line when she heard the clatter of the ambulance bell.

"Christ almighty, yer look terrible."

Bending down with her face only inches away from Ethel, she saw the grimace of pain still etched on her face.

At that point the ambulance came around the corner and stopped outside The Bell where the customers, some still holding their lunchtime beer, had come out to join the crowd which was swelling, making it difficult to negotiate around.

The ambulance men sprang into action and brought out a stretcher and a large canvas bag. Both were placed on the ground. They had not moved Stan at all. They decided it was a matter of getting him to hospital as an emergency. The first thing to do was to somehow place him onto the stretcher without re-aligning his leg. Speaking quietly and calmly to each other, they took some scissors from the canvas bag and carefully cut his trouser leg away from him to assess the extent of the damage. They both knew what they would find. It was a compound fracture. The crowd visibly drew breath as they witnessed part of Stan's leg bone protruding through the skin. In awed silence, the crowd was watching every move being made. The ambulance men quickly got to work. They carried on in silence. Very carefully, they slowly edged him onto the stretcher which had been placed directly behind him and, on the count of three, gently lifted him up and into the ambulance. With a flurry of activity clearing the road, the ambulance sped off with Stan, its bell ringing out the urgency of the journey.

The crowd began to thin out, the men from The Bell strolling back into the pub, chatting about the events of the day. They didn't know much about Stan. He had been in for a drink a few times and they knew he appreciated a good brandy. He was always on his own. He mixed well with everyone and some of the men from the factory used the pub and so there were always some familiar faces in there. Their general opinion of him was that perhaps he was from a moneyed background but that, maybe, things had gone wrong and the money wasn't there now. They wondered if he had a wife. He had never mentioned one. Come to think of it, he never talked about family.

Ethel was still sitting on the chair at the corner of the street, Churchy had stayed with her.

After finishing off her conversation with the neighbours, Liz came bustling over to Ethel.

"What do yer want ter do? Shall I come 'ome with yer until Bill comes 'ome?"

Before Ethel could say anything, a small battered van drew up and Bill leapt out of it. Someone had got word to him at the building site that Ethel had been in an accident. They had all heard the clatter of the ambulance bell and were wondering where it was headed.

Moving faster than he had for a long time, Bill reached Ethel who was now slumping on the straight-backed kitchen chair. She had tried to find a more relaxed way to sit on it but when she moved a pain shot up her arm. She could still move her fingers but her shoulder felt as though it had seized up.

"What 'ave yer done, old luv?"

His concerned expression was turning into panic.

"Oh, Bill. I don't know what I was doing. I didn't see Stan and 'is bike as 'e came along. 'E never goes fast on that thing anyway, but we collided. I only 'ope 'e is not badly injured because of me."

Pointing to the van, Liz said, "If I were yer, I'd put 'er in that and get 'er ter the 'ospital. It won't take yer long. I'll come with yer if yer like."

Churchy had the beginnings of a smile on her face, knowing Liz's motive for that suggestion was so that she wouldn't miss out on any information that could be overheard at the hospital.

As usual, when he was thinking things over, Bill pouted.

"Well, as the foreman let me take the van ter find out what was going on, I suppose 'e won't mind if I take Ethel ter the 'ospital in it."

Bill had good reason for not wanting to leave Ethel with Churchy and Liz. Churchy would be preaching the goodness of the Lord. If he hadn't been looking down on her, it could have been much worse. She would probably be asking Ethel and Liz to join her in a prayer of thanks.

Liz on the other hand would be relating other accidents she had witnessed in the last few years. She had a photographic memory of all the worst things she had seen. Her best and most related was when Ron from up the street fell off his ladder and smashed his brains out on the pavement. Head first he had landed. She made that tale more gruesome every time she told it.

Bill still had a lot of brick dust in his hair and his knarled hands were bearing the signs that he had been shovelling cement when he was told about the accident.

He ran his fingers through his still thick hair and patted his clothes down.

Although he was a manual labourer, he paid a lot of attention to what the politicians were talking about and how they were going to get the country back on its feet. The newspapers were eagerly and thoroughly read by him and his mates. The fact that a new National Health Service was now at everyone's disposal was, in his view, a good move to start with. They were concentrating initially on the health of children and, although he and Ethel had not been blessed with any, he always had a soft spot for the kids that played out in their street. He knew which ones were from loving families and which were deprived and from abusive ones. Perhaps they would benefit from this brave new world.

Ethel looked along the street. This had been their street for so long now that almost anything that happened here involved everyone. The accident would be talked about in The Bell, the butcher's, the corner shop and the market that bustled and thrived in all its efforts to give a lot of the people here the main place to get news of anything that might be worth passing on. Her thoughts went, once again, to Stan. He lived on his own with only his cat for company. In her present state of mind she felt mounting panic as she grew more and more aware that everyone would blame her for the accident and if Stan didn't recover quickly, who would look after his cat? It was a stupid thing to panic about but all the same, she felt herself getting more and more worked up.

Stan's buckled bike was still lying at the side of the road. It never had been much but it had got him from home and work every day. It was Stan the kids used to go to when they found any bits of metal or punctured bike tyres because he always found someone who needed something repaired, or a tyre could be used again once Stan had worked his magic on it.Bill called over to one of the young boys who was circling Stan's bike and gave him a shilling to go round to the bombed house he had been working on, to let the foreman know what had happened and that he would get the van back to him as soon as he could. The boy thought it was Christmas come early!

A few doors along, Vi had come to her front door. She was peering around it, having only opened it enough to see out. When she had heard the clatter of the ambulance bell getting nearer and nearer, she started to panic thinking it might be the police coming for her. She never could distinguish the difference between an ambulance bell and a police car one. She really had got herself worked up about those coupons. She quietly closed the door and collapsed into the armchair in the kitchen.

Out in the street, Bill helped Ethel into the front seat of the van.

With the drama now over, the little street soon turned into its usual free flowing tributary of people seeking to struggle with and overcome all the everyday incidents, accidents and dramas that came their way.

Angel Street was known in this area as Pilgrims' Progress because at one end of it The Bell pub was a landmark, The Angel pub was at the other end and St John's Church was in the middle. All your needs were served if you were a traveller.

Liz made her way back home. She needed a cup of tea because she had a lot to think about. Her mind was working overtime. Once in her little kitchen she filled the kettle and put it on the stove. Taking a cup down from the hook on the shelf she noticed her ration book and, behind it, her clothing coupons book. How on earth had Boss-eyed Ben been able to get hold of hooky clothing coupons? She took the book from the shelf and read the printed penalty for using them illegally. It was a fine of £100 or prison for three months. Boss-eyed Ben must have somehow got hold of some poor bugger's clothing book who had died and instead of passing it on to the authorities, he had kept it and however many others he could get his hands on.

The kettle started rattling on the stove as the water began to boil. The steam coming from it was rising into a cloud of vapour which made the small kitchen even more damp than usual. If her Jack had still been alive, he would have built her a wash house. The kettle continued to puff out its steam, rising up to engulf the laundry which was strewn along the wooden drying rack hanging from the ceiling.

Once the tea was made, she sat at the table in the middle of the room to consider her thoughts.

If Janet's husband had been given the black market coupons from Boss-eyed Ben, how much had he paid for them? Also, had Vi bought stuff with them? Janet must have known that her mum had used them. All this was turning into a right royal nightmare.

She was staring into the gloom of the kitchen light when a knock on her front door made her jump. It was Churchy.

"I thought I'd pop round because I didn't know if you'd 'eard anything more about Stan. Once I've got me 'air looking a bit more respectable, I'm going ter see Reverend Luke ter ask 'im ter say a special prayer fer Ethel and Stan. Do we really know anything about Stan? Nice enough bloke but kept 'imself to 'imself. Once 'e's 'ome from the 'ospital, we might be able ter find out a bit more."

Automatically sitting down at the table, she eyed the cup of tea.

"I could do with one of them after today's antics."

Liz went over to the shelf where she kept her cups and saucers. She liked to offer tea with a cup and saucer. It seemed to make the gesture more civilized in this area of London, where usually a chipped mug would do.

She poured the tea.

"There's also the cat," said Churchy.

Liz looked at her. She had forgotten about the cat.

"Don't ask me ter look after it because I can't abide 'em. I 'ad one once as a mouser and it brought in rats as well as mice and so I 'ad ter get rid of it."

Slurping her tea, Churchy said, "I can't 'ave it because I'm what old Dr Harris called allergic, whatever that means. I 'ad one years ago and every morning when I woke up I found meself covered in blotches. 'e said I wasn't ter 'ave anything ter do with cats or dogs."

Trying to be helpful, Liz said, "When yer speak ter Reverend Luke later today, perhaps 'e can arrange fer someone ter feed it until Stan comes 'ome."

Looking at Churchy, Liz thought she always looked half starved. She was, as they say, as thin as a whippet. The clothes she wore looked as though they had been taken from a charity bag. Her face always had a grey pallor about it which wasn't helped by the way she had her hair scraped back in a bun, revealing a complexion like waxwork. She was a good soul though. The church always looked a treat after she had arranged flowers on the altar and had polished the brass.

Reverend Luke had been transferred to them from a country parish somewhere near Rotherham, Yorkshire. He hadn't actually put a name to it but he seemed a nice enough bloke and had made quite a few friends since he'd arrived and so Churchy would work on him to find out more as time went on. He had said they were a Christian lot in his old parish and he hoped he could persuade a few more here to come to church. All the same, Churchy wondered why he would want to leave a place he liked so much. She had got this information out of him soon after he had arrived. Rose, his housekeeper, who had come with him, didn't give up much. She almost protected him. She was the one that kept him up to date with the local news. She would have told him about Stan's accident and Ethel's injury. All the same, there was something that didn't feel right with her. She never spoke much but, when she did, she didn't have a Yorkshire accent. It gave Churchy a reason to wonder why that was.

Having finished their tea, Liz got up to put the cups and saucers in the sink. Churchy hadn't quite finished chatting yet.

"Do yer know, when I think about it, I've never 'eard anything at all about Stan. Not a bad word said about 'im. On the other 'and, I've never 'eard 'im speak about family or anything else. With 'im in the 'ospital, should we find out if 'e's got any relatives or something? They'd wanna know 'ed been in an accident."

Liz sat down again.

"I shouldn't bother yerself about that. The 'ospital will be able ter get some details about 'im from old Dr Harris. That 'ouse 'e lives in could do with a bit of repairing. The front door paint is peeling something rotten and the step is beginning ter break up. I've never been in there meself so I don't know what the inside is like but I bet a bloke living on 'is own don't keep it very nice."

With that said, she deliberately looked at the clock on the wall and tutted.

"Is that the time? I've got ter go out."

Taking the hint, Churchy stood up.

"I'd better get going meself if I'm ter get me 'air out of these pins in time ter catch Reverend Luke."

The two women left the house, Liz going down to the market and Churchy going into her house along the street. There was a lot to do if she was to catch the reverend before he left his house next door to St John's.

The church house was a big red brick one. It had stood next to St John's for donkey's years. The garden of it backed onto the old cemetery which was now so full it couldn't be used any more. Some of the old upright pitted gravestones which had been put there some hundred or so years before were now toppled over and partly broken. The families who had them put there all that time ago would hate to think that in the passing of time, today's people would not want to care for them. They had their own survival to think about. Some of the local kids played amongst the grave stones, which were almost covered up by the weeds and grass around them. One of the games was who would go in there when it started to get dark. Chicken run, it was called.

Old Reverend Michael had lived in the house and had been the local vicar for about twenty-five years. He'd been married to Mary for more years than they could remember. It was on one of his visits to see the progress being made in the rebuilding of a bomb damaged local factory that he met his maker, when some loose brickwork came toppling down and killed him instantly. As Bill had said at the time, 'That was a call from on high'. Mary, his wife, was so distraught that she collapsed and died two days later. That prompted another one of Bill's comments which Ethel thought inappropriate, 'E's with the devil 'e knows'.

Some church elders came down and made all the funeral arrangements. They would both be buried together at the last spot available in the old churchyard. It was felt they should remain at the place they knew best.

The women of Angel Street who usually dealt with the task of washing and laying out of bodies were more than sad on this occasion, because everyone knew the reverend and his wife so well. A collection was taken up and on the day of the funeral the whole street turned out to pay their respects. There was no family to invite and so Ethel, Liz and Churchy put on a little spread of sandwiches and cakes for the small congregation.

Churchy liked to look her best when she went to church and, as she was going to pop into the church house first, she made a special effort by putting a clean frock on after she had done her hair. Reverend Luke was easy to talk to. She thought he was about forty. She had tried to find out a bit more about him but no information had been forthcoming. The only thing she had found out was that his parish in the country had taken in some of London's pregnant and unmarried women and anyone else who the church was willing to help. They apparently had an arrangement with a mother and child home near where his church was.

Putting some biscuits she had made into a tin, she thought that would do as a gift for him as she knew he liked a biscuit with his tea.

As she walked up the red and black tiled pathway to his front door, she couldn't help remembering all the times she had visited this house, for good and bad reasons. She noticed the windows needed a clean and the brass knocker ought to be polished. This new housekeeper, she thought, wasn't up to scratch. As she reached up to the knocker, the door suddenly opened. She was quite taken aback. Standing in the dark doorway was Rose, the housekeeper. Tall and thin, she certainly wasn't a welcoming sight. Before Churchy could utter a word, Rose stepped forward.

"Yes, what do you want?"

Churchy smiled. "I've come ter speak ter Reverend Luke about a couple of things. Is 'e in?"

"No. You've missed him."

Her rapid-fire response seemed almost like a warning not to expect to see him.

Still clutching the tin of biscuits, Churchy said, "If yer don't mind, I'll come in and wait, then."

Raising her hand, Rose said, "He's had a call from the hospital and had to rush off."

"Oh! Does that mean 'e's 'ad some news about Stan? 'E was taken in this afternoon."

Looking a bit annoyed, Rose said, "I don't know what it was about. I'm not his keeper."

Churchy smiled. No, she thought, you're only his housekeeper and by all the looks of the house, not a very good one.

Stepping back and looking at the windows, she said, "Those curtains could do with a bit of a wash. I got them from Mare Street market over Hackney, but that was a while back, when Reverend Michael was 'ere."

Rose frowned. "Is that still there?"

As soon as she said it she knew she had made a big mistake.

Churchy looked surprised.

"Yer know Mare Street market, do yer?"

Rose stepped back as though to close the door but Churchy moved closer.

"Where did yer say yer come from?"

With a frown and biting her bottom lip, Rose said, "I came with Reverend Luke and you know that. I've known him for a while and, apart from that, what is it to you where I'm from? He's not here and you can find him in the church later."

With that, she pushed the heavy door shut.

Churchy smiled. I was right, she thought. There's more to 'er than she's letting on. She felt almost pleased with herself after that meeting because she could ask around next time she was over Hackney.

As she left, she thought, I will pop into the church to say a prayer for Stan and Ethel. I can always see the Reverend Luke another time.

As she went a bit further along the street, the battered van could be seen parked outside Ethel's house. She thought, I'd better give 'er a knock ter see 'ow she got on and she might 'ave news of Stan.

The front door was firmly shut, which was a bit unusual if she was in. Everybody kept their front door ajar. Raising her hand to the black iron knocker she somehow had a feeling all was not well. She knocked once and waited.

She saw the shadowy figure of Bill coming along the passage. The door opened.

Bill was still in his work clothes. He stepped outside onto the pavement and pulled the door closer behind him.

"Ethel's not too good at the moment. She just wants ter sit quietly."

"Oh, my Gord. What's 'appened? She'll be all right, won't she?"

Churchy was becoming alarmed at the serious expression on Bill's face. She put her hand up to her mouth.

Bill knew everyone would be watching behind curtained windows. It was unusual for any man to be chatting to Churchy on the doorstep. They would all be wondering what was going on. One thing was for sure, though; if Churchy knew anything, the whole street would too.

"They've let 'er come 'ome then, so it can't be too serious. I 'ave ter say that she was a funny colour when yer took 'er ter the 'ospital."

Taking in a long breath, Bill said, "She's all right except fer a bruised elbow. Nothing broken. They've strapped 'er arm up again because the X-ray didn't show any break. She's just a bit shook up."

With that, he turned towards the door and pushed it open.

"I've got ter go in because the foreman needs me ter get the van back. I'll get me keys and go."

Not satisfied with that, Churchy was feeling very put out. She hadn't got much information from the housekeeper at the church house and now she was being short changed by Bill about Ethel's situation. There was definitely more going on that she needed to find out about. Reluctantly, she shuffled along to her own house, the tin of biscuits still under her arm.

Once indoors, her thoughts returned to Stan's cat. She had better catch up with Reverend Luke this evening to see if he could arrange for someone to feed it until Stan got back. A broken leg took a while to heal and so he was going to need some help when he came home. He was a nice enough bloke. She could, perhaps, do his shopping for him. She'd need his front door key.

With her thoughts escalating, there seemed to be so many questions to be answered. So far as she could recall, nobody had ever been in Stan's house or, for that matter, had much of a conversation with him. He'd had that house ever since she'd known him and had always lived in it on his own. She supposed as long as he paid the rent regularly, the landlord left him alone.

Putting the tin of biscuits in the centre of the table so that she wouldn't forget them later, she decided to put the kettle on and make herself a bit of tea.

The kitchen was still filled with the smell of the recently baked biscuits. She prided herself on the fact that whenever anybody had a problem, they usually ended up in her kitchen with the necessary cup of tea and either biscuits or cake.

It was only September, but she had a fire in the grate that had settled down to a low glow which could be woken up with a newspaper held over the open fireplace to draw it back into life. It was a comforting force in the dim light of the room.

Chapter 2

Churchy's mind would not stop racing. There were so many things whirling around in her thoughts. She couldn't help wondering how Rose, the housekeeper, seemed to know about Mare Street market if she said she was new to the area. The look that Rose had given her when she opened the door would have stopped a lot of people in their tracks. The woman looked as though she was in her twenties and yet she seemed very confident and almost too blowsy for a housekeeper, especially one for a vicar. The spiralling smoke from the cigarette held between her well manicured fingers had created a scene which would not have been out of place in one of those films they showed at the pictures, where a starlet was seeking only one kind of attention. There was something she needed to get to the bottom of there. Oh! well, there would be plenty of time to have a word with the Reverend later but, in the meantime, the kitchen seemed so silent. Perhaps if she listened to a bit of news and whatever programme was on the wireless while she ate her tea, it would take her mind off things. Reaching over to the polished wooden box which housed the wireless, she turned the knob which tuned it into whatever station she wanted. Earlier in the day she had been listening to some music on it but midday she had been listening to the calming voice of Alvar Lidell as he read the news. The Olympic Games were over and done and so the news now had reports of the country still picking itself up after the war and concentration on what the politicians hoped to achieve to make life better for everyone.

It didn't work. Her tea was eaten with pauses for thought.

Back at the church house, Rose was thinking, that's all I need, some busybody nosing around. The life she had left at the place outside London had been good. No one knew her there and no one had judged her. The baby she had given birth to had, thankfully, been taken for adoption and that suited her fine. She didn't want a baby hanging around.

Reverend Luke was a free thinking vicar and had understood the predicament girls like Rose found themselves in. He was a healthy young man who appreciated having a fine-looking woman like her around. She was looking for a way out of the alien countryside and back into the familiarity of London. This job was her passport to rekindle old friendships and she didn't want anything to upset that.

Churchy took the pins out of her hair and gave it a bit of a comb. She put a dab of face powder on, took her jacket off the peg on the door and made her way along the street to St John's, biscuit tin under her arm.

As she walked the short distance to the church she mulled over how she was going to approach Reverend Luke with her now increasing enquiries.

Passing Liz's front door she noticed it was slightly ajar. She was obviously back from shopping. Deciding not to stop, she continued along the street to the church. With the afternoon light slowly fading into dusk, she carefully picked her way through the groups of children running around trying to catch each other. The chalk markings on the pavement for hop scotch, only a few days old, were still quite fresh. She hadn't seen any more of Vi. She didn't even come out when Ethel and Stan had the accident. That was another strange thing. With her thoughts becoming more and more tangled, she was glad when she reached the church.

The great carved wooden doors were open. As she went in, the familiar smell of the place seemed to calm her down. The scent from the flowers mixed with the strong smell of polish was always present.

It was not a particularly inspiring building, even though the great windows above the altar were ablaze with stained glass scenes. The aisle leading to the altar with its crisscross of cream and brown coloured tiles always resounded to the sound of anyone walking on them. It was an indication to Reverend Luke that someone was coming towards the altar, if he was in prayer with his back to the doors.

It was a pleasant September evening.

Once inside, the mellowing light in the church revealed the flickering candles on the altar sending faint images of light across the tapestry which hung near the choir stalls. The bowed figure of Reverend Luke could be seen in silent prayer. Churchy looked around. There were no other people there. All the pews were empty.

The vastness of the place made her feel lost. The presence of old Reverend Michael had seemed to fill the place in the old days. She stood quietly for a few seconds, remembering the day they had discovered a newborn baby near the altar. The mother of that child was never found. The baby would be about ten years old now. A good home had been found for her. The name Mary was suggested.

Marriages had been founded, christenings conducted and burials finalized. What a special place this was. The thought that someone like Rose could have any connection with it was dreadful.

The silence made her feel uneasy, almost as though her presence would signal bad news.

She walked down the aisle, her footsteps making a muffled sound. Reverend Luke's head turned slightly to acknowledge her presence. He stood up and turned to face Churchy, a smile on his face. He was used to seeing her in the church. He silently beckoned her to come forward. Churchy hesitated.

"I 'ope I'm not disturbing yer, but I 'ad ter come and see yer."

Reverend Luke remained silent.

"Would yer mind if I sit down a minute? Me legs are playing me up."

With that, she sat herself down on the nearest pew, still clutching the tin of biscuits.

Reverend Luke couldn't help smiling because she looked so small in this lofty building.

Sitting down beside her, he thought, I wonder what I'm going to hear this time. He was always the first person she came to when there was something worth reporting in this parish. Secretly, he was quite grateful.

"Oh, I nearly fergot, these are fer yer. It's biscuits I made."

She handed the tin over.

Before she could say any more, Rose appeared in the church doorway.

"There's a call for you from the hospital. They said it was urgent." With that, she left.

Standing up, Reverend Luke said, "I've got to go, it sounds important. Perhaps you could come back later if you need to speak to me about something."

"Yes, yer must go. I was only going ter mention Stan's cat and who should be feeding it."

Reverend Luke rushed out of the church to take the call at the church house. Churchy decided that she would see him later.

Still sitting in the pews, she wondered why such a young, handsome, lively bloke would want to be a vicar. He'd be a good catch for anyone. If Rose had been with him for some time at the other place, she couldn't help wondering how he'd managed to stay so pure and holy. She seemed the sort of person who'd corrupt anyone, even a vicar.

Leaving the church, she reached the end of its pathway when a feather floated down in front of her. She paused and looked up. There didn't appear to be any disturbance in the tree above. Oh, she thought that means someone has just died and an angel has come to tell us.

She decided she would not come back this evening. She could see Reverend Luke sometime tomorrow.

Shuffling along the street, she thought of seeing if Ethel felt any better but decided against that.

Someone was calling her. Looking over to the corner she could see Joan from the greengrocer's. She was waving at her.

I wonder what she wants, thought Churchy.

Crossing the street, she could see Joan was keen to talk to her.

"Hello, Joan. What can I do yer for?"

Coming to the kerbside, Joan said, "I thought I'd better let yer know that I've been feeding Stan's cat. I've got two of me own. I found out that I could get into 'is garden round the back and found the cat sleeping in that shed of 'is. The door on the shed needs repairing because yer can't shut it. The cat 'ad been sleeping on some sacks in there. I put a dish of cat food down and left 'im to it. I'll 'ave a look in the morning ter see if the food's gone. While I was there I saw one of the winders in the back kitchen was broken and taped up. 'E really ought ter get the landlord ter fix the shed door and that winder. I thought if Stan 'as ter be in 'ospital fer a few days with 'is leg, I could look after the cat fer 'im."

Churchy hadn't expected that.

"Well, that's really good of yer. I expect 'e will be worrying about the cat."

Churchy had known Joan for years. They had been at school together but when Joan got married she started helping out in the shop with her husband. It was one of those corner shops that never seemed to close. They had a living room at the back where they could sit and listen to the wireless during the evening while the shop was still open. They simply served whoever came in. They worked very hard, opening at seven in the morning and not closing until about ten in the evening.

There were always hessian sacks of potatoes stood up in the doorway. Once inside, a permanent smell of cabbage and turnips filled the air. A wooden rack held newspapers and just beyond that, where a small counter jutted out, a line of jars held loose tobacco which could be weighed out in small quantities depending on what the customer could afford. Eventually they bought the business.

Because of this, she knew everyone in the area. Churchy was wondering if she knew anything about Stan. Perhaps she knew if he had any family they could get in touch with. This was Churchy's chance.

"While we're talking, do yer know if Stan's got any relatives? I thought someone ought ter let 'em know 'e's in 'ospital fer a few days."

Joan frowned.

"Now, there yer've got me. 'E's never mentioned any and I've never seen anyone visiting 'im. It's not that I'm nosey, but yer see all the comings and goings in the street during the day from this shop."

Churchy tutted.

"Well, when 'e does come 'ome, I'll offer ter do 'is bit of shopping fer 'im and maybe I can ask 'im about any relatives."

With that said, they parted company, Joan going into the shop to serve a customer who had come from around the corner and Churchy going home. What a day.

The next morning it was glorious. The sky was cloudless and the sun had already started to show itself. Bill leaned across the bed to reach the window and pulled the curtains open. The bedroom flooded with light.

Ethel was lying on her back with the quilt draped across her. She felt uncomfortable because the strapping on her arm had given her a very disturbed night. Bill looked at her.

"I'll go and put the kettle on, luv. It's only 'arf six so there's plenty of time fer me to 'ave a shave and get meself off ter work."

Ethel sat up. She didn't like being 'out of action' as Bill had put it. She wanted to do him some breakfast before he went.

She started thinking over the way yesterday's accident had happened.

She could hear Bill getting the cups out and filling the kettle. In the silence of the bedroom every noise seemed unusually loud.

She wouldn't need to go out today because there was always something in the cupboard she could use for dinner tonight. The thought of people seeing her with her arm strapped up made her feel even more responsible for the accident. Her mind immediately went to Stan in the hospital.

I bet he's wondering how it all happened, she thought. He wouldn't thank her the next time he saw her. Perhaps she and Bill ought to get him another bike. It wouldn't be a new one but they could probably stretch to a decent second hand one.

She could hear Bill's tread going backwards and forwards across the little kitchen. Finally, he appeared in the doorway with the tea. Handing it to her, he could see she was sitting awkwardly and was obviously tired.

"What yer need is a day's rest and time ter get yer thoughts tergether. Yer not ter blame yerself."

Having said that, he felt that was all he could do and went back into the kitchen.

Outside and along this street of terraced houses, the day was being acted out. Wives were preparing breakfasts and husbands were getting ready to go to work. There were front steps to be whitened and children to be sent to school. The war had been a terrible blight on this community for those that had lost loved ones but the future was looking better now that the government had promised better housing. Some welcomed it but others did not want to be rehoused away from Angel Street. This was the only place they could call home.

Liz was up and about. She was at her window waiting for Bill to go passed on his way to work. Once he was gone, she intended to see if Ethel was any better.

Sure enough, at half seven, Bill went passed her window.

The street was already busy, with the milkman starting his round and a coal truck could be smelt nearby. You could smell the coal streets away. It was a good smell. She didn't need her jacket and so, picking up her keys, she made her way along the street to Ethel's.

The door was firmly shut. Bill always closed it instead of leaving it ajar. She tapped on the frosted glass panel and straight away pressed her face to it to look in.

Ethel came out of the bedroom, having managed to get some clothes on with the help of Bill before he had left.

There was Liz, almost glued to the glass panel. Opening the door, Ethel couldn't hide the fact she didn't want any visitors by heaving a great sigh.

Liz moved forward so that the door opened further.

"I thought I'd pop in ter see 'ow yer are. There's gonna be something yer need from the shop and I could also get yer a bit of breakfast cooked."

She stepped into the passage and pushed the door open a bit more. Ethel, resigned to the fact she couldn't stop Liz coming in, stepped back and nodded towards the kitchen. The kettle was filled and Liz took a couple of cups down and busied herself clearing the table, where Bill had been doing himself a sandwich.

Just as they had both sat down, a loud knock on the front door echoed along the small passage. They both sat motionless for a few seconds. It wasn't eight o'clock yet. Who would be visiting at this time of the day?

Liz stood up. "I'll answer it."

Ethel had a feeling of dread come over her. Had anything happened to Bill?

Opening the front door, Liz was surprised and taken aback by the burly figure of Dave Taylor, their local bobby. Everyone knew him. The local kids were very wary of him because most of them had, at some stage, had a clout around the head from him for one reason or another. He'd been their local bobby for many years.

As surprised as Liz was to see him, he was more than surprised to see her at Ethel's home so early in the day.

"Well, Dave, I suppose yer want ter speak ter Ethel. Bill 'as already left fer work."

"Yes. I need ter speak ter 'er about a few things. I take it she's in?"

Calling down the passage, Liz shouted, "It's Dave Taylor. 'E needs ter speak ter yer about some things."

With that said, she stood back and let Dave pass her.

Ethel felt a fear wash over her like she had never felt before. Had he come about the accident? Surely, it couldn't be about anything else. She had never been involved with the police before. How important could this visit be?

Dave Taylor strode into the little kitchen. She knew him well but now he looked like a complete stranger to her.

He pulled a chair out from the table and sat down. He put his helmet on the table and seemed to settle himself before speaking. Liz followed him in. The only sound was the ticking of the clock. Ethel looked petrified.

"How are yer? It must 'ave been a nasty accident fer yer to be involved in. Yer still look a bit peaky."

Ethel said nothing.

Clearing his throat, he said, "The station 'ave sent me round ter take a statement from yer about the accident with Stan Newton. I 'ave ter tell yer that 'e passed away last night. 'E 'ad a fractured skull."

"What!" Ethel couldn't believe what she was hearing. She gasped and then, putting her hand up to her face, began sobbing and shaking. Liz quickly went around the table to where Ethel was sitting.

P.C. Dave Taylor took a notebook from his top pocket.

"I need yer ter tell me when yer stepped out and collided with Stan how that happened."

He leaned forward with his arms on the table, pen in his hand.

Ethel was still sobbing.

Liz thought, I never knew his name was Stan Newton. I don't think anyone knew his surname. Why would they? He was only known as Stan.

With Ethel sobbing and Liz fussing over her, P.C. Dave Taylor decided it would be better if Ethel came into the station with her husband to make her statement.

Seeing him out, Liz finally made some tea to try to calm Ethel.

Somehow, word soon spread that Stan had died. Churchy was one of the first to hear. Oh, she thought, that was the feather that floated down in front of me at the church. Her first mission during the morning was to let Joan over at the shop know so that she could continue to feed the cat. Her next thought was, someone ought to let the landlord know what had happened. Fred Talbot, the rent collector, would have to be told about Stan's death so that he could pass the information on to the landlord. This would make her the first to tell him, almost a feather in her cap.

She'd heard that Liz was with Ethel and that Bill had been sent for. Her next move was to go round to Fred Talbot's house to let him know what had happened. Everyone knew where he lived and she hoped she could catch him in.

As she made her way through the busy market and passed the market pub, The Railway Arms, she started to wonder who would make the funeral arrangements if Stan didn't have any family.

Knocking on the door, she didn't have to wait long before Fred's wife opened it. It was still early and she could smell something cooking.

"Can I 'elp yer?"

"Is Fred in? I 'ave come ter tell 'im that a bloke in our street 'as passed away and I thought 'e ought ter know. Tell 'im Churchy is at the door."

The woman turned slightly and called down the passage. Fred appeared in the kitchen doorway.

"Ello, luv. What are yer doing 'ere? It's a first fer me ter find a tenant visiting me instead of me chasing a tenant." He smiled.

Still standing on the pavement, Churchy waited for him to reach the front door.

"Yer know Stan in our street? Well, 'e passed away last night and I thought I ought ter let yer know. We've only just found out 'is name was Stan Newton. Did yer know anything about 'im? Did 'e ever mention family?"

Fred frowned.

"No. I just collected 'is rent along with all the others."

Churchy was determined to find out more.

"Where was the landlord that yer paid the money ter then? All those rents 'ad ter go somewhere."

Still standing at the door, Fred seemed reluctant to invite her in. He didn't want to have to answer a lot of questions about the landlord. He wasn't sure who he was anyway.

"Ter tell yer the truth, every week I paid the rents into the bank in the high street. yer know the one, Midland Bank. Where it went from there, I couldn't tell yer. They seem to be dealing with the rents for the landlord. Funny old arrangement if yer ask me. They will 'ave ter to be told about Stan and so I suppose I should go ter see them. They're not going to be getting any more money from 'im now."

Obviously Churchy wasn't going to be invited in and so she left the news with him and went home.

As she reached Angel Street Joan came out of the shop and shouted over to her.

"I've just 'eard about Stan. It's awful, poor man. What did 'e die of?"

Looking along the street as if she was going to give away a secret, Churchy moved closer to Joan and almost whispered that he had died from a fractured skull. "I 'eard that Ethel is in a bit of a state about it."

The two women carried on their conversation about the accident as though they were reporters on a local paper, revealing secrets.

Fred Talbot decided he ought to let the bank know what had happened as soon as possible. Putting on the only suit and decent tie he owned, he looked quite businesslike and felt ready to pass on this important information.

Reaching the bank building, it looked every bit as though it only dealt with people in suits. He couldn't imagine many of its customers were workmen. The grey façade was familiar to everyone but not many of his rent payers would have even been inside.

Approaching the huge double doors, he noticed for the first time that the windows either side of the entrance were patterned with stained glass. The brass handles on the doors were polished like gold and although he delivered the rent money he had collected to the bank every week, this visit had taken on a more sombre recognition because of the news he had come to deliver.

Once inside, the familiar dark wooden panelling seemed, on this visit, to close in on him. He approached the long counter where each of the staff sat behind openings which gave just enough room to pass cash or papers through.

He knew one of the cashiers and went to her position.

"Hello, Fred. What are you doing here today?"

She was always welcoming and Fred liked her. Some of the other cashiers always gave him the impression they were far more than simply bank employees. Far more important that that.

"Hello, Jane. You're right. This time I need ter see the manager about one of the tenants I collect rent from. Is there any chance I could 'ave a word with 'im? It's quite important."

"Just you wait here. I'll see what I can do."

With that, she disappeared into the back of the area, where a line of metal filing cabinets were.

Fred waited, feeling very insignificant. He suddenly realized he didn't even know the bank manager's name.

Moments later, Jane returned to show Fred into the manager's office.

With a welcome smile and a firm handshake from the manager, Fred began to feel more at ease.

The highly polished desk seemed to take up a large part of the room. A black telephone sat at one end and a wooden box, filled neatly with papers, was at the other end. The blotter in front of the manager had evidence of ink on it where it had been used when signing documents. Taking pride of place though was a sloping wooden panel placed centre of all this with the name of the manager emblazoned on it in gold leaf lettering. William Slater, and just below that the word 'Manager'.

The manager gestured to Fred to sit down.

Leaning back into his swivel chair, William Slater centred his attention on Fred.

"What can I do for you, Mr Talbot? I understand you are the landlord's agent for several tenants in Angel Street and also others further afield. A busy job."

Drawing in a long breath, Fred cleared his throat and began.

"I 'ave come ter see yer about one of the tenants, a Mr Stan Newton. 'E lives – no, lived – at 15 Angel Street. 'E died yesterday. It was an accident."

The manager moved forward in his chair.

"I am very sorry to hear that. I do know of him. He had lived at the property for some time."

Rising from his chair, he moved across the room to a metal filing cabinet. Removing a brown folder from it, he placed it on the desk and sat down.

Opening up the folder, he scanned it. He flicked through several of the papers and finally removed a few and placed them on his desk.

"Did you know him very well, Mr Talbot, because I see that you have been collecting rent from him for several years now?"

Fred leaned forward on his chair. He wanted to be as helpful as possible.'E was a man who kept 'imself ter 'imself really. I never got invited in and never 'ad any problem with 'im. 'E worked at one of the local factories, I believe. 'e was never behind with 'is rent."

The manager looked slightly surprised.

"I never knew Mr Newton worked at a local factory. It would seem that our Mr Newton had many secrets. Was anyone close to him?"

Fred wasn't sure they were both talking about the same man. What secrets was he referring to? There had never been any suggestion that Stan was anything other than a bloke who lived on Angel Street and who went to work every day on his old bike and kept his conversation with his neighbours to a minimum.

Fred drew in a long breath.

"What kind of secrets are yer talking about?"

The manager shifted in his chair.

"All I can tell you is that I have a firm of solicitors to contact in the event of Mr Newton's death. It states clearly in his file that they are his family solicitors. I am not at liberty to divulge any more information at this stage. One of the procedures mentioned in these instructions is that a representative from the solicitors, Brewer, Barnett & De'Ath would be required to attend the property with an official from this bank, together with a neighbour of Mr Newton or a close friend. As you seem to be the only person who was in regular contact with him, can I ask that I put your name and details forward as a friend?"

As a friend, thought Fred, I don't want to get involved with something I don't know about. It might cost me money.

Fred was speechless and feeling very confused. Why did the bank have a file about Stan? Why would this family he had never heard of have their own solicitors? Why would these people have to visit Stan's home?

He then had an awful thought. Surely he wouldn't be needed to help clear the place out. That's the last thing he would want to do. It would mean a lot of work disposing of his furniture and stuff. It was all probably on its last knockings anyway because as a bloke living on his own he wouldn't have bothered about the condition of the stuff. If necessary, he thought, he could ask Boss-eyed Ben to help out with his cart to shift stuff.

The manager was patiently waiting for Fred to say something.

"Yes, I suppose yer can put me name and address down if yer 'ave ter. As long as I don't 'ave ter do any sorting out. I can't shift any weighty furniture and I don't know anything about ornaments and if they're worth anything. If something went missing, I don't want to be held responsible."

He was getting a bit agitated now.

The manager smiled.

"I don't think you need to worry about any of that. They just want an independent person present when they enter the property to take an inventory."

"An inventory. That's a list, isn't it? There can't be much in there and so I don't know what all this fuss is about."

Fred felt even more confused.

Taking down Fred's name and address, the manager said that he would be getting a letter from the solicitors with a time and date to meet at Stan's house.

With the meeting over, the manager shook Fred's hand and ushered him out of his office.

Fred looked at the large clock which was fixed in a prominent position, directly over the area where the cashiers were sitting. It showed eleven thirty. He had been at the meeting for an hour. It surprised him. He'd have to get back home to let his wife know about the meeting.

Meanwhile, Churchy, having said all she could about the situation to Joan, felt it was time to approach Reverend Luke. After all, he may be asked by any family that might come to light to make funeral arrangements. That could shed some light on a few details. She wasn't getting any information from anybody else.

As luck would have it, she saw him from a distance, going into the church. Quickening her pace, she soon arrived at the entrance and almost glided in, making no sound at all. There were several people speaking to him, all in a huddle. They had, like her, obviously been waiting for his return.

Walking up to the group, she stood silently waiting for him to see her. She was, of course, trying to pick up bits of the conversation going on in case it was about funeral arrangements. It was, after all, her job to keep the church looking nice despite the fact that the budget for flowers was small. The last time she had asked for money she thought she would have to get it from Rose the housekeeper but, unlike in the past, she was getting it from Reverend Luke and not the housekeeper. The old arrangement had worked well and she didn't understand why that had changed.

There was still something troubling her about this new housekeeper.

Finally, the small group said their goodbyes and left.

"Hello." Reverend Luke had turned to face her. Churchy moved closer.

"Yer know about Stan then. Terrible business. I was wondering if anyone found out if 'e 'ad any family ter speak of."

With a sigh, Reverend Luke shook his head.

"I don't think so. At the hospital all he had in his pockets were a few coppers and his front door key. I was with him when he died but he never regained consciousness. I believe the police took what belongings he had on him. I expect they will find out a bit more about him once they have spoken to his landlord, whoever that is."

Churchy immediately thought of Fred Talbot. He'd soon enough hear from any landlord when he could't collect the rent.

"Oh, well then, yer will let me know if the church needs doing fer 'is funeral?"

She decided to stop wasting her time and go home.

Chapter 3

It had only been a few days since the accident but with everyone talking about it, the whole sorry tale seemed to have been going on forever. Ethel was recovering from her fall. She had visited the police station with Bill and given her version of events, which seemed to satisfy P.C. Dave Taylor. She was, however, feeling very low. She had been responsible for Stan's death. Although Reverend Luke had visited her to try to help her through her mental turmoil, she couldn't get the sight of Stan lying in the road out of her mind. Bill hadn't been much help to her, especially when Reverend Luke arrived on the doorstep. He had no choice but to invite him in but he didn't hold with all that sympathy talk, which he thought made things worse. It had been an accident with a sad end but Ethel would get over it and it would appear that Stan didn't have any dependants, The vicar hovering in his doorway was, he thought, not needed. He decided this was all women's stuff and he was better off out of it. He was only too pleased to be able to get to his job on the building site every day because Liz seemed to have adopted Ethel as a sympathizer. Most days she had come round to go shopping with Ethel, on the assumption that she needed a companion in her hour of need.

A couple of days had passed when a letter dropped through the letterbox at 16 Rushbrooke Street. When the letterbox clattered, Fred's wife, Mavis, stopped washing up and went to investigate. The envelope was a crisp white one and along the top of it in red was the name of a company. It was addressed to Fred. As he had told her about the meeting with the bank manager and that he would be hearing from some solicitors, she was a bit surprised that the letter had come so soon. Whenever people mentioned anything to do with solicitors, they always complained about the slow pace they seemed to work at. Fred wouldn't be back until late afternoon and so she put the letter in a prominent position on the mantelpiece.

During the course of the day, while he was on his rounds, Fred had been asked about Stan. Everyone seemed to know him but nobody knew anything of his background and Fred couldn't enlighten them.

By one o'clock he had collected rents from the properties in the area of Hackney, which was not his favourite place to be when asking for money. There were many homes which were overcrowded and money was tight. Some of the properties were rented out to groups of women who worked in the clubs in the West End. They were always good payers and although they worked late into the night, they made sure they were around on rent days to have a quick chat with him.

Looking at his watch, he decided to stop off at the nearest pub for a pie and a pint. The Red Lion wasn't too far away and he knew the landlord there. As usual, the place was full.

'Ow yer doing, Fred?"

The landlord was pulling pints and keeping an eye on who was coming in. The Red Lion was a very lucky pub for some, because during one of the nights when bombs had devastated many of the homes around it during a particularly heavy bombardment, the Red Lion had only suffered slight damage. A lot of people had sought shelter in its cellars and had been thankful that the building, being a Victorian one, had been so well constructed, (possibly by some of their grandparents, who were builders at the time) that it would take more than that bugger Hitler's bombs to wreck it.

Fred made his way through the crowd and settled at the bar with the other lunchtime drinkers.

"I'm fine, thanks. And yerself?"

The beer was slopping over the top of the pint glass that the landlord had put in front of him. That was the good thing about using this pub, the landlord always knew what you wanted before you asked for it.

Fred took a sip.

The noise in the pub, with countless conversations all going on at the same time, reached quite a pitch. Smoke was filling his lungs as he drew in a breath. Cigarette smoke had, over the years, stained the ceiling a mustard colour and had coated the walls with a stain that had darkened the wood panelling.

The landlord leaned towards Fred and said, "I 'ear Stan Newton 'as copped it. We 'eard yesterday. Nice bloke. Very quiet. If yer 'ear when the funeral is, can yer let me know because some of the blokes want ter get a wreath made up fer 'im."

Fred was a bit taken aback. Just how many people knew Stan? he thought.

The landlord continued to pour pints and shout orders for food through the small open hatch behind him. Fred put his order in for a pie while he still had the landlord's attention.

A few minutes later, the landlord beckoned Fred to go to the other end of the bar. Finding a space near the far wall, he managed to put his pint down. A plate with his pie swiftly appeared but, before he could get stuck into it, the landlord obviously wanted a word with him.

"I 'ear that Rose is back on the manor. They say she's over your way. 'Ave yer seen 'er?"

Fred frowned and pursed his lips.

"I'm not sure I know this Rose. Yer say she's back, but if she was 'ere before, I don't think I knew 'er. What did she do?"

The landlord stood back and smiled.

"What did she do? She did anything yer wanted fer a few bob. Very popular, she was. She used ter work over Soho way fer an oriental. Chinese, I think. 'E taught 'er ways ter make a parson chuck 'is collar away."

He paused and chuckled.

"She left the area about a year ago. The word was she got knocked up by some sailor. 'E sailed into the sunset and she parted the ways from 'ere, but we don't know where she ended up."

Fred still didn't know who he was talking about.

"I'll ask around fer yer and let yer know if I find anything out."

With people calling for drinks, the landlord left Fred to his pie and pint.

The afternoon rent collections seemed to go on for ever as he made his way from Hackney back into his own area. The nearer he got to the docks, the more hard luck stories he was told and he ended up taking only a few pounds from some of the tenants instead of the full rent. Good job, he thought, that he was allowed by the absent landlord to give them a chance to catch up with the money owed when they could.

By five o'clock he decided to call it a day and was glad when he reached his own home.

As soon as he put his key in the lock Mavis came to the door and told him there was a letter waiting for him and the envelope had the address typed on it.

Once in the little kitchen, he put the leather holdall down that he kept his rent payment ledger in and then carefully removed the small black and red metal box which contained the cash he had collected, the coins rattling as he placed it on the table.

Hanging his coat on the hook on the back of the door, he then, in his usual methodical way, made his way through the scullery and out to the toilet in the small shed in the garden.

Mavis took the envelope down from the mantelpiece and placed it on the table next to the tin. She was feeling very impatient and wished that Fred, for once, would just get on and open the envelope but, being a man who had a regular routine on his return from rent collecting, she knew she would just have to wait.

She filled the kettle and put it noisily on the stove in the hope that Fred would hear the clatter of the kettle and hasten his routine for once.

Fred emerged from the shed and made his way back into the scullery.

Standing by the cooker, he had to tell Mavis how surprised he was by the number of people who seemed to know Stan.

"They even want ter 'ave a whip round to get a wreath fer 'im from The Red Lion."

Finally, he went into the kitchen and sat down at the table.

Putting a cup of tea in front of him and, at the same time, placing the letter to the side of it, Mavis sat down and waited.

He picked the envelope up and saw the name printed along the top of it: Brewer, Barnett & De'Ath.

"Yes, that will be the solicitors."

He tugged at the fold along the top of the envelope and, opening it up, took the folded letter out. He read it to Mavis.

'Dear Mr Talbot,

In the Estate of Stanley Bartholomew Newton deceased.

As Solicitors for the Newton Family Estate, I write to enquire if you would be able to attend at the property 15 Angel Street, Leytonstone on Friday the 28th September at ten o'clock. Your name and address have been supplied to us by Mr William Slater of Midland Bank Limited. Please telephone the writer on the above number to confirm if you are in a position to meet this request.

Yours faithfully,

Bartholomew Brewer'

Fred fell silent. He put the letter down and looked at Mavis.

"The Newton Family Estate! What's that when it's at 'ome?"

He scratched his head, took a deep breath and looked up to the ceiling.

"There's obviously a lot about Stan that we don't know. I'll 'ave ter speak ter Churchy. She'll know people 'e used ter talk to. In the meantime, I'd better get over ter the phone box on the corner and let this bloke know I'll be there on the 28th."

With that said, he took the necessary coins for the call out of his pocket and left.

The next morning, P.C. Dave Taylor could be seen pedalling along Angel Street. He had been asked to make sure Stan's property was securely locked up, both back and front. As usual, Churchy was chatting to Joan at the corner shop and, on seeing him she cut the conversation short and made a bee-line for him. He leaned his bike against Stan's front wall.

"'Ello, Dave. Why are yer 'ere?"

It hadn't taken her long to get over the road to where he was. Like a whippet, she certainly could move fast when she wanted to.

"Good morning, Churchy."

He pushed on the front door and tugged at the window frame for a minute.

"That all seems secure. I'd better check round back."

He made his way to an opening between the houses and disappeared into the garden. Churchy followed and, seeing him pushing on the back door, decided she would give the back window a bit of a push and pull.

"Well, it all seems to be shut up tight."

He stepped back and looked up.

"We've 'eard at the station that some solicitors are coming on the 28th ter look around the 'ouse. We've got the keys. I believe Fred Talbot 'as bin asked ter be 'ere."

Churchy looked amazed.

"What solicitors? Why is that necessary? Are they 'oping ter find something valuable in there? The 28th, yer say. I'd better be around then, ter see fer meself."

She rushed off, leaving P.C. Dave looking in the shed.

Churchy was now in a bit of a quandary. She was annoyed at the slow progress she had made in the local information she was hoping to gather. One of the lines she thought she would pursue was getting more information on Rose, the housekeeper. With her thoughts searching for an excuse to quiz Reverend Luke about her, she thought she would tell him that she needed some cash to buy a new tin of Brasso to polish the altar candlesticks.

Making her way along the street, she saw a car pull up outside the church house. Now, to see a car in this street was unusual, but to see one outside the church house and it wasn't for a funeral was queer. She held back and pretended to search for something in her pocket while secretly watching who was going to get out of it.

Almost immediately a woman came out of the church house and, walking very fast, made her way to the car. She was slim and wearing a colourful summer dress which showed off her figure. She had on stockings and very high heeled shoes. Her loose auburn hair was bouncing onto her shoulders.

The rear door of the car opened and the woman looked into the car and, smiling, stepped inside pulling the door closed behind her. Within seconds the car was gone.

Churchy was still standing in the street where she had been watching the car. She was trying to make sense of what she had seen. The woman who came out of the church house had been Rose, she was now sure of it.

The day for the solicitors to visit Stan's property soon came round. Mavis had washed and ironed Fred's best shirt and had even pressed his suit trousers to give them a proper crease. Fred himself was getting a bit agitated because he didn't know what all the fuss was about. Perhaps, he thought, because Stan's rent would be lost, they wanted to see if there was anything worth selling to get some money back.

As he made his way along Angel Street, Churchy was hot on his heels. Her turn of speed wasn't wasted on him.

As they reached No. 15, Fred turned to her.

"What are yer doing 'ere? There's nothing ter see. The bloke from the solicitors will be 'ere in a minute. They're never late when there are possessions ter be valued."

At that moment a black car could be seen at the top of the street. As it made its way to where Fred and Churchy were standing there seemed to be a lot of net curtains being shifted about in a lot of windows.

The car came to a stop. The gentleman who stepped out was wearing a pinstriped suit and carried a brown leather briefcase. He looked to be in his forties and had a sallow complexion. Perhaps someone who spent most of his working life in an office, Fred thought. His ready smile was not what Fred had expected.

He was followed by the ample-bodied William Slater, the bank manager.

As Fred observed the two men, he thought who would have ever imagined that the death of Stan would have involved a bank manager and a solicitor meeting to discuss the contents of his home.

The small gathering on the pavement looked very official.

Bartholomew Brewer approached Fred with his hand outstretched.

"Good morning Mr Talbot. I am pleased to meet you."

Fred shook his hand.

"You do, of course, know Mr Slater from Midland Bank."

Fred nodded.

"We have obtained the keys from the police station and so I think it best if we enter the property to see what we can find."

Churchy looked at Fred, who gave her a nod that meant it was time for her to go. Reluctantly, she took the hint and walked away.

William Slater promptly unlocked the door and they all entered.

The small passage was dark and seemed very uninviting. The first two doors were shut and Fred guessed they would be the front room, reserved for 'best' and the next room would be used as a bedroom, if a property was shared. In this case, though, Stan was the only tenant. At the end of the passage was a door leading to the small kitchen.

The solicitor turned and said, "Why don't we start in this room first?" pointing to the room at the front.

The door was pushed open, only to be blocked by something. Another push and it wouldn't budge any further. He put the briefcase down and with a firm hand on the door, tried to ease it open a bit more. Looking at Fred, he said, "Mr Talbot, could you see if you can edge yourself into the doorway, enough to be able to move the obstacle just a little?"

Fred felt he wasn't in a position to refuse and so he stepped forward and with his slender body, wedged himself in the opening, putting his arm around the space in the doorway and managed to wrestle a box away from the door, enabling the rest of his body to ease into the room.

The musty smell which permeated the area made it obvious that nobody had been in here for some time. The room was full of boxes of every size and shape. There did not appear to be any furniture in there, just boxes.

The solicitor was getting impatient.

"Can you make some room for us to get in?"

Fred didn't know which way to turn. There was hardly room for him to shift anything, let alone make a space for two more people.

"You'll 'ave ter give me a minute. I'll 'ave ter see if I can push a couple of these boxes aside so that yer can 'ave somewhere ter stand."

The bank manager peered around the door as far as he could, his bulky body preventing any more movement.

"Good God! The room's full of boxes. There must be dozens of them."

There was a scraping sound as Fred was attempting to push and pull the box nearest the door to one side. It seemed an impossible task. With his back against the wall, he placed a foot against the side of the nearest box and pushed as hard as he could.

The box moved away slightly. He thought, I knew there was something odd about this visit. Why was it necessary?

Eventually there was enough space for the others to get in. Opening some of the boxes, it seemed they were all full of books. These were not ordinary books, thought Fred; they seemed to be leather bound and some had gold lettering on the front of them.

As the men couldn't investigate any further, they all decided it must be a room where Stan stored stuff and so they made their way out into the narrow dark passage and leaned against the wall where the stairs were.

Fred brushed his suit down and thought Mavis wouldn't be pleased about him wearing his only suit to a house that needed cleaning.

The door of the next room was also hard to open. This time William Slater put his bulk to good use and forced the door so that they could all get in. It wasn't a bedroom. The first object they saw was a huge wooden hall stand with intricate carving across the top of it and a mirror in the centre. A zinc drip tray was at the bottom and at least a dozen walking sticks could be seen standing to attention on the tray. Some of them seemed to have silver finials which had been engraved. Others appeared to be topped with ivory.

Glancing around the room, there were huge gilt-framed mirrors leaning against the walls, some taller than the three men. They all just stood still, observing what was there.

Along one of the walls they saw what seemed to be very large carpets which had been rolled up for storage. In the centre of the room was an item of furniture covered with a blanket. They went over to it and slowly pulled the blanket off.

Fred and William Slater gasped as they saw a circular table, which was black with beautiful inlaid flowers of all colours, which seemed to be made of small stones. They shone and glinted even in this dull light.

Bartholomew Brewer had not said a word.

They had seen enough in this room.

Entering the small kitchen at the end of the passage, the room couldn't have been more ordinary. It was a simple kitchen, no different from any other kitchen in this street. A well worn wooden table and a couple of chairs were in the centre. A cooker was near the blackleaded fireplace and a shelf above that had a clock and two vases on it. There was also a tall kitchen cupboard with two glass windows in it, where tins and packets of food could be seen. At the place where the back door was, a sink and draining board stood atop a cupboard with gingham material covering the space which probably housed saucepans. They were all quite relieved at the sight of familiarity.

A small grubby window next to the door had been broken and was taped up.

They had all seen enough.

At last, Bartholomew Brewer spoke. With a strange look on his face he said, "I think we should see what is upstairs. Let's hope it is not in the same state as down here."

Fred couldn't put his finger on it but he knew there was something odd about the solicitor. He hadn't said very much and also, he hadn't shown as much surprise as he and William Slater had when finding all this stuff.

It was agreed they would make their way up the well trodden stairs.

There was an unspoken unease about this situation. William Slater was the first to break the silence.

"Well, our Mr Newton certainly seemed to live a simple life, despite the fact that his background and family prestige would indicate he should be enjoying the benefits he's entitled to."

He immediately knew he had said too much.

Fred noticed his almost look of panic. There was something going on here that was downright strange. Had he been the only one who didn't understand what they were finding? The silence in the house was almost unbearable. For three men to be investigating these contents, it was odd that none of them was making much conversation.

The threadbare carpet runner on the stairs made their steps almost echo in the silence.

Bartholomew Brewer was first to reach the landing which was very dark because all the doors here were, once again, closed. By the time they were all up there the small landing was crowded.

Fred held back. He felt he shouldn't be here anyway. It was intruding.

Bartholomew Brewer stepped up to the door which was the room at the back of the house. He turned the door knob.

This time the door opened easily. He stepped in. The others followed. The first to speak was William Slater.

"Good God!"

That was all he uttered.

Before them was a room which appeared to be a sitting room, which could have been in a fine house. The walls were papered with an oriental design which had cranes and exotic birds seemingly flying around the room. Gilt framed silk worked pictures hung over the fireplace. There was a long, low, couchlike bench which had a stack of embroidered cushions along the length of it. A low red lacquered table was in front of it with what appeared to be Chinese ceramic dishes on it. A bamboo screen with silk panels covered in painted designs stood next to a full length mirror with gilt serpents entwining its frame.

With all this opulence before them, they had only just noticed that the floor in the room had floorboards which were stained and polished to a burnished gold.

They were all still standing at the entrance to the room.

Fred was the first to come out of their dumbfounded silence.

"What the hell is all this? 'E couldn't 'ave nicked it all. Where's it all come from?"

William Slater's eyes were slowly taking everything in as he glanced around. He had never seen anything like this before.

Bartholomew Brewer simply smiled.

It was jointly agreed that they should go into the next room.

As soon as they entered the next room it was obvious it was a place of comfort and learning because three of the walls were lined with bookcases, which were fitted from the ceiling to the floor. Volumes of beautifully bound books were displayed, some behind glass panelling. Next to the fireplace was a wing backed chair which seemed to be placed exactly right for anyone seeking a place to read. In a recess stood a leather topped desk with gold tooling around its surface. A brass lamp stood on it and focused their attention to the brass handles which adorned various drawers at the front of the desk.

In the same recess, the walls were hung with countless framed silhouettes, the black outlines on white backgrounds creating a memory for someone.

Bartholomew Brewer walked over to the desk, his tread muffled by the thickness of the carpet which covered the floor.

Staring for a minute at the silhouettes, he sighed and scratched the back of his head. It was as though he was lost in thought.

Turning to the others, he found William Slater sitting in the wing backed chair with a broad smile on his face.

Fred was overawed by this whole experience. He didn't know what to do or what to say.

He glanced at his wrist watch. They had been in the house less than an hour and, yet, he felt he had somehow walked through time into another age. He didn't like it. None of this made any sense. He didn't like being in a situation he couldn't control. He stood with his back against the wall as if wanting to find something firm and real to lean against.

William Slater strode across the room and suggested they look into the front room of the house. He seemed to be keen to find out what other surprises they were in for.

Looking at Fred, Bartholomew Brewer asked if he was all right. Fred nodded.

One after the other they entered the next room. It was dark because the only window in there was covered by curtains that reached the floor. William Slater walked over to them and pulled them open. It was a sunny day and the sunlight streamed in. They were in a bedroom.

A brass bedstead dominated the room. It was made up for use. The only other item of furniture was a chest of drawers.

Bartholomew Brewer went over to it and ran his fingers over the top of it and along the front beading. He was treating it as though it was something very special and almost an old friend.

There were some framed photographs on it, six in all. They seemed to be family photographs. Who could they be?

Fred walked over to the window and looked out. He wanted to make sure he hadn't imagined any of this and was relieved that what he could see was Angel Street with all the familiar people he expected to see walking along it.

He turned.

William Slater was smiling. "I knew there was something funny about Stan Newton because of the file of papers I had to keep on him."

Looking at Bartholomew Brewer he said, "His connection with your firm of solicitors always puzzled me."

At this point, it was decided that they would leave the property and arrange a time when they would meet up at the solicitor's office. It was also agreed that what they had witnessed was to remain a closed secret.

The property was, once again, locked up and would be checked each time P.C. Dave Taylor was in the area.

As they parted, Fred said, "This really is a house of secrets."

Chapter 4

It was a few days later that Churchy decided she would make her way over to Hackney to make a few discreet enquiries about Rose. The arrangements for Stan's funeral still hadn't been made which was, in itself, a bit strange. Reverend Luke hadn't been able to find much out about Stan or any family he might have. She was relying on the solicitors and Fred Talbot to give her any bits of information. For the moment she wanted to steer clear of Reverend Luke until she had found out a bit more about Rose.

On her way down the street she decided she would pop in to see Ethel, now that she was back to normal. The door was, as usual, ajar. She was washing up.

Ethel looked over at the small figure of Churchy who seemed very tidy for a change. Obviously she was en route to somewhere which wasn't just Ethel's kitchen.

"Ow are yer, Ethel? Yer look almost back ter yerself. I'm just going over ter Hackney ter see a few people."

Wiping her hands on a towel, Ethel walked over to Churchy and smiled. She knew she just wanted to find out if there had been anything more said that hadn't filtered through the street gossip yet.

"It's very good of yer ter pop in as yer busy."

She didn't want to encourage too much conversation because that was always the start of rumours about people being passed on.

"It's a nice day fer a trip if yer going over ter Hackney. I 'aven't been there fer a while."

Churchy was still standing by the table and Ethel was thankful that she hadn't planted herself down hoping for a cuppa.

"Yer can see I'm on the mend and the whole situation seems behind me now. Obviously, once we 'ear when the funeral is going ter be, me and Bill will arrange fer some flowers fer Stan. If 'e didn't 'ave family it will be nice ter give 'im some sort of a send off. We might even 'ave ter arrange a small tea fer the neighbours ter come to. I think that's the least we could do."

Churchy looked at Ethel and realized she was still feeling the whole incident had been her fault and that she was trying to put matters right by Stan.

"Oh, that's a really nice thing fer yer to do. I expect everyone will want ter contribute something ter the tea."

Stepping back, she said, "I'd better get me skates on if I want ter get over ter Hackney in time ter see me mates."

With that she showed herself out.

The journey to Hackney didn't take long.

Churchy decided she would make her way first to the market. She knew a lot of the stallholders there and, besides, she hadn't spoken to them for a while and so it would be good to catch up.

The first stall she made her way to was the one her cousin was working. It had the familiar smell about it of cabbages and fruit. Eddie had worked the stall for years.

As she made her way along the street she had to keep dodging the discarded leaves of vegetables that had been cut off to make them look better. Eddie was proud of his stall's display and he had placed the fruit on it in lines, which looked very inviting.

As she approached him, Churchy called out.

"'Ow are yer, me old mate?"

Eddie looked up and a broad smile showed off his weathered but still handsome features which had not left him, even though he was now in his forties.

"Well, what a sight fer sore eyes."

He stepped out from behind his stall.

"What do I owe fer this visit? I don't owe yer any money, do I?"

His smile was getting broader.

"No, yer silly sod. What I need is a bit of information."

His eyebrows shot up and he turned his head to one side.

On seeing Churchy, one of the other stallholders came over.

"'Ello, Churchy. I thought it was you."

She looked at him and was trying to remember his name.

"Yer don't want ter get anything off him. My stuff's better."

All three of them were laughing now and the customers that were trying to pass them were wondering what was so funny.

"Now, boys," she said. "Does the name Rose mean anything ter yer?"

Eddie and his mate just looked at each other.

"Now, there's a blast from the past."

In between serving his customers and shouting out that his stall was the best for fresh fruit and veg, he told her that he could have a chat when he took a tea break.

They arranged to meet at half past eleven under the clock on the Town Hall but it would only be for about ten minutes.

Oh, well, at least, she thought, I may be able to find something out.

She strolled off to have a look around the market stalls but didn't expect to buy anything. She'd done her shopping at Joan's the day before and wasn't planning to splash out on any extras.

Her legs were beginning to play her up and, seeing a bench near the Town Hall, she made her way over to it. A brass plate on it had been paid for by the local British Legion to honour the dead from the area. A suitable resting place, she thought, for the living weary.

With all the usual paper and wrappings from some of the stalls swirling around her feet, the light breeze picking them up and carrying them off, only to rest again somewhere else, she wondered where it all ended up. The dustbin men weren't due round for a few more days.

The Town Hall clock sounded the half hour. She looked across the dozens of stalls and finally saw Eddie coming towards her, still smiling.

The tea stall was a few feet away and already had a queue forming. She could smell the sausages frying and wondered what might be in them. The tea stall customers didn't seem to mind what it was. They were just hungry as they had been in the market since seven that morning.

"I'll get 'em in, shall I? What do yer want? Is it just a cuppa?"

"That'll be fine. Two sugars," she said, smiling, knowing that wouldn't be possible because of rationing.

With two steaming mugs of tea, Eddie sat on the bench next to her.

"Now, what's this about? Information, yer said."

Churchy took a sip of tea and winced. It was strong and had barely any sugar in it.

"It's nice ter see yer, anyway," she said. "What I wanted ter ask yer is, do yer know a woman 'oo used ter live around 'ere? 'Er name is Rose and there must be loads of women with that name but I'm only interested in one of 'em."

He looked into his mug of tea and gave it a bit of a swirl, possibly hoping that would improve it.

"'Aven't yer got more than that ter go on?"

Churchy put the mug of tea down on the bench beside her.

"I believe she was very popular among you blokes."

Eddie looked puzzled.

"If yer referring ter the Rose I think yer are, she's not the sort of person I would want yer ter know."

With that kind of response from him, she knew she was on to something here.

He laughed out loud.

"Rose was offering something what wasn't rationed, that was fer sure."

He took a couple of gulps of his tea.

"She used ter work fer a Chinese bloke over Soho way. 'E paid 'is girls very well if they kept 'is customers 'appy, if yer know what I mean. I think 'is club was called The Paradise. I never used 'er though. It was a bit too risky. She entertained a lot of sailors. She left the manor about a year ago."

With ten minutes gone, he took both their mugs back to the tea stall.

"I've gotta get back now, but it was good ter see yer."

Churchy continued to sit on the bench. She now knew she was right about the housekeeper.

I wonder, she thought, should I ask Reverend Luke about her? He must know what sort of person she is. If she was one of the unmarried mothers who went to stay away until the

66

baby was born, he would know about it. Her next thought was, does he know she still seems to be on the game? It was definitely her that got into that car.

With the sun now beginning to lose its heat and the constant noise of the market beginning to get on her nerves, she decided to make her way back home.

As she walked along Angel Street she could see the ample figure of Liz cleaning her windows. This, of course, was a regular occurrence, not because they always needed a clean but just to be out there in case anyone was passing by with anything worth passing on.

As Churchy approached, she dropped the cloth into the pail of water, some of it splashing onto her well worn slippers. She turned to Churchy.

"'Ello, luv. Nice day fer a stroll. Been anywhere interesting?"

Drawing in a long breath, Churchy said, "I've been over Hackney way. I wanted ter see me cousin Eddie about a few things. I'm glad I've seen yer because I wanted ter tell yer about that business at Stan's 'ouse. I was there when the bank manager from the Midland and some solicitor bloke that Fred told me about all arrived. It all looked very official. Poor ol' Fred was wondering what was going on. 'E'd been roped in because they wanted someone there that 'ad known Stan. Talk about a fish outa water. Anyway, they all went in and I 'ad ter go on me way. Next time I see Fred I'll ask 'im about it."

Liz looked up the street.

"'Ave yer 'eard any more about when the funeral's going ter be? Yer know I don't get ter church much – births, marriages and deaths – that's me and so I can't really arrive at the church 'ouse and ask because that would seem strange."

"As far as I'm concerned," said Churchy, "the whole bloody thing seems strange. I'll let yer know if I 'ear anything."

Liz bent down and picked up the cloth from the pail and wrung it out. Churchy went on her way.

At Fred's house, Mavis couldn't get her head around the fact that Fred wouldn't tell her anything about Stan's place. She liked reading crime stories and so her imagination was up and running. Fred had said it was more than his job was worth to mention anything about it. He did tell her though that there would be another letter from the solicitor soon and that he would probably have to go to their office in the City.

Strolling along, Churchy could hear laughing and shouting. Looking towards the church, there seemed to be some kids playing in the graveyard.

I'm not having that, she thought. It don't seem right.

Sure enough it was a local boy, Ben, who was often in trouble, with his mates and they were trying to catch some poor cat that had found itself between gravestones and bushes. It was a wonder Reverend Luke hadn't heard the commotion and come out.

"Leave the poor thing alone, yer little buggers, or I'll get Dave Taylor after yer."

She wondered if it was Stan's cat.

At that moment, something caught her attention at the window of the church house. What was it? She could have imagined it but, no, she was sure it was Reverend Luke who had come to the window and moved the net curtain to one side to look out. It appeared in the short time she saw him that he was undressed, the pale skin on his chest clearly visible. He turned his head as though he was speaking to someone in the room.

Churchy felt almost embarrassed at what she was imagining. This was a man of the cloth and yet, here he was, in a state of undress in the afternoon when he should be available in the church for anyone who might want to speak to him. She didn't know what to do.

Trying to think of a reason to knock on the church house door, she turned to find Ethel standing there.

"I 'ope I didn't make yer jump. I thought I'd 'ave a word with the reverend to find out if there was any more news 'e could give me about when I could arrange Stan's funeral tea. Bill won't be 'ome fer a while yet and as 'e doesn't like anything ter do with the church. I thought I'd see 'im now if 'e's at 'ome."

Churchy thought this couldn't have come at a better time.

"Why don't yer knock, then?"

It wasn't long before Rose opened the door. She was looking a bit flushed, her auburn hair hanging untidily onto her shoulders and the dress she was wearing looking creased.

Ethel stepped back from the door as though reluctant to speak.

Looking directly at her, Rose said, "What do you want?"

Her abruptness took Ethel by surprise.

"I'm the one 'oo was involved in the accident in the street and I need ter speak ter the reverend about some things. 'E said I could call on 'im when I needed ter."

Rose turned to look along the passage as though she was expecting Reverend Luke to be coming down the stairs, but there was no sign of him.

"He's out at the moment but he should be back soon."

Her voice had softened.

Ethel felt as though she should almost apologise for being here. She wasn't usually such a nervous person but, at this moment, she had a feeling something wasn't right.

Before she could say anything else, Churchy stepped forward.

"I think if yer check, yer will find Reverend Luke is upstairs because I saw 'im looking out of the winder when all that noise was going on."

Rose drew in a deep breath.

"Are you calling me a liar?"

For her small stature, Churchy could put on a brave stance.

"I know what I saw. Give 'im a shout, then if 'e appears, we'll know, won't we?"

Ethel was shrinking by the second.

Looking at Churchy, she said, "I'm going now. I'll try ter see 'im another time."

She turned and hurried down the path like a frightened cat.

Churchy was still staring down Rose.

With a move so swift it only took seconds, the door was slammed shut, leaving Churchy alone on the step.

With no choice but to leave the matter there for the time being, she decided to go around the back of the house to see if that poor cat got away.

She followed the well trodden path along the side of the house and saw, emerging from the back kitchen door, two young women. They were quite small. They definitely were not children. As they hurried away across the garden and into the graveyard they were obviously making their way to the back gate. Churchy did notice, in the short time she saw them, that they both had short cut black hair which gave them an oriental look. Now she was even more confused.

Forgetting about the cat, she decided to head home with her thoughts. Perhaps she ought to share this experience with Liz. She might as well get her tuppence-worth in once the story had been told.

She realized that she hadn't eaten all day. It was time to get some dinner on and mull over this eventful day.

It had been good to see Eddie again. He, of course, didn't know it, but his reaction to the question about Rose had given her a lot to think about. She liked Reverend Luke but couldn't understand why he had brought that woman with him. What was going on?

The light was beginning to fade now and she was ready to settle into her armchair by the oven. The little kitchen was still warm. She had left the oven door open, which filled the room with the smell of the meal she had just eaten. A cup of tea was the finishing touch to a strange afternoon.

As she settled back into her armchair, the room was full of shadows. She glanced over to the wooden crucifix which hung on the wall over the fireplace. She could feel herself dozing off.

Chapter 5

The letter arrived. There was no mistaking who it was from because the envelope had a franking mark on it with Brewer, Barnett & De'Ath across the top. Mavis was, once again, feeling impatient because it had arrived while Fred was out rent collecting.

Although she knew of Stan, she couldn't say she knew him because Rushbrooke Street was a fair way from Angel Street. Fred sometimes mentioned tenants' names if there was any illness or death. He had told her that Stan's body had been taken to a chapel of rest but it wasn't one she had ever heard of. He had also said that the solicitors would be making the funeral arrangements and they would tell him when that would be so that he could let Stan's neighbours know. There was nothing she could do but wait for him to get back. I wonder, she thought, if his place is better than this one and if we could do a swap? Fred would know if it was in a better condition.

Her next thought was, if she did him a special tea, perhaps he would give her a bit more information about what was going on.

Looking over at the clock on the shelf, she decided she just had time to get down to the fish stall in the market. She'd get him a nice bit of fish.

The weekend had arrived and the flowers in the church would need changing.

Liz was, as usual, on her knees, donkey stoning her front step and Vi had, at last, emerged from her self imposed captivity, having decided that the coupon business had gone away. Even so, she would be keeping away from Boss-eyed Ben from now on.

As Churchy approached, Vi she could see her chatting to Ethel. Both women were speaking very quietly.

"Well, this is nice, ter see the two of yer out in daylight."

Looking at Ethel, she said, "Are yer going ter see if Reverend Luke is about this morning? I'm going ter 'ave a word with Liz on me way before I get up ter the church."

Ethel was still a bit subdued but managed a smile.

"Yes, I'm going ter try ter see 'im this morning."

As Churchy approached her, Liz stood up.

"Nice day, Churchy. 'Ave yer got time fer a cuppa?"

"I'm glad yer said that, because I've got something on me mind that I want ter unload on yer."

Picking up the donkey stone and the pail of water, Liz wiped her hands on the floral apron she was wearing and ushered Churchy in.

The kettle on and the chairs round the kitchen table pulled out, the scene was set for Churchy's tale to be told.

"I think Reverend Luke is keeping an immoral 'ouse. There are young women visiting the place and I've found out that 'is 'ousekeeper used ter work on the game fer a Chinese bloke over Soho."

Liz sat down with the freshly filled teapot in her hand.

"What do yer mean?"

Leaning forward and speaking in a hushed voice, as though she didn't want to speak her thoughts out loud, she said, "I meself saw Reverend Luke in an upstairs room. He was undressed and I don't think 'e was alone."

Liz put the teapot down with a thud.

"Yer must be mistaken."

Churchy pushed her cup forward as though it was long overdue to be filled.

"I know what I saw and me cousin Eddie over at Mare Street market said Rose 'ad bin away fer a while but when she was 'ere, she was very good at teaching these young girls 'ow ter please the men, if yer know what I mean." She patted the side of her nose and smiled. "I tell yer, Liz, there's something going on over there and it's not right."

They both sat looking at each other across the table in unusual silence.

"Reverend Michael would be turning in 'is grave if 'e knew," said Churchy.

"Right," said Liz with a determined look on her face. "If yer not doing anything ternight, we'll get ourselves over there at about ten o'clock and if we see people in the church 'ouse that don't belong there, we'll ask 'em what's going on. It's corrupt, that's what it is."

With Churchy nodding her head and looking a bit alarmed at what she had started, the two of them finished what tea was left and finalized their plan.

Back at Fred's house on this Saturday morning, the only clue that he had given to Mavis about what the solicitors were planning was that they were arranging Stan's funeral at the City of London Cemetery, Little Ilford, for the following week. This wouldn't please the neighbours, he thought, because it would mean a journey, probably by train, to get there. He knew they were all looking forward to lining their street when the horse-drawn carriage carrying Stan in his coffin would pass. Now it wouldn't, because the Chapel of Rest wasn't their local one. No, this wouldn't go down well.

The letter had also requested his presence at their office in the City. This shouldn't be necessary, he thought, because Stan wasn't even family. However, to find out what all the fuss was about, he felt he would have to attend. Stan's house had remained locked up.

He decided that, to give the neighbours a chance to attend the funeral, he would let Churchy and Ethel know what the funeral arrangements were. That way it would give everyone time to arrange any flowers they wanted to get and, as the funeral was to be on the Friday, people might have to take the day off work to attend. The City of London Cemetery was known to most of them and they would know how to get there. If Ethel and some of the other ladies wanted to put on a tea at the end of the day, they would have to decide whose front room it should be in.

He then remembered what the landlord of The Red Lion over in Hackney had said about having a whip round for a wreath. He would have to let him know about the funeral.

After a lot of goading from Mavis, Fred had told her that he was due to go to the solicitor's office in the City on Wednesday and that they were arranging for him and William Slater to be collected from the bank at 9 that morning. This was all becoming very unusual and seeming more important by the day. His curiosity about Stan was at fever pitch now. This whole situation was like something in a book or a mystery you saw at the pictures.

Joan at the corner shop was still feeding Stan's cat. It was a nice little thing and she didn't think Stan had ever given it a name. She was trying to think of one.

With everyone knowing when the funeral was to be, plans were being made for a tea to be put on at Liz's place as she had a nicely decorated front room. If she borrowed a table from the Salvation Army for a small donation, that would be big enough to put all the food on that people were offering to come up with.

The day seemed to go worryingly slow for Liz and Churchy because of what was on their minds. Were they doing the right thing? Should they doubt the reverend? It now seemed an intrusion into someone else's life.

As the day wore on, they both came to the conclusion that with such serious doubts about the reverend, they had no choice but to satisfy their curiosity in case rumours started.

The September evening was a wonderful one. The light was just failing by ten o'clock and the warm air carried the scent of the flowers which surprisingly survived in the church garden, despite the number of people who used it as a short cut to both the graveyard and the next street.

As they made their way in silence they passed the church, whose huge wooden doors were firmly closed and reached the back of the church house. There were lights on in the kitchen and also on the stairs. They went in and immediately could hear voices. They looked at each other.

"We'll 'ave ter go upstairs now if we want ter know what's 'appening up there."

Liz had a determined look on her face. She went first with a now nervous Churchy behind her.

All was well until half way up, hearing laughter and at least one male voice swearing very loudly, the sound of a creaking stair made them quicken their pace to reach the landing. It seemed that no one had heard them.

They now both cowered in a corner, not knowing what to do next. Second thoughts were going through Liz's mind, but they had got this far.

Both bedroom doors were open. The swearing from one of the rooms was getting more fevered. The sound of laughter followed every expletive.

Churchy and Liz inched forward, holding their breath and hoping they would be able to see into the room without being detected. The light on the landing being switched off, there were no shadows to give them away.

The swearing was now muffled and as they peered in, they could see the slim figure of a young girl sitting astride a man lying on the bed. Each time her silent, rhythmic movements paused, a low groan could be heard. Another woman's voice was heard and they saw her kneeling at the pillow on the bed, leaning forward, offering her breasts as a comfort.

Liz and Churchy were frozen in disgust.

Suddenly, from the other open doorway the naked figure of a young Asian girl appeared. Her body, the colour of amber in the light coming in from the landing window, was that of a very young girl. Her long black hair glistened like silk as it fell over her shoulders.

With no attempt to shield her naked body from their gaze, she smiled. She was holding what seemed to be a cat-o'-nine-tails, its leather thongs hanging limply by her legs.

She silently beckoned them to her and pushed the bedroom door open further. They inched forward. There were candles in the room which gave off a perfume as the smoke from them spiralled upwards and disappeared into the shadows of the dimly lit room. Lying face down on the bed was the naked figure of a man, who appeared to have his outstretched arms tied to the metal bars of the bedstead. His back bore healed scars and what seemed to be fresh strips of blood where he had been whipped. His flesh was quite pale, as though it had not been in any sunlight for a long time.

Immediately, Churchy felt her heart thump. What had she done? What dreadful secrets would she have to live with now?

Her thoughts were in turmoil.

The figure on the bed turned his head to one side and she could see it was Reverend Luke.

He called out in panic, "Oh, no!"

His voice echoed around the room. The Asian girl went over to him and raising the cat-o-nine-tails once more, brought it down onto his back. He flinched and cried out. She was smiling and watching the reactions of Liz and Churchy.

They both screamed and turned, heading for the stairs with tears streaming down their faces.

With her vision partly marred by tears, Churchy felt her legs collapsing under her and, before she could reach the bottom step, she fell forward and hurtled down the remaining stairs. As she landed on the floor, her small crumpled body seemed to fold up and shrink. She lay there silently.

Liz called out her name but there was no response.

The dim light on the stairs made it difficult to see if Churchy was conscious. Her head was turned and facing the wall.

"Help me someone. Help me." Liz's cries echoed in the now silent house.

Two of the young women appeared at the top of the stairs, now wearing silk kimonos.

"Fer Christ's sake, get me some 'elp. She may be dead or something."

From out of the shadows Rose appeared.

Liz didn't know what to do. Should she move Churchy? No, she thought. That might be dangerous.

Churchy groaned and moved her arm in an attempt to touch her head. She was also trying to move her legs, but gave out a sharp cry as her foot reached the wall.

Rose remained silent, as though her very presence was only a shadow.

"Get a doctor or something 'ere. She needs 'elp." Liz was becoming more demanding and the panic in her voice as she called out was not wasted on Rose. She heard the telephone dial whirling as Rose dialled for help.

With the arrival of an ambulance, the whole street seemed to have become aware that there was something going on that needed to be explained. The light, now fading, was being given a boost by all the little houses along the street opening their doors and pulling curtains aside in order to see what was going on.

People were now milling around the garden of the church house, trying to see who needed an ambulance.

Several of the women, with curlers in their hair and some still holding the cups of tea they had been enjoying, were now forming groups to chat about what all this could possibly mean.

Liz could be seen walking to the ambulance, followed by Churchy on a stretcher, covered with a blanket, her tear-stained face contorted with pain as she tried to talk to one of the stretcher bearers.

Bill was standing near the ambulance as Churchy was about to be put into it. She called out to him that she had fallen down some stairs.

He turned and told the group nearest him that there had been some sort of an accident and probably Churchy and Liz had been having a meeting with Reverend Luke about Stan. What he didn't say to them was that he was wondering why they would be upstairs in the church house.

Once the ambulance had sped off, the crowds dispersed, all with their own thoughts about what had happened. None of them, of course, could ever have realized the truth.

At the church house, Rose closed the door and its other occupants melted silently into the night as though they had never been there. Only Reverend Luke could be heard, in prayer, begging forgiveness to an unseen god.

By midday Monday Churchy left the hospital, with her leg partly in plaster as she had broken her ankle in the fall.

Liz was still trying to come to terms with what they had witnessed. She just didn't want to think about it but nothing she did would clear her mind. She felt sick at the memory of it. She decided, after two sleepless nights, that she would see how Churchy was and would suggest they didn't tell anyone about what had happened. She was sure no one would believe them anyway. Perhaps Reverend Luke would request a move to another parish and take Rose with him. She didn't care what excuse he gave. It would just be best if they left.

Wednesday morning arrived and Fred was up early. Hopefully, he would today find out what all this mystery about Stan was about.

Angel Street was buzzing with talk of Stan's funeral tea. Vi, Madge, Liz and Ethel had decided between themselves who was going to make sandwiches and who was going to find enough ingredients to put a few cakes on show. With limited sugar, as it was still rationed, the cakes would have to be plain with perhaps some fruit and a bit of jam for sweetness. There was always someone in the street who could help out with the odd treat. They were on a mission and wanted to do their best for Stan, to show how much they had all liked him. Liz's front room was definitely the place where the tea would be held.

As Fred made his way to Midland Bank to be picked up for the meeting, he still wondered why Bartholomew Brewer hadn't shown surprise at what they had seen in Stan's house.

Glancing at his watch, he quickened his pace as he didn't want to keep everyone waiting.

William Slater was outside the bank looking up and down the street. As soon as he saw Fred he stepped forward to meet him.

"I think we're going to find this meeting very interesting and, hopefully, we'll get to the bottom of the mystery."

Just at that moment a car drew up and the smiling face of Bartholomew Brewer could be seen. He leaned over and, winding the window down called for them to get in.

"Thanks for being on time. There's a lot to get through at the office this morning."

Fred and William Slater sat in the back and, for a few moments, savoured the opportunity of travelling in a car.

Not having had much time to chat at their last meeting, the conversation during the journey inevitably turned to the war and their experiences while in the army. They had both learnt to drive during that time and now, with the war over and everyone making the best of things, the idea of being able to buy a car of their own seemed a long way off, but it was a dream they both shared.

The journey travelling to the City was a stark reminder of how much rebuilding there was to be done. The shattered remains of what used to be bustling streets filled with families who had probably lived a lifetime there, now seemed half full – or was it half empty – with some families trying to continue to maintain what houses were still habitable.

As they neared the centre of the City, the office buildings loomed above them, each one probably teeming with life behind all those windows. It was almost reassuring that they, in their own world, were still continuing on their quest to get the country back on its feet again. It made Fred feel very small and insignificant in the scheme of things.

Bartholomew Brewer had been silent during their journey, leaving the two of them to chat.

The car came to a halt and they all got out. The buildings along this street were uniform and gave no indication of the importance of the countless companies negotiating and dealing in ways to get the country restored and rebuilt again after the last few devastating years. Fred was suddenly very aware that he was in the heart of a wonderful city.

They entered a building not far from the parked car.

The reception area was quite small, the red tiles on the floor bearing the signs of years of constant use. On the wall to the right of them Fred noticed a series of brass plates with Company names on them.

Bartholomew Brewer stepped forward.

"We are on the top floor in this building and so we should take the lift."

The black wrought iron guard doors which stood closed across the lift shaft rattled as a gust of air travelled invisibly towards the ground floor, bringing the lift cage with it. They all entered the lift and immediately the smell of oil on the lifting gears which were hauling them up to the top floor filled their nostrils.

The top floor seemed comprised of a long corridor with countless doors bearing company nameplates. They dutifully followed Bartholomew Brewer without speaking.

Turning to them he said, "These are our offices," and, opening the door, ushered them inside.

The room was sectioned off in three areas with typewriters clattering in one of them and the secretaries could just be seen over the partitions. One of them looked up from her typewriter and smiled, her flying fingers resting for seconds.

Walking forward, passed another section, Fred noticed a man sitting at a desk, his head bowed as he concentrated on a file in front of him. A neat stack of brown files could be seen on his desk held together with red tape or ribbon. That, thought Fred, was .how he remembered seeing offices like these in the films he and Mavis had seen at the pictures. The large black telephone on this desk could just be seen among other papers which were spilling out over the corner of the desk.

William Slater was making mental notes of the room as the shrill ring of a distant telephone was heard. As he scanned the room, the first thing he was aware of were the bookshelves, which appeared to surround him with countless volumes of books which seemed almost on parade. How many times, he wondered, were they taken down to be read for necessary precedents?

A further partitioned section held filing cabinets and another two desks. Bartholomew Brewer guided them into this area.

A neat and tidy desk was under the window with an orderly stack of papers on it and a shallow wooden box marked, 'Post.'

He stood behind the desk and pointed to the chairs near the desk.

"Please take a seat while I get the file out which we have on this case."

Both men drew the chairs nearer the desk and sat down.

While the solicitor was getting the file out, William Slater leaned over to Fred and said, "I don't think I could work in these cramped conditions. It's too claustrophobic."

Fred smiled. He didn't know how to react. The only other office he had been in was William Slater's.

The silence was broken when the sudden shrill telephone bell rang out in the adjoining area and the man who had been pondering the paperwork there, started speaking to the faceless voice down the line.

Turning around, Bartholomew Brewer placed a full file of papers onto the blotter on his desk. The printed name on the file could clearly be seen as Stanley Bartholomew Newton. It was only then that both men suddenly realized the name 'Bartholomew' had been running through this whole tale of mystery from the start.

Sitting down, the file was opened up and the papers spread out. Leaning forward and looking directly at both men, he pouted and placed one hand on top of the other.

"I have brought you here today to explain what the death of Stanley Newton involves.

"As you both knew the man, or thought you knew him, I have to tell you that he was, in fact, a cousin of mine. The name 'Bartholomew' runs through our family and has done so for several generations." With barely a pause, he continued, "The family owned a very large and impressive house on the outskirts of Wanstead, which is now part of a London Borough but was, at one time, many years ago, in an area of parkland. On the death of our grandparents the house was sold and the many and valuable contents were distributed among direct family members. The considerable sum of money received on the sale of the property was shared by some family members, one of which was Stanley

Newton. His share was invested in property and, at his request, many of the terraced houses in Angel Street and some of the neighbouring streets were purchased. He is, in fact, landlord to many of the people he lived amongst, but we were sworn to secrecy about that."

Both men sat silently, listening to all of this.

"When we visited his home in Angel Street I recognized many items remembered from my childhood when visiting the big house in Wanstead. That is why I was silent about what we found, because it was quite an emotional reunion for me."

Fred was deep in thought and now realized why Bartholomew Brewer had shown no surprise.

William Slater had often wondered why a firm of solicitors should be involved in Stan's death and now he knew why.

Chapter 6

While the two of them were listening in silence to the amazing facts being divulged as a result of Stan's death, the atmosphere at the meeting was one of secrets being explained. Luckily, both William Slater and Fred were level headed and, in their own minds, without speaking of their thoughts, they realized that no one could be sure of people they knew and what their backgrounds may be. In their neck of the woods you took people at face value unless they stepped over the line.

Observing the expression on the men's faces, Bartholomew Brewer realized that all this unexpected information was coming as a shock to both of them.

Pausing and, sitting back in his chair, he said, "Perhaps a cup of tea is called for. We need a short break before I continue."

Adjusting his position on the chair, William Slater said, "Before you continue, how much more is there to be said?"

Bartholomew Brewer rose from his seat and said, "The rest of the details I can tell you will be of great interest and they are details you can pass on to the community."

He left the two of them looking at each other, but speechless in their reaction.

The telephone on his desk sprung into life. The closeness of it made the demanding sound for attention seem urgent.

Bartholomew Brewer swiftly came around the wooden partition in a well practised move. Putting the receiver to his ear, he silently listened to the caller. With no visible reaction to the message he had received, he replaced the receiver and sat down.

With the clatter of cups on saucers, two of the secretaries arrived with the tea.

Fred's thoughts were that a stiff drink would have been more appropriate on this occasion.

Settling back into a comfy position, Bartholomew Brewer began the second phase of the instructions left by Stan.

"The generosity of Mr Newton seems to know no bounds. In his instructions, should anything happen to him which resulted in his death, he has made provision for all the properties which make up his estate to be repaired and renovated to a reasonable standard. Further, no increase in the rents should come into force until five years following his death."

Suddenly there was silence. The clatter of the typewriters seemed to have stopped. No intruding telephone bells were ringing. Not even the distant echo of a door closing could be heard. They seemed to be on an island with no communication. Fred and William Slater were lost for words.

Looking at his watch, Bartholomew Brewer shuffled some of the papers about.

"The contents of Mr Newton's home will be given to various members of his remaining family. The wish is that they stay amongst relatives. Those silhouettes found in his bedroom are a particular favourite of mine."

Fred remembered how he had paused for ages to look at them when they were at Stan's.

"The house will then be rented out and Mr Talbot you will be, as usual, required to collect rent on it each week in the usual way. My company will find a suitable tenant and we will let you know about that." He paused. "Do either of you have any questions?"

They were both silent, suddenly Fred remembered that Mavis had dispatched him with the explicit instructions to find out if they could move into the house once it had been emptied.

"There is one question. Once the property has been cleared and is ready for a new tenant, would it be possible for me and the wife to take up the tenancy?"

He thought, if you don't ask, you don't get.

Immediately Bartholomew Brewer responded. "I wasn't expecting that sort of question, but I will certainly enquire for you."

With the meeting over, they all stood up.

"I will leave you to let the tenants on your book know what the situation is regarding their homes. You will, in the near future, be asked to accompany this firm's choice of local builder to each home to ascertain what remedial works need to be carried out."

With the meeting over, they all left the office and headed for the car. The journey back was made in dumbstruck silence.

Back in Angel Street, there almost seemed to be a party atmosphere building up.

Liz called in at the Salvation Army Hall and had chosen a table she thought would fit into her front room once the furniture had been either shoved to one side or taken out. Vi, Madge and Ethel had agreed between themselves that there would be sandwiches made up with a couple of ounces of ham from Vi, three ounces of cheese which Madge had saved over the last couple of weeks and Ethel would provide the bread, now off ration, and some margarine. Joan kept chickens in the small garden behind the shop and so she could let them have a couple of eggs for cakes. Boss-eyed Ben grew rhubarb in his back garden and that, with a bag of broken biscuits from Churchy, bought in Mare Street market, would do nicely to make a rhubarb crumble.

Fred's wife Mavis had been invited to the 'do' and she said that she would contribute what sugar she could from her rationed eight ounces that week. Tea was going to be provided by Dave Taylor, the local bobby, because he wasn't married and so, with the allocated two ounces he was entitled to, there was no wife to keep brewing cups of it.

The landlord at The Red Lion had told Fred that he would contribute a bottle of sherry to toast Stan on the day.

This was all coming together nicely.

With all the arrangements in full swing, Fred decided that he would wait until after the funeral on Friday to let them all know the outcome of the mystery meeting he had attended at the solicitor's. It would be a treat to give them all the good news.

Because Stan was to be buried at the City of London Cemetery with the remaining members of his family attending, Reverend Luke would not, of course, be asked to officiate.

Strangely, at this point in time, no one had thought to seek out Reverend Luke to let him know about all the arrangements. It had been taken for granted that Churchy had, with her walking stick for support, been over to the church house to update him on the situation. Nothing could be further from the truth.

Thursday, the day before the funeral, Liz made her way along Angel Street hoping, for once, no one would stop her for a chat. She had still not got over what she had seen at the church house. She knew Churchy had not been over to the church at all. She'd used her broken ankle as an excuse.

Her luck was out. Vi came shuffling along the street waving at her.

Oh, no, thought Liz, I can't be doing with this now. 'Ere, Liz. There's a note on the board outside the church. 'Ave yer seen it?"

With a sigh, Liz thought, I'm about ter be told what it says, I expect.

Coming to an abrupt halt, her face red with the effort of walking, Vi puffed her cheeks out.

"It says Reverend Luke 'as been called away unexpectedly. That's a bit strange. It's a good job 'e wasn't going ter see poor old Stan orf."

Pausing for a few seconds, she stuck her hand into her blouse to adjust a strap or something.

"I was over there the other night when Churchy got carted orf. Come ter think of it, I didn't see 'im then, either."

Looking at her, Liz said, "I'm on me way ter see Churchy and so I'll ask 'er if she knows where 'e's gorn."

They parted company, Vi continuing her struggle on the way to Joan's at the corner shop; Liz, thankfully, giving nothing away. She continued on to Churchy's house to pass on the news that Reverend Luke, in her view, had done a runner.

This Friday morning was going to be one to remember. The whole street seemed to be making their way to the City of London Cemetery to say their goodbyes to Stan.

Everyone had found something black to wear and the sombre occasion brought tears to many of the residents of Angel Street, especially Ethel. She still felt guilty for causing the accident and always would.

90

The presence of Stan's immediate family at the cemetery, including Bartholomew Brewer, gave the occasion a sense of businesslike formality.

Ethel looked down at the ground. The gravel path which ran through the cemetery was well trodden by the families who had delivered their loved ones here. She couldn't bear to be anywhere near the group standing around the coffin. Instead she raised her tear-stained face and looked across at the horizon of bunched flowers and wreaths which seemed to meet the sky. Such beauty in solemn silence had to be seen. Why, she thought, does all this beauty have to be wasted? Stan would never see it.

After acknowledging the members of Stan's family, the group of friends and acquaintances made their way back to where they felt they belonged – Angel Street.

Liz's front room looked a treat. The room had been decorated with bunting by Madge, who felt that Stan's passing should be thought of as starting a new chapter in his life rather than a tragedy. Not everyone agreed. To Churchy the afterlife didn't exist.

With everyone arriving back from the cemetery, the whole street seemed to be ready to shake off the sadness of the occasion.

With the September evening turning into a golden sunset, Fred decided now was the time to tell everyone about Stan's background and his subsequent generosity.

"That can't be right. Surely he would have said something."

Ethel looked at Bill. She couldn't believe her ears. Why was he so ordinary when really he was posh?

Vi and Madge immediately started talking about what improvements they were going to ask for and one of them was going to be a decent scullery. The old butler sink in

Madge's was cracked and leaked. All the time she was adding other repairs that were needed, to the ceiling in her bedroom and the guttering at the back. They were both nodding every time something else was thought of.

Bill went over to Fred Talbot.

"What's the inside of Stan's 'ouse like, then? Does it need doing up? I could be able ter 'elp out there if me boss agreed. Nice little earner that would be and on me doorstep."

Fred Talbot put his drink down on the window ledge and leaned towards Bill so that their conversation couldn't be overheard.

"I tell you, I was more than surprised at the contents in there. It's a good job he kept quiet about it or it would all have been lifted by some thieving bugger."

Joan had managed to leave the shop and had popped in. With a quick glance around the room she saw Churchy sitting by the table, her walking stick propped up against her chair.

"Ow yer doing then? Are yer on the mend?"

Churchy was just about to take a bite out of a sandwich when Joan had appeared.

"This is a bit of all right. It's a shame it takes a funeral ter get us all tergether. Are yer still feeding that cat?"

Joan managed to squeeze herself next to Churchy, although there wasn't room to sit down.

Looking around the room, she said, "Where's that vicar bloke? I 'aven't seen 'im yet. 'E's missing out on a free tea. 'As he got the 'ump because 'e wasn't asked ter do the service?"

Churchy didn't answer.

Liz came over and started rearranging some of the food on the table. Turning to Joan she said, "Well, that's the free of 'em. What with Ethel's shoulder, Stan's passing and

Churchy's ankle, we can relax a bit now. They say things 'appen in frees."

Joan was still curious about the missing vicar.

"Do yer know why the reverend 'asn't shown up? It's a bit unusual, that is."

Liz looked at Churchy, who seemed to be almost cowering in her seat.

"I fink 'e left a note saying 'e was needed somewhere else."

Somewhere like 'ell and damnation, Churchy thought.

With people coming and going all the time, it was difficult to pin anyone down for a chat.

Fred saw the landlord of The Red Lion come into the room. He wasn't expecting him to show up. The pub had arranged for a wreath to be sent to the funeral people and it had taken its place with the other flowers around the burial plot.

Fred raised his arm in the air and the landlord saw it. Making his way across the room, the landlord was smiling and being greeted by some of the men who sometimes used The Red Lion.

"I came on the off-chance of seeing Rose. Is she here?"

Churchy, hearing him mention Rose, struggled to her feet and grabbed his arm.

"Did I 'ear you mention Rose?"

He looked quite surprised at the way she had grabbed his arm. He didn't know who she was.

Fred seeing this, moved closer.

"Churchy is the woman who looks after the church and is friendly with the Reverend Luke's housekeeper."

Of course, Fred had no idea of what had gone on at the church house. He had only just found out that Rose was the housekeeper there.

The landlord laughed out loud and several of the people in the room looked at him.

"Housekeeper! Is that what they call it now? She certainly 'elped run a very popular 'ouse in Soho."

Fred looked puzzled.

"What are you talking about?"

Liz was listening to all this and took hold of Churchy's arm. She wouldn't budge.

"I'm going nowhere until I get some answers."

With everyone else locked into their own conversations, it was lucky that Churchy was in a corner of the room. Liz gave her a look that would have frozen water and was determined that Churchy was not going to get the opportunity to wreck this get-together with one of her set tos.

Looking at the landlord, she then raised her eyes to the ceiling and then at Churchy, as though she was telling him that she was a bit funny.

He got the silent message.

Breaking away from Churchy, he edged his body towards the door. As he went, he called out to one of the men he recognized and was thankful that he was there.

Churchy slumped back down on her chair.

Fred was still there, looking a bit bemused. There were people milling about outside and, seeing Mavis chatting on the pavement to Vi, he took the opportunity to make his getaway.

Liz was beside herself with anger.

"I thought we decided we were going ter keep the reverend thing a secret. What do yer think yer doing? No good will come of it if yer let the cat out of the bag."

Churchy pursed her lips and knew Liz was right. If Reverend Luke had gone and taken that brazen hussy with him, at least her last memory of him would fade in time.

Outside, Boss-eyed Ben and P.C. Dave Taylor were locked in conversation.

"I knew that girl Rose before she teamed up with the Rev, yer know. She 'ad quite a reputation, that one. Did yer know that she was old Flo's daughter? I remember 'er when she was a nipper. Flo used ter clean in The Bell and Rose used ter get friendly with a lot of the blokes in there, even when she was only just out of school."

P.C. Dave Taylor was a good listener. It was part of his job.

"I 'ear the Rev and Rose 'ave gorn missing. Do yer think there's anything in that story? Maybe I should check the silver in the church," he said with a smile.

"No," said Boss-eyed Ben. "The only thing that will be missing will be 'er tricks of the trade, which pleased everyone."

They both stood there laughing.

Fred decided now was the time to raise a glass of sherry to Stan's memory and called everyone to order.

With no appropriate glasses about, the sherry was dispensed into anything there was to hand. A cheer went up and everyone present took a moment to dwell on their own recollection of Stan.

The evening was coming to a close and people were gradually dispersing.

Bartholomew Brewer had attended a tea at a local hotel with the rest of the family. They had politely declined the offer to come to Angel Street, saying they wanted to get talks under way about clearing out Stan's house and distributing the contents.

When Fred had been told about this arrangement he immediately thought it was business as usual, even on an occasion like this.

P.C. Dave Taylor came over to Fred.

"I gave the keys of Stan's place ter that solicitor feller. Do yer know when they'll be clearing the place out? I think I ought ter be there as all the stuff in there, I 'ear, is not yer normal old contents."

Fred looked alarmed.

"Where did you hear that? I was very careful not to let on about what we found in there. I haven't told a soul."

The bobby tapped the side of his nose.

"Yer can't keep anything secret around 'ere. Yer should know that."

He continued on with the rumours he had heard.

"Let's face it, unless they take the stuff out under cover of darkness, everyone in the street will be watching."

"Yeh, I suppose so," said Fred. "Me and Mavis wouldn't mind being able to move in there. She's been on at me for ages to find us another place. I have mentioned it to the solicitors and we'll just have to wait and see."

"Now that surprises me," said the bobby. "I did 'ear that the family 'ave already got someone lined up fer it. It's one of their old aunts, so I 'eard. She's a clairvoyant and felt it would suit 'er because she also uses a Ouija board and so perhaps she's hoping to 'ave a word with 'im."

He stood there chuckling while Fred looked glum.

Chapter 7

It was now a week since the notice appeared on the board outside the church. People wanted to know what was going on, even the non church goers.

Churchy was being asked awkward questions and she didn't know how to answer them. She hadn't been into the church since that Saturday night and the huge wooden doors remained tightly shut. She knew that, once she had access again, it would be a sorry sight in there, with the brass needing cleaning and the flowers would all be wilting or dead.

The first indication something was up was when a car arrived with a load of boxes in the back of it. Suddenly there was a lot of activity at the back of the church house and although it was early, eight o'clock, the street was buzzing into life. They had had two Sundays with the church closed. Surely they would soon be seeing someone arriving to answer their questions.

Monday morning started with the usual chaos at No. 5 Angel Street. Freda and Harry were trying to get their two eldest boys to get out of bed because, if they wanted something to eat before they made their way to school, they would only get a breakfast if they were in the kitchen in the next ten minutes.

Tony, who had just recovered from a broken arm, had spent most of his eleven years getting into physical scrapes and was finding his luck was still holding, even after his latest escapade. He was a climber. Walls, fences, trees. You name it and he had tried to scale it. His circle of friends knew he was the dare devil and together they always found something in their neighbourhood to investigate, to see if they could find anything worth retrieving. Harry, his father, was an ambulance driver and, on more than one occasion, had been called out when a child had been injured and, each time, he had wondered if it was going to be Tony he would find. So far in his eleven years he had sustained a blow to the head which had needed stitches, a couple of broken toes when the wheel of the winkle man's cart had run over his foot and a cut lip when he was in a fight with one of his schoolmates, which livened up the playground games on that Friday afternoon. The latest accident resulting in a broken arm had occurred when he decided to clamber over the remains of a bombed out house only a couple of streets away. He was convinced he could find something in there worth retrieving while being urged on by his friends.

Nine-year-old John was always the messenger. He was the son who was part of the gang but he held back a bit and observed. His school reports had indicated that he was a thinker and very bright. Freda and Harry hoped that when he took the eleven plus exam which weeded out the clever kids, that he would pass it and go on to better things.

Little Tom was only four and came as a bit of a surprise to them.

Shouting up the stairs, Freda's voice had now taken on a sergeant major tone and this, the boys recognized as trouble.

"We're coming. We're coming."

The noise of them coming down the stairs, which only had a thin carpet runner on them, echoed into the small kitchen. They both came crashing into the room, shirts hanging outside their short trousers, the knees on both of them bearing the scars of grazes and healed cuts from the past. They both wore school jumpers but, needless to say, there had been many occasions when repairs had been called for.

The kitchen was small and now crowded. With cut bread on the table, a half empty jar of jam, an open tin of condensed milk and mugs of tea, both boys dived in, spreading some of the condensed milk over the bread and with broad grins, they munched as fast as they could, still standing, drinking the tea which was already poured.

Freda just stared at them.

"You'd better down that lot quick or there will be trouble if you both get to school late again."

Harry was trying to look annoyed at the pair of them but the whole scene reminded him of when he used to get into trouble about being late. One thing though that they didn't try, was ducking out of classes altogether. His poor old mum had a hell of a time with him and his brother for that.

He felt a bit sorry for Tony because he had been born at the end of September, which meant he had to wait until after Christmas before he could move on to the secondary school. Really, he was ready to join the older children now. Perhaps that would calm him down a bit and stop him constantly getting into trouble.

"I'm off now, luv."

He put his uniform jacket on and slung the first aid bag over his shoulder. It was only a ten minute walk to the ambulance station, which gave him a chance to catch up with some of his neighbours along the way.

With the boys finally gone and Harry on his way, Freda looked across the kitchen to where little Tom was playing. Nothing seemed to bother him.

Clearing the table of the breakfast wreckage, she looked at him.

"We've got a busy day, Tom, and so I'd better get the boiler on for all that wash that needs doing."

He looked up from the battered cars he was playing with.

A tap on the already open front door brought Liz down the passage and into the kitchen. Her large frame, complete with patterned wraparound apron, seemed to fill the kitchen doorway.

"I've just got the boiler on fer me wash and thought I'd pop in ter see yer. Last night I was awake fer ages making a list of the repairs me place needs, thanks ter Stan's generosity."

Freda smiled but hid the fact she really didn't want this right now. It would mess up her morning.

Pulling a chair out from the table, Liz smiled at little Tom and plonked herself down.

"The other thing I was keen ter let yer know was that those 'ouses round the corner, yer know the ones that are almost completely gorn, are being demolished in the next few months. I 'eard the council said they were too dangerous ter leave standing."

Freda knew them well because that site had been the subject of more than one argument when Tony had been caught clambering amongst the rubble.

"That'll be a good thing. When I go past them on the way to the shops, the remains of a tattered curtain in one of the windows always seems to be flapping in the breeze like a distress flag. I used to know the people in some of them. I think they were all killed during that raid. It's almost as if their memory lingers on."

Liz had sat quietly while Freda was saying all this.

"That sounds like what Churchy would call deep thinking, that is."

For Liz to say that, thought Freda, she knew her view on the bombed houses would be passed on.

Standing up, Liz said, "Well, I've got ter go. I thought I'd just let yer know about the demolition. That'll be a few days we won't be able to put the wash out."

She saw herself out.

Joan from the corner shop was in Stan's back garden, feeding the cat. From the alleyway which ran along the side, P.C. Dave Taylor emerged.

"'Ello, Joan. I see yer still feeding the cat. 'E don't look bad on it."

Joan finished putting some food in the dish in the dilapidated shed.

"I'm only giving it scraps but it seems ter be surviving. I 'ope the next tenant takes care of it."

The bobby looked up at the back of the house.

"We've bin told at the station that there are a few lads on this patch doing a bit of breaking and entering. They will be looking fer stuff ter sell on quickly. Make sure the shop is secure when yer close. The cigarettes yer sell will be of interest ter them."

Joan interrupted him.

"It's the kids coming 'ome from school we 'ave trouble with. They come in as a group and while one of 'em buys sweets, the others slip stuff in their pockets. Them not getting any sweets money means we lose money."

The bobby leaned against the back wall.

"We're not troubled too much with kids stealing stuff. Over Hackney they're always rounding up the little tikes. They seem ter work in gangs. So far, they say, they avn't progressed ter stealing anything valuable. Mind you, there's not much they don't 'ear about and that might change things."

He was, of course, thinking about the contents of Stan's house.

Back at the station, P.C. Dave Taylor was going over the latest crime figures for their district. Some new names were added to the list. They were young men who'd been involved with housebreaking in the area near the local golf course. They were professional and quick. Jewellery was what they were after. The pawnbrokers in the area had all been alerted but, so far, none of the jewellery had turned up. They seemed to be getting away with it.

What he didn't know was that they were on the look-out for any young lad who was willing to take a chance to earn some pocket money and who could keep a secret.

At the end of a working day, The Angel was always a place to have a beer before going home. Bill was still working on one of the nearby houses and decided to drop in for a quick half. It would wash the dust from his throat after all that bricklaying.

Most of the men in there at this time were old mates and the few minutes they spent there before going home was just enough to catch up with anything that might be happening locally.

This pub had been so central to the residents of this street. It was a meeting place.

A lot of news had been spread from this pub. When they heard the unbelievable news that the king was going to abdicate, they heard it from here first. When war was declared, the implications of that on the country were discussed for weeks. Only this year the Olympic Games had been held in London and they had all joined forces to get the residents of this street interested in the event by arranging for coach parties to take them to the stadium, all arranged through the men using this pub.

It was now a not so well kept secret that the astonishing contents of Stan's house would be cleared out this week.

Among the many workmen standing at the bar was a new face. Reg Green was from out of the immediate area and had decided to scout around for any money-making deals he might hear about.

Smartly dressed in a grey suit and fresh white shirt, he was noticed by the drinkers he was almost mingling with. With his head slightly bowed, his hair had the shine of Brylcream on it which made Bill smile. The only time he used such stuff was if Ethel tried to smarten him up for a family get-together. He appeared to be enjoying his beer while catching bits of the conversations of the rest of the men propping up the bar.

The chat was still about the get together after Stan's funeral. Inevitably, the word 'valuables' crept into it, although the men were careful to speak in low tones as a stranger was in the pub.

Harry from No. 5 was in there, as his stint of driving the ambulance for the day was over. The talk turned to kids and Harry was talking about the progress young John was making at school, much to the surprise of the men. They joked that if he was so bright, he couldn't be his. They all seemed to be enjoying their few minutes in the pub before heading home.

The landlord asked about Tony and what new scrapes he'd been in. They had all known Tony since he was born and the joke was that he should join the circus next time it came round. He could be their high wire act, or perhaps the one who got shot out of the cannon.

After a good laugh all round, the men began to disperse to go home.

Reg Green had lasted his beer out while all this chat was going on and, finally, put his glass down.

Looking at the landlord, he said, "I think I'll have a whisky before I go. Have you got a decent one?"

The landlord finished wiping along the bar and turned to take a bottle from the shelf behind him. Taking a glass from the back, he poured him a generous double from the Dimple Haig. Returning the bottle to the shelf, he turned to face the stranger.

"I 'aven't seen yer in 'ere before, 'ave I?"

Reg picked up the glass and savoured the smell of the whisky before he drank.

"You certainly know a good whisky."

Putting the glass down, he leaned on the bar.

"That Tony they were talking about sounds a bit of a handful. Reminded me of my brother. He was always the one who'd give my old mum the most trouble."

Smiling, he picked up his glass, finished his drink and settled up.

Leaving the pub, he thought, I bet that kid goes to the local school.

Ever since the funeral tea, when Fred Talbot had heard the Newton family already had someone in mind as a tenant for

104

Stan's house, he had been dreading telling Mavis. Luckily, she had not yet heard about it. He decided to pay a visit to the bank, where he could have a word with William Slater to see if he knew any more.

Arriving at the bank, he asked if the manager was available for a few minutes as he had a matter to raise with him about one of his deceased customers. There was no other way he could word it. Intrigued, William Slater came into the reception area, all smiles, quite pleased to see him.

Stepping forward, he extended his hand to greet Fred.

"What can I do for you?"

Fred wanted to be taken into his office but it would seem that the manager was quite happy to discuss Fred's visit where they were.

"The new tenant of Stan Newton's house is, I believe, an aunt of his and I wondered if that was right? I had hoped to be able to rent the place myself."

William Slater nodded.

"I've only just received a phone call from the solicitors this morning to say the house will be cleared out tomorrow. Once that has been done, the new tenant is due to move in at the weekend."

"Oh, so it is true. Will I be collecting rent from the new tenant or, as it's a family member, will she be living there rent free?"

William Slater looked at his watch.

"I'll have to let you know about that."

The men then shook hands and parted company.

Wednesday morning was going to be very interesting as far as Liz was concerned. Standing behind the net curtain in her front room, she looked up and down the street for any sign of a removal van. As soon as she saw a large van with the name of a local removal firm on the side of it, she wanted to make sure she was about when they started moving the things out from Stan's because she still wasn't sure what had been found in there. Another reason she wanted to be about was to ask if anyone was needed to clean the place through before the next tenant arrived. By offering ter do that, she thought, I might be able ter 'ave a gander at what all the secrecy was about.

Making herself look respectable, she took her turban off and her hair pins out. She ran a brush through her hair. It was showing quite a bit of grey now but she still liked to keep it tidy. The lisle stockings she had put on this morning were rolled down to her ankles. She pulled them up and fastened them to her suspenders.

She pulled the front door almost closed and padded along the street to where the van was parked. She hadn't bothered to take her battered slippers off because they were the most comfortable thing to wear as they didn't give her bunions too much trouble.

Before she had a chance to speak to the men unloading loads of blankets and sacks from the back of the van to wrap things in, she looked behind her and saw a young woman who appeared to be looking at door numbers. She had come to a stop at Churchy's door.

Doing a quick turn around, she made her way back to her place.

"Can I 'elp yer?"

The woman looked to be about thirty-ish. She was slim and had short brown hair which framed her suntanned face. She was new to this street where everyone was known. It was a warm day and she had a simple cotton frock on, which neatly fell over her young figure. The yellow and white flowers on it made her seem chaste and pure. She had a chain around her neck with a crucifix on it which caught the sunlight.

With a big smile, she genuinely seemed pleased to have found someone to talk to.

"I'm looking for someone everyone calls Churchy. My name is Christine."

"Well dear, I'm Liz and I can 'elp yer there. Churchy is me mate and she lives 'ere, where yer've stopped. She's 'ad a bit of an accident and so she won't be about much terday. If yer come in with me I can introduce yer."

Pushing the already open front door, Liz called out to Churchy that she had a visitor.

The kettle was on the stove and had just come to the boil. Looking at Liz coming into the kitchen with a stranger, Churchy hobbled over to the table and leaned her walking stick against a chair.

"Well, yer timed that right. I was just about ter 'ave a cuppa. I 'aven't 'ad me breakfast yet. I 'ad such a sleepless night with me ankle, that I just lay there fer longer than I usually do and now I'm all behind."

Liz stepped forward.

"I think yer 'ad better sit down and I will do yer a bit of breakfast and pour the tea.

Looking at the young lady, who was by now wondering what to do, she pulled out another chair and pointed to it for her to sit down.

Feeling a bit awkward, she blurted out, "My name is Christine and I have come to move into the church house with Reverend Michael. I was asked to find someone called Churchy who apparently does the polishing and cleaning in the church."

She stopped speaking and suddenly the room was quiet.

"Reverend Michael, yer say? We 'ad a Reverend Michael fer years, until 'e was killed by falling masonry."

Churchy leaned on the table and looked directly into the face of the young woman.

"I do the flowers as well, in the church."

Liz turned and put the now filled teapot squarely in the centre of the table. Churchy had a nice set of cups and saucers on her little dresser and Liz took three down.

"Before I pour the tea out, what do yer want me ter get yer ter eat?"

Churchy just waved her hand in the air and pursed her lips. She didn't feel like eating and wanted to know more about this Christine.

"Yer say yer moving inter the church 'ouse with a new vicar. Where is 'e, then?" Her tone seemed quite aggressive and it surprised both Christine and Liz. "We 'ad a bit of trouble with the last one and so I want ter know a bit about the pair of yer."

Liz leaned over the table, giving Churchy a steely stare, and poured the tea out.

Christine sat upright on her chair and took a deep breath.

"Reverend Michael has asked me to speak to you as we are, at the moment, still unpacking our things. He hopes to meet you later. Perhaps you both could come over to the church house this evening, when he will be able to introduce himself."

The mood in the room lightened just a little, but not much.

"Where are yer from?" Churchy was already getting impatient to find out more.

Christine took a sip of her tea. She smiled.

"We've been travelling abroad, but have now been asked to settle at St John's."

She picked her cup up and took another sip.

"Can I let the reverend know you will come? He has said nine o'clock would be a good time."

Churchy was fiddling with the spoon in the sugar bowl.

Liz couldn't stand much more of this.

"Yes, tell 'im we will both be there. Is anyone else going?"

"I'm glad you asked that because the reverend thought it might be a good idea if your local bobby could come as well. He likes to meet people who can tell him about the community. The trouble is, of course, I don't know who that is."

"Don't yer worry about that," said Liz. "'Is name is Dave Taylor and I will get in touch with 'im."

With the arrangements now settled, Christine wished Churchy better and made her way back to the church house.

Damn, thought Liz when she looked at the clock over Churchy's fireplace, I've missed a lot of the clearing out of Stan's.

Looking at Churchy, she said, "I've gotta go. I'll see yer tonight."

She hastily left Churchy still sitting at the kitchen table with a lot of questions to be answered.

Shuffling along the road, she was aware of a lot of curtains twitching and moving. Were they watching the removal men or her, as she had been seen with a stranger?

I'd better get round ter the cop shop, she thought, ter see if Dave is there. She was a woman on a mission.

Reg Green had returned to base as he called it. Base, being a flat over a hairdressing salon in Woodford High Street, was only a temporary home. He had better things in mind. His friend, Dick, was the one with the knowhow and he considered himself the brains. They had both had a few narrow escapes with the police but had, so far, managed to escape any formal questioning about local incidents. Between them they had made a living on a small scale when they knew a property would be without its owners. The few things they had got away with had been sold, with no questions asked, on the other side of the Thames.

They now had a new target to concentrate on. There was a big house over Epping way and they had heard it was going to be closed up for a couple of months while the owners took a holiday.

The local police knew about the owners going away and it had been arranged that a patrol car would go past it every evening to check that the iron gates leading to the driveway were still locked and that there were no lights showing from inside. Their only problem was getting in. It would have to be around the back, probably through a small kitchen window.

Reg had told Dick what he had heard about the kid who could handle himself in a situation which needed a bit of scrambling about. Perhaps if they offered him some pocket money after school one afternoon, he could get into the house for them and then let them in. They could, after they'd found anything worth taking, then deliver him back to near his street, with his reward, and he could then walk home just a couple of hours later than normal. His mother would probably think he was playing out.

It would be best to do the raid in daylight with no police patrol about until the evening.

If they persuaded the kid to help them out, it could all be over and done with during an afternoon. They would make up some story to convince the kid it was all legit.

Chapter 8

Liz had managed to get in touch with Dave Taylor and had arranged with him that she and Churchy would meet him at the church house at 9.

Churchy, in her impatience, was almost making a list of questions she wanted to ask. She was not going to be fobbed off with just any old answers. She was almost on a collision course with the new Reverend Michael and this Christine woman even before the meeting.

P.C. Dave Taylor came strutting along the street just before 9. Liz hurried along to catch up with him.

Panting to keep up with his marching walk, Liz said, "I 'ope this new vicar can offer us a decent cup of tea. Yer can tell a lot by the strength of the tea offered by them people. Them, and the Salvation Army, 'ave 'ad a lifetime of dishing enough of it out. They should 'ave got it right by now."

P.C. Dave Taylor chuckled as he strode the few more paces to reach Churchy's place.

"I thought I'd come along a bit early in case Churchy wanted assistance with 'er walking. The ankle must 'ave slowed 'er down a bit."

"Well, that's real thoughtful of yer, Dave."

Pushing the front door open and going in, they found Churchy with her best frock on and wearing a small hat.

Liz was a bit taken aback.

"I didn't know we 'ad ter get dressed up."

Churchy smoothed her dress down and grabbed her walking stick.

"I wanted ter let 'im know I'm not just the cleaning woman but someone what can put on a good show fer meself."

P.C. Dave Taylor smiled and said, "That's right, luv, yer should start off the way yer want ter go on."

With that said, the three of them made their way over the road to the church house.

The familiar pathway leading up to the front door still held mixed memories for Churchy. Would anything ever be the same again since Reverend Michael had died? It seemed strange that they had been sent another Reverend Michael.

Perhaps that was a good omen.

The three of them reached the front door but didn't have to knock because Christine appeared in the doorway, all smiles. She certainly was a welcoming sight and Liz was quite surprised that she already liked the young woman, even though she didn't really know her.

Stepping forward and looking at Churchy, Christine said, "I remembered you had an injured ankle and didn't want to leave you waiting for me to answer the door and so I must confess that I have been looking out for you."

Liz thought, she is already one of us.

Glad to be the centre of attention, Churchy smiled and said, "That's really good of yer. Thanks a lot."

As they entered the hallway of the house, they all had mixed feelings. They could smell that some baking had been done. It was a friendly smell and seemed welcoming. Liz looked at P.C. Dave Taylor and smiled.

"It smells as though we're going ter be offered more than a cuppa."

He thought back to the last time he was in here. It was the night of the accident when Churchy fell down the stairs. He still didn't know why she had been upstairs. Still, that was history now, and the place certainly smelt a lot better. That night, there had been a sweet smell of incense or something in the air and there had been a stillness which he had sensed, even though the situation had called for the medics being needed and a lot of commotion and questions being asked.

As they were shown into the living room, Churchy could see some things had already changed. The only times she had to come in here before was to collect money for flowers or cleaning stuff. It was usually a dark room and always had a musty smell. The old desk was still under the window but now had a tidy look about it.

Now, the old net curtains had been taken down, and about time too, she thought, because the room was brighter and didn't seem quite so sinister. The dark leather settee which was usually in the middle of the room had been pushed against the wall and had a bright coloured cloth draped over it. A table and chairs had been brought in and there was a jug of flowers in the centre of it. As she silently scanned the room she noticed that some of the dreary old paintings had been taken down and replaced with bright pictures which seemed to be of strange flowers or, at least, flowers Churchy didn't recognize. Good, she thought, he obviously likes flowers. Perhaps that'll mean he'll get me to plant some in the church garden. In her mind, things were looking up.

Liz couldn't put her finger on it but there was something she couldn't get her head round. Perhaps all this change and the colour he was introducing into the place was a good thing. The war was over and things needed change, even the church. Maybe he was young.

Christine, eager to make them welcome, was fussing about, getting them to sit around the table. She wanted to get the tea tray in and offer them some refreshments, which included her home baked cakes.

"Reverend Michael will be down in a minute. He's trying to fix a dripping tap in the bathroom. We're not used to having a bathroom."

Oh, my Gord, thought Churchy, where 'ave they bin living? None of us is used ter 'aving a bathroom.

With her eyes darting around the room, she noticed several wooden ornaments had replaced the old china vases. She nudged Liz and looked over at them. Almost whispering, she said, "Funny old things ter 'ave on yer sideboard. I wonder what else 'as changed."

The telephone bell rang out, which gave them all a shock. It did, thankfully, break the silence.

Christine went over to answer it, smiled, and called up the stairs, "Reverend Michael, there's a phone call for you."

The sound of him coming down the stairs made them all look towards the doorway and the small table where the telephone was.

On seeing him, Churchy sat wide-eyed, Liz was speechless and P.C. Dave Taylor stood up.

The short conversation on the telephone ended and Reverend Michael came into the room. Walking over to them, his smile lighting up his face, quite literally, he offered his hand to P.C. Dave Taylor, then Churchy and finally Liz. His handshake was firm, he was tall and slim and his welcome was one of genuine pleasure that they had accepted his invitation. The expression on their faces made him smile even more broadly.

114

He pulled a chair up and sat down as Christine poured the tea and offered cakes. Not a word had been spoken. He broke the awkward silence.

"I expect I have come as a bit of a shock to you. A new vicar in any parish takes some time to get to know, but I hope you will all find me helpful to you and the other people who live in these streets. It has taken me a long time to reach you and I don't just mean my journey from the West Indies, where I have been a missionary for a number of years."

All Churchy's thoughts, at this moment in time, were that he was black. This was a first.

Liz was enjoying this little outing. There would be so much to tell everyone. She sat further back on the chair and finished the cake she had been eating.

P.C. Dave Taylor wanted to know more about him but didn't want to make it sound official. He would have to catch up with him on one of his patrols.

The next morning, having satisfied herself that the vicar seemed a nice enough bloke, Churchy sat at her kitchen table, smiling. He had told them that he and his helper, Christine, had spent the last four years on a mission in Jamaica where they had the job of teaching the children at the Mission School and helping with health matters. His flock had been widespread and so he had set up a small bible class in each of the outlying villages. This had meant his work had taken him into areas where disease was rife and, as a consequence, his own health had begun to suffer. The church elders had decided to relocate him back to London, which was where he had studied years earlier at theology college. Yes, she thought, he would do nicely.

Back at the flat, Reg was putting a plan together for the raid on the house he had found out about. Dick was not sure about using Tony but, with no other way they could gain entry into the place, it seemed the only option they had.

He wanted to see the boy first, just to get to speak to him in a casual way and find out whether he was as willing to help them out, without asking too many questions, as Reg thought he was.

They both decided that it would be good to hang about outside the school in the hope Tony wouldn't mind them stopping him for a chat. They would have to be very careful.

Reg decided to talk to him about the bomb sites and how the local kids spent time clambering over the wrecked houses. He would say how clever they were not to get too many scrapes when doing it.

Dick suggested they made a game up, where Tony had to see if he could get through a small window in a friend's house and then let them in through a back door so that they could play a trick on their friend. It would all be a bit of a laugh, if they could take something away with them to make it really funny.

Reg thought that idea might work. He was a bit surprised that Dick had thought of it.

They decided Monday would be a good day to try to speak to Tony and then, perhaps the next day, they could collect him from school. Hopefully, he would think it was all a bit of a lark and he would earn half a crown as a reward for helping them out. He would also get a ride in a car. Reg and Dick had pooled their resources and bought an Austin A40. It was a two door and suited them whenever they picked any girlfriends up. Also, as Tony wasn't very tall, he would have to sit up straight in the back to be able to see out of its windows. As he wouldn't know where the house was, he wouldn't be able to tell anyone where he had been taken.

If this works, thought Reg, we could do well out of this.

Over the weekend, Reg wanted to have a final look at the house in daylight to see if it would be easy to get around the back by climbing over a wall. Also, he wanted to get it straight in his mind where they would be able to park the car off the lane. He wanted somewhere a short distance from the house and somewhere in a small clearing but with bushes and trees shielding it.

Dick pointed out that they could find themselves short on petrol if they made an unnecessary trip. With petrol still rationed they would have to make sure they had enough to get them there and back. This bloody rationing was doing their little schemes no good at all. With everyone being urged to pull together and get the country back on its feet, they were being stopped in their tracks at trying to make ends meet. What items they managed to get their hands on were probably surplus to requirements to the sort of people they had burgled. What were a few bits of jewellery and silver to them? The finds had mostly been in cupboards or drawers and weren't what Reg had called 'essentials'.

It was finally decided that they wouldn't make the trip out over the weekend but would concentrate on priming the kid on Monday.

Saturday morning and Freda and Harry were in their kitchen wondering what was wrong with John. He had been sick a couple of times in the night and had complained about his stomach hurting.

"He's only eaten the same stuff as us and so he can't be suffering with food poisoning."

Freda was trying to remember what they had all eaten.

"He keeps crying in pain and that's not like him."

Harry was thinking that he would see how it went for another hour and then he should get round to old Dr Harris. Perhaps he could work out what was wrong.

He was his usual calm self and was trying to get Freda not to worry but just to wait and see for a bit longer.

Liz was having a good weekend. With Churchy still hobbling about with her walking stick, it was, she thought, up to her to let everyone know about Reverend Michael and Christine.

The church had been opened up. She had done Churchy a favour by polishing the brass candlesticks and dusted about a bit. The one thing she wasn't going to get involved with was flower arranging.

There will be a few new faces in there on Sunday, she thought. It's going to be curiosity that will bring them in.

She made her way over to Joan at the shop. The place smelt terrible. She had been cooking beetroot which Boss-eyed Ben had given her from his garden.

"Christ almighty, Joan, it smells as though someone 'as died in 'ere. I might come back later when it's cleared a bit."

Rushing out from behind the little counter, Joan almost sprang at Liz.

"I 'ear the new vicar is black, then. Where's 'e from?"

Liz stood in the open doorway.

"'E's bin in the West Indies. 'E was a missionary out there but 'e got sick. The church people needed ter get us someone fer our church and so they sent 'im 'ere. I shook 'ands with 'im."

Joan leaned against the door.

"I wonder what 'e eats. I don't 'ave anything from them parts."

Taking a deep breath and looking up to the sky, Liz couldn't believe the ignorance of Joan.

"What do yer mean? 'E eats the same as us. Don't be so bloody daft. 'E's an educated man. Went ter college and all that."

Joan seemed a bit put out.

"I was only asking."

Liz decided it was time to go.

"I'll see yer around. I've got ter get on."

She sauntered away, smiling.

John's yells were getting louder.

That's it, thought Harry.

Looking over at Freda, he said, "I'll pop round to Dr Harris to see if he can come and see him. I won't be long."

He wasn't sure, but he had seen someone in the back of his ambulance who was suffering from appendicitis and all the signs were there with John. If that was what the trouble was, he would need an ambulance but he was off duty. The whole time he was walking round to the surgery, he was trying to remember who was on the rota for today.

Luckily, Dr Harris was at the surgery. After a short explanation for his visit, Dr Harris picked up his old battered leather bag and the two of them made their way back to No. 5.

After a brief check of John, it was decided that he was suffering from appendicitis and that he would have to get to hospital as soon as possible. If the boy had been in pain since the night before, there was a chance it could perforate.

Harry knew the implications of that.

It was decided that they wouldn't ask the new vicar to phone for an ambulance but Harry would nip along to The Bell and use theirs.

Tony and little Tom were agog with excitement. It looked as though they were going to get a ride in an ambulance when John got taken away.

That thought was short lived.

With Freda putting some pyjamas and things into a bag for John, Harry had gone along to Madge to ask her to give little Tom and Tony some tea while he and Freda went to the hospital. They would be back as soon as possible. Like the good neighbour she was and having had three sons of her own, she didn't hesitate.

It wasn't long before the ambulance pulled up outside No. 5. As usual, on seeing an ambulance arrive, the street suddenly became a very busy place, with the usual passers by being outnumbered by concerned neighbours spilling onto the pavement and upstairs windows being opened to look out of for a better view.

It's not fair, thought Tony, I've missed out on a ride in an ambulance.

Harry knew the ambulance driver and, once John was settled in the back and he and Freda were on board, they speedily took off, the sound of the clanging bell deafening them.

Once at the hospital, it was confirmed that the appendix would have to come out. Freda had calmed down a bit now, knowing that John was in the right place.

The operation would need to be done straight away and they could stay until he had been brought back to his ward. There would be no more visiting then until Monday afternoon, because they wanted John to rest after the operation. Harry understood that but Freda didn't.

Sunday arrived and, without his brother around, Tony was getting bored. He was looking for a bit of excitement. He was beginning to feel left out. His mum was going to the hospital to see John tomorrow and his dad would be working. Madge was going to look after little Tom and all he had to look forward to was school.

As predicted, Monday was a rotten day at school because the lessons that day were boring. He felt thoroughly restless. To top it all, it was a day that, in all the goings on about John, his mum had forgotten to give him any money so that he could buy a slice of cake from the bakery on his way home. Tea was going to be a bit late this day because Freda wouldn't be back from the hospital until about five o'clock.

Reg and Dick were already at the school boundary. Reg knew what Tony looked like and was on the lookout for him. He would try to get him chatting in the hope he could find something the kid was interested in. Football maybe. He had seen him earlier, kicking a ball about with some friends.

Sure enough, Tony found himself chatting to them about football. They said they supported Arsenal.

The conversation continued on and Tony told them about his brother in hospital and that he had missed out on a ride in an ambulance.

Dick's mind was ticking over at quite a speed.

I wonder, he thought, if this kid is ready for our little job this afternoon? He had told them that he wasn't going home straight away.

When Tony went back to playing with a couple of his mates, Dick mentioned to Reg what he was thinking. If the kid was annoyed at missing out on an ambulance ride, he might be keen to get the chance of a ride in a car. Their Austin might impress him.

They needed to do the job in daylight and so why not spin him the story about playing a trick on a friend this afternoon? It could all be over and done with today. They could have him back by about six. They would have their loot and he would have some pocket money.

They both thought, why not?

As Tony decided he'd had enough of kicking a ball around, he left the playground.

Reg walked along the street with him, telling him about the car he and his friend had bought and also about the practical joke they wanted to play on their friend. He told him the shiny half-crown he had in his pocket could be his and asked if he could help them out. The bonus was that he'd get a ride in the Austin.

Tony was mesmerized with the thought of getting half a crown and a car ride. He could, they told him, be home by teatime.

All his friends had now dispersed and, as the three of them walked away from the school, his excitement was mounting.

Reg told him that he thought the window at the side of the house was just big enough for him to get through. As he was such a good climber, he should be able to manage it. Once inside, he wanted him to open the kitchen door so that they could get in and find something they could take. Their friend would think it was really funny.

Tony was hooked. This was a real adventure.

The car was parked not far away. As Tony got into the back of it, the smell of the leather seats and the look of the gleaming dashboard really excited his young mind.

When I tell John about this, he won't believe it, he thought.

As they sped along the street, Tony sat on the edge of the back seat, trying to take in as much as he could. They were passing houses he didn't recognize and they were travelling along lanes now bordered by trees. Finally, they came to a stop.

"Where are we, mister?"

Reg turned the engine off and opened the door. Once outside, he pulled his seat forward.

"This is where my friend lives. You have to get out here. I told you it wasn't far."

To Tony, it seemed as though they had been travelling for ages.

Dick got out and looked up and down the lane.

"Our friend's house is just along here." He pointed to a stone wall which had ivy growing over it, Tony noticed there were quite a lot of stinging nettles around the base of it. Those he didn't want to go anywhere near because he'd had a bad time in the past with them.

"We'll help you get into the garden and then all you've got to do is climb through the kitchen window."

Reg looked at his watch. It was quarter past four.

Reg guided Tony along the lane until they reached a part of the stone wall that was crumbling a bit. He had got an old blanket from the boot of the car and threw it across the wall.

"That should make it easier for you to get into the garden. If you go around the side of the house you will see the kitchen window. I'll follow you round."

Tony never questioned any of this, having swallowed the story hook, line and sinker.

Making his way across the lawn, he could see the kitchen window at the side of the house. Looking at Reg, he said, "Your friend must be very rich to live somewhere like this."

Reg smiled.

Chapter 9

The grass was wet from the overnight rain.

Tony hurried over to the side of the house. He couldn't believe this was someone's garden. It was so big! To his young mind this place was somewhere perhaps a film star lived. The adventure was getting more and more interesting. This was much better than going to Aunty Madge's for tea. Even his new found friends seemed to have a lot of money. They had a car, they both wore suits and the family he came from only wore suits at weddings and funerals and none of them had a car. Reg reminded him of his Uncle Dave, who had a dress shop in the high street. He always gave him and John a couple of bob when he came round to see his sister. He'd often heard his mum talking about him. She didn't like all the girlfriends he had and the money he seemed to waste on them.

Looking at the side of the house he said, "I can't reach that window. I'm not tall enough. You'll have to give me a leg up."

Reg looked around and, seeing a dustbin nearby, pulled it over and stood it under the window.

"If you stand on the lid you should be able to reach the window ledge easy. I know these kind of windows. If I hit the frame where the latch is, it will usually bounce open."

Tony stood back.

Sure enough, after a clenched fist hit the window frame, the latch on the other side of the glass jumped up. Reg pushed on the metal frame and it slowly opened up.

With a look of total surprise, Tony blurted out, "How did you do that?" He was now really impressed.

"Never you mind. All I want you to do is get up there and in and then unlock the kitchen door."

His voice didn't sound quite so friendly now.

Tony felt like he was one of the people he was always reading about in his comics. He thought of Gnasher and the Bash Street Kids in the *Beano*. They were always doing daring things.

Pumped up with excitement, he climbed onto the lid of the dustbin and leaned through the window. After a bit of a balancing act, he got one of his legs in and got a foot in the sink that was just below the window lodge. With a hand hanging onto the frame, he managed to lever himself through the window and landed on the draining board.

Reg was now standing with his head and shoulders in the window space.

"Good lad. Now get yourself over to the door and unlock it for me."

Tony, still high on his success and the thought of the half-crown he was going to get, jumped down and went over to the door. There was a lock in the centre of it and a slide lock at the top. Looking up at the top lock he said, "I'll have to stand on a chair to slide that lock over. It's like our one at home."

Looking around, he saw a stool in the corner of the room. Picking it up, he put it against the door and clambered onto it. The top lock was no problem, it slid along easily.

Getting down, he turned the handle on the other lock but the door remained closed.

Reg, watching all this, said, "Look for a key on the dresser over there," his voice now sounding impatient. He was keen not to break any windows or leave any damage. That was not his style. So far in their career, he and Dick had got away with some petty thefts without getting detected. The fence they used to sell the stuff to wasn't fussy about how they obtained their bounty. He knew the pair of them weren't violent and left no trace of their 'visits'. The police were only really interested in burglary if the victim got beaten up or injured in any way. Reg and Dick weren't the sharpest knives in the drawer, but at least they had the sense not to arouse suspicion by boasting about violence.

Tony could see a huge cupboard with lots of shelves which had plates stood up on it. He went over to it but couldn't find a key. Reg, now getting a bit anxious, called out to him to look in the drawers for one.

Tony was getting flustered now but did as he was told. Sure enough, a set of keys was in there. Finally, he managed to get the right one, which unlocked the door.

Reg was in straight away. Dick had stayed with the parked car but was now outside the house. He was carrying a large bag.

Tony didn't know what to do next.

Dick didn't want Tony to see them at work.

"Why don't you wait outside for us? We won't be long."

Immediately both Reg and Dick disappeared and could be heard walking from room to room. One of them had obviously gone upstairs because the ceiling was creaking. They must know their friend's house well, Tony thought, because they seem to know their way around.

He went into the garden. Going further around the back of the house, he could see a pond. As he got nearer it he could see some large fish. He stood watching them for some minutes. They were smashing and nothing like the fish he had seen in the local pond.

The silence was soon broken as Reg and Dick came into the garden.

"Come on, Tony, it's time we got going."

They hadn't been long. All three of them hurried back to the car. The bag, with its contents, was placed carefully in the boot. Almost pushing Tony into the back,, they took off slowly at first but then gathered speed as they left the lane.

Before leaving the house, they had closed the window and shut the door, leaving no indication they had ever been in the house. There was nothing to tie them to this robbery.

Dick was driving this time. As they sped along the country lanes, Tony was rocking about in the back.

"We'll soon have you home. You did very well for us today. Our friend will be very surprised."

Reg looked at his watch. It was half past five. Later than they had hoped for.

He turned around and held out the half a crown.

"You deserve this." Handing it over his shoulder to Tony, he could sense the boy's excitement.

Just as they thought things had gone well, the car started spluttering and slowing down. It finally came to a halt. Dick had managed to coast for a while and got it to the side of the road. The petrol gauge showed almost empty.

"Bugger," shouted Dick. "We're still about two miles from home."

Tony, sitting in the back, realized something was wrong.

"What's the matter, mister?"

After a short low voiced discussion which bordered on an argument, it was decided that Reg would try to find a petrol station where he could buy a can of petrol to bring back to the car. That would, at least, get them back to drop

Tony off. They had seen a small garage with a couple of pumps about a mile down the road from where they had been. Dick would stay in the car with Tony.

This was going to be a nuisance. He had lined up a busty bird he had met in one of the pubs they used and she was ready for it. If he didn't get to the place arranged to meet her by eight, she would be off the boil and he might not get another chance with her. Worse still, his reputation was at risk. All his 'lady friends' were glad of his attentions. He always delivered what they each in their own way hoped for.

The sun had disappeared and Tony realized it must be getting late. He had no idea how late.

Harry had met Freda at the hospital to check on John's progress and all was going well. He was now sitting up in his bed and seemed to be enjoying himself. He had been given some biscuits with a drink and was looking forward to getting a bowl of ice cream. The discomfort he was in didn't seem to matter. He was being spoilt rotten by the nurses and he would be having quite a time off school. All this, he thought, was much more important than his brother's stitches in a cut and a plaster cast on a broken arm. He'd even had a proper operation.

Freda and Harry were relieved to find everything had gone well and that they could collect him in a week's time. He would have to rest at home though. If they couldn't get in to see him in the next few days, they could telephone the hospital for an update. Harry, being an ambulance driver, would be able to see him briefly at various times if he could come to an arrangement with Matron.

Now, she was a formidable woman. She had been on the medical team at various stations during the war. Her experience with countless war casualties had not softened her approach to nursing. She still demanded strict control over the patients in her care. John, being only nine, had been put into a ward for adults at the time of his admittance because beds in the children's ward had been filled with some seriously ill youngsters, mainly due to an outbreak of scarlet fever.

With no worries about him, they made their way home. Madge had arranged to give little Tom and Tony some tea before they got back.

The first indication something was wrong was Madge standing at her front door, holding little Tom's hand. She was anxiously looking up and down the street. It was now seven o'clock and Tony was not home from school.

On seeing them, little Tom ran to meet his mother. Harry looked at Madge and immediately knew something was up. Turning to Freda, his expression said it all.

"Where's the other one? If that little bugger has played up and not gone to Madge's, I'll be more than annoyed."

Madge was almost in tears.

"Tony never came round after school. I took little Tom out and we went around a couple of streets to look for him but he wasn't playing out with any of his usual mates. I feel so responsible."

Freda could feel the panic in her stomach rising. She was grasping little Tom's hand so tightly that he cried out in pain.

"It's not your fault."

Harry didn't want Madge to feel she had let them down. She was a good neighbour.

"I'll go and have a word with the lads playing footie and see if they know where he's gone."

Barging into their game and rounding them up, he fired questions at them as to why Tony wasn't with them. None of them remembered which direction he went in when he left the school playground.

Freda watched their response to Harry's questions and put her hand up to her mouth.

It was now half past seven and the evening light was beginning to shadow everything.

It wasn't like Tony to not come home from school. He always reported in before grabbing something to eat and then racing out.

Freda looked at Harry. "I'll go indoors and see if there's any food missing. He might have decided he would go on one of his pretend camping trips. You know when he made a bit of a den in that bombed out house in Beechcroft Road? That Saturday he was gone all day and, remember, we had to go and look for him."

She was trying to convince herself that it was just one of his games, but somehow she felt it was more than that.

Harry was turning things over in his mind and trying to hide his concern from Freda.

Little Tom, watching his mother's frantic search in the kitchen cupboards, began to cry. Freda could find nothing missing. It was then she remembered she had forgotten to give him any cake money.

Harry was now standing on the pavement in front of The Angel. A crowd was gathering. Word had got out that there was a young lad missing. The people in these streets were like a close knit family. Any problem, no matter what, was something to be sorted by all of them.

The Town Hall clock struck eight.

Harry was due on an ambulance shift at eight but had completely forgotten about it. He had better let the ambulance station know why he wouldn't make it.

P.C. Dave Taylor had heard about the problem when he had come off duty and was having his usual pint in The Bell.

Churchy was standing in her doorway and Liz and Joan had joined her. When they saw Reverend Michael and Christine crossing the street, they all felt a feeling of foreboding. It was almost a sign of something terrible having happened.

It was decided that with the street filling with neighbours and strangers, it would need a bit of organizing if a street search was to be undertaken.

At No. 5, Freda was sobbing. Madge was with her. The kettle was on and there seemed to be a continual funnel of steam rising. Neither Freda or Madge wanted to be in the kitchen drinking tea. They both wanted to be out looking for Tony.

It was decided amongst the men that they would go street to street checking through the bomb sites. Maybe Tony had been on one, messing about, and had slipped. Perhaps, they hoped, he was trapped. Even that would be better than not found at all.

Reg was still not back with any petrol. Dick was losing his temper and swearing about it. He was out of the car and pacing backwards and forwards. The car door was open.

"I need to do a pee, mister. I can't wait any longer."

That was all Dick wanted. A kid who was getting fed up and wanted to do a pee.

"You'd better go in those bushes," he said, pointing to a line of trees along the side of the path where they had stopped the car.

"Where are we, mister? I think I've been here before."

Looking around, he noticed a dilapidated farm building.

"Yeh, I've been camping here with my Scout group."

He was going off this adventure fast now. Also, he was really hungry.

"Have you got anything to eat, mister? I'm starving."

Dick was more concerned about the date he was supposed to be on. When Reg gets back, I'm going to lay into him good and proper, he thought.

Tony started wandering away from the car.

"My dad will have me guts for garters when you take me back home. I'm not allowed out on me own when it gets dark."

The locals from Angel Street had now formed themselves into groups. P.C. Dave Taylor had organized several parties of about six in each. Some of the off duty police had shown up as well.

Churchy and Liz had brought out an old pasting table and stood it outside the church. It was soon filled with an assortment of cups and several chipped tea urns. A few chairs were brought out and now, with the lights of the lamp posts breaking the gloom, there was a feeling that with the usual routine swinging into action in an emergency, Tony would soon be found.

Freda didn't know what to do with herself.

"Don't yer worry, dear, 'e can't be far." Churchy was trying to think of something more comforting to say but nothing came into her mind.

"I 'ope that bloody vicar don't ask us ter pray fer im. That would put the kybosh on things. Gloom before doom, my old mum used ter say."

Liz was not helping with that sort of comment.

The other kids in the street were being quizzed by a couple of policemen. They had been on duty and the sight of them in their uniforms made it seem more serious than anyone wanted to think.

With all suggestions of where he may have gone and every reason explored of why he would have taken off, the thought he had simply run away because he was in trouble was ruled out. Everyone was desperate to solve the problem before nightfall.

Reg was still not back and it was now half past nine. Dick was raging. Looking at Tony, he said, "If you know where you are, kid, do you think you could find your own way home?"

He knew this was dicey, but he would rather the kid got back to where he belonged than the police thought he had been kidnapped or something.

"My dad always told me, if I ever got lost in a wood, I should find a main road and follow it. Someone would come along in a car and wonder why I'd be walking there."

Dick perked up a bit on hearing this.

"Your dad sounds a very wise man. I think you should do just that. We can't be far from a main road because I can hear traffic. I'll walk with you over there," he said, pointing to a lane beyond the next field.

Even Dick didn't like the idea of walking about here in the dark, but he'd rather guide the kid in the right direction than be accused of taking him away.

Tony was a bit apprehensive but wanted this little adventure to end now. He'd had enough.

"All right, then, but you'll have to come with me till I get to a proper road."

After thinking about it, Dick wasn't too sure it was a good idea after all. He was quite at home driving around

London streets but beyond that he'd be lost. What if he went with the kid and then couldn't find his way back to the car?

This was turning into a nightmare.

Reg had managed to find a small petrol station and bought a can of petrol. His coupons were, luckily, on him. This purchase was going to put a dent in his social spending money and he was not pleased.

After returning along the road he thought he had taken, he now found himself lost. He couldn't see the car anywhere. Christ, where was the bloody car? His mind was in turmoil. Like Dick, out of London, he was a fish out of water. He stood by the side of a track he now found himself on.

Calling out, he hoped Dick and the kid would be able to hear him. There was no response. The only sounds were of trees rustling in the evening breeze and the occasional crack of twigs falling and who knew what scuttling about on the ground. He was as scared as a lost child which, in the circumstances, seemed ridiculous for a grown man.

The air was turning damp and he had his best suit on. He'd be bloody mad if it got ruined.

This sodding job was not working out.

Back in Angel Street, two of the groups of men had already checked out half a dozen bombed houses. They had even managed to look into the old air raid shelters in some of the gardens. There was still no sign of Tony. Little Tom was now sound asleep in the back room of Joan's shop. Freda had insisted on helping with the search, even though she was dreading finding Tony in some terrible state and badly injured.

The torch lights of all the searchers could be seen flashing in and out of the streets.

A group from the local Salvation Army could now be seen talking to the residents of Angel Street.

Liz looked at Churchy. "'Ow do they do it?"Churchy was puzzled.

"Do what?"

"They must 'ave some system of 'earing about trouble. They always show up. I'm not saying it's a bad thing, but it gives me the creeps. It's almost as though they are expecting a bad ending."

Vi had decided to help by giving some of the kids milling about some of her homemade biscuits. They, in turn, were having a marvellous time, oblivious to the seriousness of the situation. They were just pleased to still be playing out this late.

P.C. Dave Taylor had decided to extend the search and had contacted the local fire station. The men there had passed on the news of the problem and quite a few off duty firemen had turned up.

They decided to search in one of the streets that was due to be cleared because almost all the houses there were so badly damaged they had been roped off.

By now, every shed and outside lavvy had been searched but there was still no trace of Tony. It was now seven and a half hours since he was last seen. Freda was in a state of collapse and Ethel, Churchy and Liz were doing their best to comfort her.

A tap on Harry's shoulder made him turn around quickly. It was John Simmons, the headmaster of Tony's school.

"I've come with some colleagues to see if we can be of any help. There are several of our teachers here. We heard about the situation and had to come. Is there any news yet?"

Freda had recognized him straight away. She was the one who always had to deal with smoothing over some of Tony's antics when he was in trouble at school.

Henry looked serious.

"I'm afraid not. He's really done it this time. Was there any trouble at school that you know about?"

"No, nothing. He was seen playing football when school finished and that was that."

It was now ten o'clock. The firemen had decided between them that before it became too dark, they would start looking in the wrecked houses. They had told P.C. Dave Taylor what their intentions were and that only they should make these searches because they were equipped with ropes and tools on their belts if needed, plus they were all wearing helmets which would give them some protection against falling masonry.

Dr Harris was trying to persuade Freda to take a sedative to calm herself down but, of course, she wouldn't.

Reverend Michael had had what he called 'a baptism of fire' having only just arrived in the parish and finding a lot of distressed people to deal with. A lot of them didn't know who he was and so it was a present from heaven to be able to introduce himself. He was mingling with some of the Salvation Army people, who were dispensing their own words of comfort.

"Blimey, look at that," said Liz. "We've got a missionary chatting ter the ladies from the Mission." She allowed herself a little chuckle.

Suddenly, there was a rumbling and crashing sound, followed by the ground shaking beneath them. A huge cloud of dust rose into the night sky and the distinct sound of glass smashing brought all conversation to a halt.

Churchy stood up from her chair by the tea urns.

136

"What the bloody 'ell was that?"

Immediately, what men had remained in the street ran to where the sound had come from. It was two streets away. With the firemen scrambling among the wreckage of the roped off houses, something had triggered a wall to collapse. It had been an upper wall. With a fireman caught in the bricks and rubble, the dust was slowly settling. There was now an ominous silence.

A cry went up.

"It's Jack! He's been brought down by the wall."

The other firemen all converged on the area, directing the light from their torches into the rubble. Some of the policemen had run to the street and they were followed by several of the men from the Salvation Army group. They now had a serious situation on their hands.

Harry and Freda were amongst the onlookers. They knew what Tony was like and they had always dreaded him getting into a scrape that was beyond his control. They stood silently, watching.

Two of the Salvation Army men already had their jackets off and their shirt sleeves rolled up. They had, during the not so distant war years, had many occasions when their help had been needed in rescues similar to this.

The landlord at The Bell had telephoned for an ambulance.

Liz and Vi had decided to abandon handing out cups of tea and would make their way to the crash site to get some information they could relay back to Churchy. When they turned into the street, Liz could see it had been Phoebe's house which had finally collapsed.

Turning to Vi, she said, "That 'ouse, I am sure, is bad luck. I've spent more hours than I care ter recall in there.

When Phoebe's 'usband was killed in the war, she stayed on in the place on 'er own. I used ter go round fer a cuppa. She managed fer quite a while until bloody 'itler came calling."

She was telling all this to Vi, even though Vi knew the story. She had been about when the bomb struck. She was in an air raid shelter with a lot of other people at the time. When the all clear had sounded, they all emerged and were amazed at the damage. Phoebe had refused to go to the shelter and had stayed in her home.

Looking at the blokes nearby Liz said, "What's 'appened? Is the boy in there?"

"We don't know. They are trying to assess the damage. One of the firemen is trapped. His mates are doing the best they can for him. I think they said he was talking and so, at least, it looks like he's survived the fall."

Liz and Vi looked on.

In the wooded area where the car was parked, Dick was still having second thoughts about leading Tony onto a main road, even if he could find one. It was dark now and anything could happen to the kid. He thought about leaving a note for Reg to say what he had decided to do but then that wouldn't solve anything. No, he decided, he and the kid would just have to hope Reg found his way back to the car.

It was now half past ten. His date would be telling everyone she'd been stood up and that would do his reputation no good at all.

Looking around him, he said, "The noises in this place are bloody unnatural. It's all creaks and groans."

Just at that moment some bushes seemed to come to life all on their own and out of the thick of them came Reg, looking very dishevelled with his jacket open, his tie sticking out of a pocket and a petrol can in his free hand. The other

138

one he had been using to push branches away from his face and precious suit.

"Where the bloody 'ell have you been? We've been here for hours. The kid is pissed off and I won't tell you in front of him what I am thinking."

With the engine running and the headlights on, they slowly drove along the wooded lane, no one saying a word. Tony was worried what reception was waiting for him back home. A good hiding probably.

As they eventually got near a pub not too far from Tony's home, Reg told him to get out and walk the rest of the way. It would only take him about ten minutes and they felt their consciences were clear. With that, they sped off in the direction of Reg's flat, the stuff they had in the boot being the only good thing about the whole afternoon's work. It was going to take more than a few quid to wipe this little episode from their memories.

Chapter 10

As Tony approached the familiar streets, the lights illuminating the area were not normal. Also, why was there so much noise and why were there so many people around? Before he reached Angel Street, a shout went up.

"He's here!"

The first person he saw was Mr Simmons. He wasn't sure if he wanted to see his father first or his headmaster. Coming home at this time of night was bad enough, but with his headmaster and his dad to explain things to it would be a nightmare, especially as he had been told the adventure was supposed to be a secret mission and he shouldn't tell anyone about it. Panic hit him like a football being slammed into the back of the net. What was going on? None of this was normal.

He could hear the shrill and tinny sound of a bicycle bell getting nearer. Coming at great speed along the centre of the road, he spotted his friend Dave. He had noticed Tony as soon as he had rounded the corner. Yelling at the top of his voice, all you could hear was, "Cor, blimey. You are not 'alf for it. Everyone's been looking for you. There's also been a lot of trouble a couple of streets away. Some fireman has been hurt. There's an ambulance, firemen and police round there. You've nearly missed it all."

He was breathless with all this news, sitting astride his bike in the middle of the road. It was strange seeing him there when it was dark.

Tony looked in a bit of a state. His school clothes seemed he'd had them on for a week.

"Well, all that is nothing to do with me. I wasn't even here."

He knew he'd get blamed if anything was wrong.

At Phoebe's collapsed house, frantic efforts were being made to get Jack safely out of the ruins.

With the ambulance parked in the middle of the street, the firemen were carefully removing debris from around Jack until they were able to reach him. His grin when they got to him told them that he was all right. His helmet was dented and at a tilt on his head but it had saved him from terrible injury. Two ambulance men carried a stretcher across the rubble and helped him onto it, while he was trying to convince them that he didn't need to go to hospital. They were having none of it and secured him in the back of the ambulance and sped off.

Mr Simmon's shout when he saw Tony brought P.C. Dave Taylor, some of the regulars from The Angel and about a dozen of Tony's friends to the scene.

Harry stepped back from where he had been helping at the collapsed house and, seeing Mr Simmons frog marching Tony along the pavement, gave up a silent prayer that he had been found. He just didn't know what to do next.

"Dad, what's going on?"

Tony's shrill voice could be heard over all the confusion of noise as people in the street relayed the news that Tony was back.

Mr Simmons stopped short of where Harry was standing and urged Tony to go forward.

With a scream from the other end of the street, Freda could be seen running towards them. She grabbed Tony with such force they both almost fell over.

"Mum, why are you crying? Has something happened to John?"

A large crowd had now formed as everyone that had been in Angel Street converged around them. For no apparent reason, someone began applauding. Within seconds everyone was cheering and clapping.

Harry was still standing silently in the middle of all this release of tension. Finally, he prised Tony away from Freda's grip and, without saying a word, slapped him around the back of the head.

P.C. Dave Taylor stepped forward and put his hand on Harry's shoulder.

"I think yer ought ter get the boy 'ome and let 'im tell yer why 'e went missing. I'll come round ter your place tomorrer and get some details from 'im."

Harry just nodded.

With the crowd now retreating, Harry went over to where some kitchen chairs had been brought out. He pulled one forward and stepped up onto it. With everyone now staring at him, he said, "I just want to thank everyone for their help with all this. We don't have any details about why it all came about but, thankfully, the little bugger is back safe and sound. Once again, thanks."

With that said, he stood down and, almost dragging Tony with him, they met up with Freda, who had collected little Tom from Joan's shop, and went home.

"I 'aven't bin up this late fer years."

Liz was in no mood to call it a day. She was annoyed that she'd have to wait until the morning to find out where Tony had been.

Looking at Churchy, she said, "If it don't give yer indigestion eating at this time of night, we could 'ave a drink and a bit of something to eat round mine. I won't be able ter settle on an empty stomach and I missed me tea when all this palaver started."

Churchy and Liz made their way down the street.

"As long as yer don't give me anything with cheese in it, I'll be all right. Me innards can't cope with cheese after four o'clock. Yer didn't know me gut could tell the time, did yer?"

With a broad grin on her face, she followed Liz along the now empty pavement thinking, well that's another problem solved by the residents of Angel Street.

At No. 5, after Tony had downed two thick slices of bread and a tin of baked beans, it was decided the questioning would start in the morning. Everyone was so exhausted and confused that they didn't know where to begin. It was obvious Tony had not been hurt or harmed in any way. In fact, he seemed his normal self.

With his clothes discarded on the bedroom floor, he was asleep in minutes. In the silence of the room Freda looked at him, stretched out in his bed and then at the empty bed next to his, where John usually was. She suddenly felt guilty for letting John out of her thoughts for a while. She had been so consumed in grief that something bad had happened to Tony that everything else had gone out of her mind.

She bent down and picked up the bundle of clothes on the floor. They were in a right old state. They had the smell of a garden and earth about them. Also, the soles of his shoes were caked in mud.

As she picked up his trousers there was a clatter on the wooden floor. Something had dropped out of his pocket.

In the half light coming in from the landing, she saw what looked like a coin. She bent down and saw half a crown. Picking it up she felt a surge of panic consume her. Someone had given it to Tony. There was no other way he could have got it.

She stood rigidly in the dim light. She was blinking rapidly in an effort to clear her mind. Had he stolen it and then run away because he was scared about the trouble he would be in? Had he found it and felt guilty because he hadn't tried to find out who'd lost it?

Looking at the state of his school clothes and the smell of them, she felt herself struggling for breath, her thoughts of the length of time he had been missing converging into blind panic of someone having persuaded him to carry out some terrible act.

From standing rigidly in the shadows, every muscle in her body seemed to suddenly collapse and, with a thump, she hit the floor.

Tony slept on.

Harry, hearing the unfamiliar sound, came bounding up the stairs. Freda was in a crumpled heap on the floor.

With his first aid training coming to the fore, he checked her breathing and felt she had fallen in a way that was, luckily, relaxed. In a faint.

Slowly, he sat her up. The colour began returning to her face. She opened her eyes as he supported her head. Wiping the sweat from her face, she looked at Harry. Without saying a word, she released her still clenched fist and revealed the half-crown in the palm of her hand.

The night dragged on endlessly.

The light of day finally arrived. Tony opened his sleepy eyes and searched the room for his clothes. Harry came into the room.

"I want you downstairs now." By the tone of his voice, Tony knew he was in trouble.

Freda was sitting at the table, the usual clutter of cups, saucers, milk bottle and bread board with some cut slices on it. He looked at the clock on the shelf. It was half past seven. His dad was usually leaving for work now but he looked as though he was going nowhere.

"Sit down and listen to me. P.C. Dave Taylor will be here soon but before that happens, I want some answers. Where were you after school? Where did you go? You know you've caused a lot of trouble and so don't mess me about. Let's hear it."

Freda sat frozen on her chair. She was dreading what he was going to say.

He looked down, staring at the table top. His lips were pushed into a locked position. His face seemed to shrink as he tried to control the tears that were building up.

Freda wanted to stretch over and cuddle him but Harry broke the silence.

"Well? Start talking or I will really lose my temper."

Tony looked up.

"They said they wanted to play a trick on their friend and asked me to help them. We would have been back by five o'clock but the car ran out of petrol."

"What! You've been taken away in a car? Who are these people?"

"They gave me half a crown for helping them get into the kitchen. They said they couldn't have done it without me."

Freda broke into hysterical laughter, the tension and unbearable thoughts that had kept her awake all night being released in a torrent of emotion.

Harry paced backwards and forwards across the kitchen.

145

"Where did they take you? What did they do when they got there? Was it someone's home?"

Firing all these questions at him in a stream of disbelief, anger and relief that the story, so far, seemed to indicate Tony had not been used in any other way than to gain access to a property. In fact, it sounded like he had been used in a robbery. Why else would they want to break into a house?

"Who were these people? How do they know you?" The questions kept coming.

There was a loud banging on the closed front door. It was P.C. Dave Taylor. He was a big bloke, his stature giving him the necessary look of authority.

"I've come round, Harry, ter ask the boy some questions and get some answers."

Harry took him into the little scullery. Keeping his voice low he said, "I think he's been used in a robbery. They even gave him half a crown for helping them."

They both smiled.

P.C. Dave Taylor stood at the table, all six foot two of him towering over Tony.

"I am going ter ask yer some questions and I need yer ter tell me the truth. I'll know if yer lie. Do yer know 'oo these blokes are?"

"No."

"Where did yer meet 'em?"

"At the playground. They said they'd heard I was a good climber."

"What did they want yer ter climb, then?"

"They said they wanted to play a trick on their friend and if I helped them they would give me half a crown."

"Where did they take you then? Was it very far away?"

"No, it was near where I went camping with the Scouts last year. Do you remember the place, Dad?" He nodded. He

146

was trying to get on Harry's good side by hoping he could join in with the answers.

Harry looked at Dave and said, "It was in the Epping area, near that old farm called Bridges Farm."

P.C. Dave Taylor continued. He was filling quite a few pages of his notebook with all this information.

"What did yer do when yer got there?"

"I had to climb in a window and unlock the kitchen door. It was a very posh house. They even had a pond in the garden, with some smashing fish in it." Looking at his dad, he continued, "They were like them fish we looked at in that library book."

Harry looked at Dave and said, "They were Koi Carp."

P.C. Dave Taylor sat down at the table.

"Yer doing very well so far. Do yer remember what their names were?"

Tony frowned. "I think one of them was called Reg, but I don't know about the other one."

"Would yer know them if yer saw them again?"

Sitting up on his chair, Tony said, "One of them had a suit on like Uncle Bob's. You know the one, Mum. Sort of brown."

Looking at his mum, he said, "Can I have something to eat? I'm starving."

Freda went into the scullery and, filling the kettle, she put it on the stove to boil. She started making Tony a cheese sandwich and called out, "Do you two want a cuppa?"

P.C. Dave Taylor continued questioning Tony.

"Yer said they took yer ter the place in a car. Do yer know what kind it was?"

Now munching on his sandwich, he was getting a bit fed up with all this. With a mouthful of cheese, he swallowed hard.

147

"It was black and I know it was an Austin because one of our teachers has got one."

P.C. Dave Taylor closed his notebook. The mention of a school teacher reminded him that Tony was due at school and he didn't want him to get into any more trouble. The headmaster had told him that he was going to hold a special assembly to warn the children about talking to strangers.

Having drunk the tea Freda had offered him, he said the matter would be investigated now they had something to go on and then left.

As Harry showed him out, they both heard Tony asking his mum if he could have the half-crown he had been given.

With Tony sent to school, Harry clocked in at the ambulance station and heard that Jack, the fireman, had been discharged from hospital.

With things seeming to be returning to normal, Madge arrived at No. 5. She had been sitting up all night worrying what the outcome was going to be, once Tony had told them about where he was. She looked dreadful. Freda sat her down and made her a cup of tea. Little Tom came into the kitchen and stood by her chair.

Freda quietly told her what they had found out and that she wasn't to blame herself for what Tony had done. After calming her down, Freda found she had also calmed herself down.

Word soon got out of what had happened.

Churchy's ankle was now greatly improved and so she had made her way over to the church to do her usual tidying up and brass polishing. Seeing Reverend Michael at the altar, she made her way towards him. He turned round.

"Ah! Churchy. What a good outcome we had last night. I got to chat to so many people I'd never met before. I can't say I converted any of them, but at least they know where to find me now."

Churchy sat down at the end of a pew. She ran her finger along the back of the next line of them as though getting rid of some invisible dust.

"Yer know what we was all thinking." She paused. "It wasn't said, but if a kiddy goes missing and it turns out he'd bin taken by a couple of blokes, well, yer 'ear some dreadful things."

"Yes, but it wasn't a case of that, was it? I hear the police are already making progress with their investigation because the landlord at The Angel said some stranger had been interested in Tony. It seems they have also been checking large houses in the Epping area, because Tony mentioned he recognized the place he was at as he'd been around there with the Scouts."

"Well, reverend, it all seemed queer ter us that they was allowed ter be near that school and up ter no good. What's the world coming to?"

Reverend Michael had to hide a smile by feigning a cough.

Churchy stood up. "I can't be sitting 'ere talking, I've got me cleaning ter do because nobody else is going ter do it."

With that, she toddled off to collect her cleaning stuff, disappearing into the darkness of the cupboard at the back of the church.

Standing at her front door, Liz was feeling restless. Who did she know that might be able to give her some information about strangers drinking in The Angel? She wouldn't go in

149

there herself because she didn't hold with drinking. While she was still pondering the question, she saw Boss-eyed Ben shuffling along. She looked at him as he approached. He always wore the same clothes whether it was summer or winter. In fact, she was convinced they were the only ones he owned. They seemed to have moulded around him. He always had the tell-tale yellow stain under his nose after years of using snuff and this had left him with a permanent sniff.

She knew he had black market connections because of the clothing coupon fiasco but, luckily, that had stayed in the street and no one found themselves in trouble over it. He was harmless really. Those coupons hadn't been stolen, only acquired by devious means. The only people who lost out on that little caper was the government. Perhaps he might know of anyone coming in from the outside, so to speak, asking questions.

As he neared her front door, Liz stepped forward.

"Mornin', Ben."

He looked up from his usual head-down pose.

"'Ow are yer, luv? 'Ows yer luck?" He wasn't sure what else to say.

Liz launched her inquisition.

"What a to-do that was last night. I've 'eard the police are looking fer a couple of blokes 'oo do a bit of thieving. If that's not bad enough, they used young Tony."

She waited for a response. Nothing. She'd try a new approach.

"If yer don't mind me saying, Ben, yer know a few 'oo make a living 'elping themselves ter other people's stuff. Does anyone come ter mind?"

Ben had always been in the know about what was going down and who was involved. He had quite a few old lags who kept him informed, just so that anything that came his way could be disposed of without alerting the police.

He'd heard from one or two pawnbrokers over the other side of the Thames that a couple of blokes from the Woodford area were making quite a few appearances with some silver and, sometimes, jewellery. None of it had been high class, just easy stuff to pass on.

"I don't know what yer mean, Liz. I keep me nose clean, yer know that."

She laughed. That was the wrong thing to say.

"Oh, come on, Ben. Yer must 'ave 'eard something."

Eager to pass by, he gave her something to think about.

"The Old Bill will be checking the pawnbrokers ter see what's new in. That might give them some leads."

With that said, he shuffled off, leaving Liz a bit put out that she was none the wiser. Things were changing. No one was being helpful about who was out for a quick quid. She was sure Ben had some idea who those blokes were.

At the station, P.C. Dave Taylor was having his notes typed up. They were very informative. Young Tony had been helpful.

As was the case in all local robberies, the usual known fences and pawnbrokers were being contacted. The main problem the police had was identifying what house had been broken into. They didn't even know what had been stolen. It was strange that no one had reported a robbery.

They'd have to get Tony to show them the area where his camp site had been.

A couple of days later, it was arranged that Tony and Harry would go to the area the scout camp had been in some months before.

Tony was over the moon. His adventure was getting better. He was now going to get a ride in a police car. John wouldn't be able to beat that.

Harry had some idea where the scout camp had been but it would be a long shot. It had been some way into the forest. The area had some pretty decent properties in it. He could understand why it had been targeted for a robbery but why hadn't one been reported?

The car made its way to the land where Bridges Farm started. They stopped. This was where the forest in all its mystery had been encroached upon by moneyed families from the Victorian age, who had built some impressive properties. It had been when these families had chosen to escape the deprivations of the London streets and chose to use their wealth to impress, in the form of large houses.

Now out of the car, Tony didn't recognize any of it.

"We were on a track, not a road. I do remember that. The house where their friend lives is down a track. Their front wall is a bit broken, but I didn't do it."

He was beginning to feel a bit worried in case he got blamed because the stone wall had partly collapsed. Tony didn't know the constable they were with and he was a bit scared of him.

Harry suggested they all stay together and walk a short way along the track. There was a dilapidated farm building in sight now and as they neared a line of bushes, Tony recognized that as the spot where he had done a pee.

"We can't be far off now, because I remember those bushes."

They continued on. There were three large houses along this track. Tony stopped outside the first two. They were nothing like the one he remembered.

He hadn't noticed before, but the first of these houses had a board by its gate saying, 'Dogs patrolling.' He was glad Reg's friend didn't live in that one.

They were now some way from the car. As they turned a bend in the track Tony saw the crumbling stone wall.

He gave a loud yell. "That's the one!"

The constable decided to take Harry and Tony back to the car. He would then go into the garden of the house and scout around to see if there was anybody about. Tony had told him about the dustbin being pulled over to the window at the side. Sure enough, it was there. He tried the front door of the house but it was securely locked. Walking around the side where the dustbin had been placed, he turned the handle of the kitchen door. It opened. Entering the house, he called out but there was no answer.

The property showed no sign of disruption in the kitchen, at least.

He decided he would return to the car and report back. It was then that he remembered Tony had told P.C. Dave Taylor about the fish pond in the garden. He went around to the back of the house and, sure enough, there was the pond. This was the house all right.

The atmosphere at the Cobden Road Police Station was one of uncertainty. The sergeant there had pointed out, in no uncertain terms, that they didn't have anyone in the one cell that their station kept open and ready. He felt the efforts being made in this case were not very good. Also, the subject of the boy, Tony, being involved could not be ignored. He had, in fact, been paid for his part in the caper. At eleven years old, he should have known better than to have joined in with this little scheme. There had been a phone call from 'higher up', as the sergeant had said that the boy should tell his side of the tale in detail to Sergeant Buxton at the station and it would then be decided whether to take that part of the robbery any further.

As he knew the family, P.C. Dave Taylor was told he would have to inform them of this decision. He dreaded it.

Along this street views and opinions were regularly expressed behind the net curtains. Ethel and Bill were never blessed with children, as they put it but, after this latest skirmish with Tony, they were secretly pleased they had never had such an upset to deal with. Madge along the street had raised three boys but luckily, none of them had given her much trouble.

In the neat little kitchen which Vi had created for herself, everything looked orderly. She wasn't a particularly fussy person but did like things to run like clockwork. She had been widowed years before and had come to like her life, where she could please herself what she did. She had been at school with Churchy and Liz and they were good friends. The only thing she didn't like was their ability to include everyone in the rumours which abounded in the area. They had often commented on how Janet managed to be able to get hold of more than her share of clothing coupons. Vi used to defend her but found it was a pointless thing to do. Everyone knew that Boss-eyed Ben could be relied upon for little extras and Vi imagined both Churchy and Liz had used him as well. Now she found herself getting worked up, dwelling on all this.

She looked at the wrist watch Janet had bought her. It was four o'clock.

She decided she would go over to the corner shop to see if Joan had any bread left. With all the fuss the day before, it had completely gone out of her mind to get some in. If Janet decided to pop in, she wouldn't be able to do a sandwich.

She calmed herself down a bit and, in her naivety, was glad her husband seemed able to get most of the things they wanted to furnish their home. Her son-in-law seemed very well connected. She hadn't thought much about how well connected he was and, if she knew, she wouldn't sleep again.

The shop door was, as usual, cluttered with sacks of potatoes, onions and firewood. Boss-eyed Ben was the one who supplied the firewood.

"It's only me." Vi called out because she couldn't see anyone in the shop. Joan appeared from the back room.

"'Allo, luv. Yer not usually out and about this time of the day. What about all that burglary business and young Tony being involved? They couldn't keep that secret. Yer couldn't make it up."

Vi started to feel alarmed. The word 'secret' made her, once again, feel bad about the clothing coupons. She was petrified that they would come back to haunt her.

She had her purse in her hand and she felt herself gripping it tighter and tighter. She was getting worked up again.

"If you ask me, it's not always your fault if you get caught up in things that are not really legal." She could feel herself getting hot. "When people offer you something and, in young Tony's case, some pocket money, I can understand why he agreed to help them blokes. There are all kinds of ways little extras come along and, if it isn't doing any harm, why wouldn't you take them?"

She was now breathless.

"Are yer all right, luv? Yer ought ter sit down a minute. I'll fetch yer a chair."

Releasing the grip on her purse, Vi opened it and took out the necessary coins.

"I'm all right, Joan. I'll just take the loaf."

She hurried out of the shop leaving Joan wondering what all that was about.

Chapter 11

The atmosphere in The Hare was always good. Reg and Dick felt more than at home here. With the volume of conversations going on, it was a wonder anyone understood what was being said. This was a pub which welcomed everyone and yet, not many strangers would be found in here. It was a huge family of regulars.

Reg and Dick were happy. They had managed to disperse the goods they had acquired among all their contacts, mainly in South London, well away from the area they had been taken from. Also, they had got some good prices for them. They were always careful not to take anything with names engraved on them and they had been doing this for long enough to know what sold.

Dick was quite happy standing at the bar. Several of the darts team were there, talking about the away game they had just won. Reg was more concerned about his suit getting splashed by the pints being precariously carried around them. He had only just got it back from the cleaners after getting it in a state in that bloody forest.

"Come on, let's get over there," he said, pointing to a free table under the window. They manoeuvred their way over to it.

Reg put his beer down.

"I saw Brian's wife the other day. Janet. Nice. How he keeps her happy, if you know what I mean, I don't know. The stuff he helps us out with must make a difference."

He picked his beer up and swallowed hard.

"Now, don't even think about it. The last thing we want now is woman trouble. Remember, the Bill are sniffing around Angel Street at the moment."

Janet's husband, Brian, was an insurance agent who collected policy payments every month from quite a range of houses on the borders of London. He was particularly chatty with some of his customers and almost became a friend to them. He was very good at casual conversation and found out a lot about the contents of the houses. An additional bonus was they told him when they were going to be away. Janet, of course, had no idea of his unlawful involvement with Reg and Dick.

Standing up, Dick said, "I'll get another one in."

Leaving Reg sitting at the table finishing his beer, Dick couldn't help smiling when he thought about the fact that their place was over the hairdresser's in the high street, where Janet had her hair done.

P.C. Dave Taylor knew he couldn't put off the inevitable and, knowing what time Harry got in from work, he chose to go to No. 5 around six o'clock.

Freda had got the bus to the hospital, with little Tom, to find out what day John could be collected. With Harry's shift ending at six, the family should be together so that he could question Tony again to see if he had remembered anything else. The sergeant had suggested he was brought into the police station as that might be a lesson in itself for the boy. P.C. Dave Taylor thought that would frighten him and he would be scared to say anything.

The day couldn't have gone any slower. Now that the property had been identified, the owners had been contacted and the police from the station local to it had confirmed that they had done a regular patrol of the lane but had seen nothing. Whoever these two blokes were that had done the job, they obviously were not amateurs.

He made his way along the street, hoping Freda, Harry and Tony were in. Reverend Michael could be seen striding along the pavement ahead of him. He was carrying a battered cardboard box. As they finally met up, his face shone with his broad grin, revealing clear white teeth and his dark eyes seeming to glint in the end-of-the-day sun.

"'Ello, reverend. Yer seem ter be in a bit of a 'urry. What's so important at the end of the day?"

"It's nice to see you, constable. I'm on my way to the school. John Simmons and myself have been chatting about what happened with Tony and we jointly thought we could explain to the children that it was wrong to take someone's possessions. The idea we came up with was, if a box was left at the school, the children could bring a toy or something in to put in the box and they could be taken to a hospital for sick children to play with. The lesson here would be to give and not take."

P.C. Dave Taylor was almost lost for words.

"What a good idea, reverend. It's even more relevant because young Tony's brother is in 'ospital at the moment and could probably do with a toy or two ter play with."

As they were both eager to get on, they said their goodbyes and walked on.

As usual, the door of No. 5 was ajar. Tapping on the woodwork, he called out. Freda came along the passage. As soon as she saw him she wanted to close the door and not let him in.

"Harry," she called out, "it's Dave Taylor."

Coming to the kitchen door, Harry was a bit surprised he was still standing on the pavement. Freda had, so far, not invited him in.

"Come in then, Dave. What's the matter with you, Freda?"

Tony was in his bedroom. He had been told he couldn't play out for two weeks. He wouldn't be getting his half-crown back either.

"'Ello, folks. The sarge 'as asked me ter 'ave a word with yer about Tony being asked more questions. 'E thought if yer could bring 'im round ter the station, that might make 'im realize 'ow important it is ter remember things. We don't want ter scare 'im, just make the questions more formal."

Freda glanced at Harry and drew in a deep breath.

"I suppose it wouldn't do any harm."

Harry nodded.

"We'll bring him along to the station tomorrow, after school, if that's all right."

With the arrangements made and the usual cup of tea offered and declined, P.C. Dave Taylor left, a lot more relieved than when he had arrived.

Reg and Dick didn't have a phone in the flat. They had to go to a phone box down the street if they needed to make a call. They had been told they could use the one in the hairdresser's if they had an emergency. This, of course, would be no good for the type of business they were in because their conversation would be overheard.

One of the pawnbrokers they used had taken in some of the items. He didn't know how to contact them and he liked it that way. If anything went wrong with the stuff they brought him, he would plead innocent about Reg and Dick's whereabouts. Now he wanted to let them know that the stuff

160

they were spreading around was quality and so causing some problems. The police had a list of the stolen items and were asking a lot of questions while systematically doing the rounds of the pawnbrokers and known fences. This particular pawnbroker, Benny Reynolds, knew Reg well. He had been at school with him. They had both, over the years, taken chances by dealing with some very dubious people in order to make a few bob. They had just stayed short of getting involved with the real villains that frequented the East End.

Benny had got his long term girlfriend pregnant and had been told by her docker father that he was going to get married. There was no way out. That was three years ago and things seemed to have worked out. His father-in-law was besotted with his granddaughter. He had set Benny up in the pawnbroker business, not because he liked him, because he didn't, but to keep an eye on him. He owned him. All money going in and out of the business was accounted for and his father-in-law employed a legit accountant to safeguard his investment.

When Reg brought some silver and jewellery in to him, he didn't ask questions. He didn't want to know where it had come from.

Reg and Dick, of course, were very careful about the houses they broke into. They relied on Brian, Janet's husband, to do the groundwork for them. So far, he had not let them down.

Benny decided he would have a pint in The Hare. Reg and Dick often used it and the landlord could know what evenings they would be in. He could only make the visit at midday, which would give him reason to shut the shop up for an hour or so on the pretext he was needing a break. His father-in-law seemed to know his every move. He was in no position to fall foul of the man. The police had asked Benny to look out for certain goods, one of which was a twelve inch tall silver cup, engraved with a carp and the date 1946. It was on a black base.

This was one of the things Reg had brought in to him and it was still in the back of the shop. If the suspicions of the police heightened, it would only take a search warrant and he would really be in the shit.

Making the journey to The Hare, he felt like a criminal on the run already.

As soon as he went into the public bar, he saw Dick. He was deep in conversation with the landlord.

Walking swiftly over to him, he tapped him on the shoulder and said, "I want a word with you."

Dick turned around. He looked startled by the way Benny had approached him and he had noticed the tone of his voice.

"What's up? You're not usually in here."

With a turn of his head, Benny said, "Outside, now."

Once on the pavement, the two men walked a few feet away from the pub. With no time to waste, Benny told him that one of the items on the police list was the silver cup Reg had brought in. He didn't want anything more to do with it or any of the other stuff from that haul. The money that had changed hands would have to be sorted between them but the main thing was either he or Reg would have to come round tonight to his place to take the stuff back. He didn't want it on his premises.

"Bloody hell! If that bugger Brian has dropped us in it, we're not going down quietly."

Benny was now sweating heavily. He wiped the moisture from his top lip.

"I want one of you to come round to mine tonight at ten. I can tell the wife it's business. I'll have all the stuff you dropped off at the shop ready for you to take back. The money I gave you for it, thinking I could easily unload it, will have to be paid back. I was hoping to sell the stuff for more. If my father-in-law finds out I've taken it in, I won't be around for long and neither will you and Reg."

Dick was now looking up and down the street. He didn't want anyone seeing him talking to a pawnbroker. People were quick to put two and two together.

He'd got the message and, on reputation alone, he knew Benny's father-in-law didn't take kindly to being used. Fear was mounting in his mind. His breathing was becoming laboured.

Dick knew where he could find Reg. It was back at the flat. He was entertaining Dawn, the busty bird from the market. She knew a few tricks and, after a couple of gins at lunchtime, she was the perfect end to a busy few days for Reg.

Half an hour later and in a blind panic, Dick was bounding up the stairs to the flat. He could hear Dawn's voice as she called Reg's name. He roughly pushed his key into the worn lock and swung the door open.

Looking across the room, directly into the bedroom Reg used, he could see the naked, disgusting, ample form of Dawn, crouching on all fours on the floor at the side of the dishevelled bed. The years and drink hadn't been kind to her and she looked what she was, a woman who was out for pleasure and didn't care how the once slender figure which had attracted men in the past had now become bulk. Reg was sitting on the edge of the bed waiting for her to pounce.

The whole scene completed the nightmare scenario which was running through Dick's mind. He was panicking and wanted to swear and lash out at anybody.

Staring at Dawn, he shouted, "Out, out, out!"

The look of complete surprise on their faces froze in the moment.

As fast as she could, Dawn scrambled to her feet to gather her clothing, which was scattered around the room. Within a couple of minutes she had been able to drag some of her clothes over her now sweating body and, swearing at Reg, she rushed out of the flat, slamming the door behind her. She left carrying her shoes but could still be heard thumping heavily down the stairs, swearing and cursing as she went.

Reg was now standing by the open window with a look of thunder across his face. His eyes were almost slits as he angrily yanked a pair of trousers on.

"What the hell do you think you are doing? Have you gone mad or something? Call yourself a mate? Get out of my way."

Dick stood his ground.

He pulled his jacket off. He was now sweating so much after his rush to the flat that he felt his shirt sticking to his back. Throwing the jacket onto a nearby chair he stood directly in front of Reg.

"We could be in trouble with that last job. The Police have been sniffing around pawn shops and finally reached Benny Reynolds. From the description of goods they gave him to look out for, one of the things was that poxy silver trophy with the fish on it. It looks like Brian has led us to the house of some bloke who's connected and he's not happy."

Reg sank down onto a chair.

Dick told him about the meeting with Benny and what they had agreed between them. The problem was, what were they to do with the stuff once it had been handed back to them. They were on a loser here.

The next hour they spent walking around the local park. They didn't want to be in the flat in case, after word got out that this latest robbery was more by someone reasonably local because they knew of the location, someone might put two and two together and think of them. The police were being pressured to find out who'd carried it out because if they didn't get answers, the owner of the goods would find the buggers and their lives would be in danger.

Before they met up tonight at Benny's place, they would pay a visit to Brian. They wanted a serious word with him.

They parked the car a couple of streets away and were soon at the block of flats that Janet and Brian had moved into. They were on the second floor.

Janet opened the door. As usual, she was looking good. She recognized them as being friends of Brian but, other than that, she didn't know them.

With a smile which he usually reserved for his lady friends, Reg said, "Is Brian about? We're business friends of his."

At that moment Vi came up to the front door.

"Who is it, dear?"

"It's all right, Mum, it's some friends of Brian." Looking along the passageway, Janet said, "He's just got in. I'll give him a shout."

Before she got the chance, Brian appeared and, seeing Reg and Dick at his own front door, he immediately pushed past her and was almost out of the door.

"I'll just see what they want, Jan. You and your mum finish your tea."

All three of them stood on the balcony leading along the block. With a heated argument going on, they all had trouble trying to have their say without making it obvious to any neighbour who might be observing them, that this was serious.

Brian hadn't know how well connected the owner of the house was. He only ever dealt with the bloke's wife and she never gave anything away. This was a serious mistake.

Reg and Dick had already decided they would get rid of the stuff they were going to collect tonight and then leave the area first thing in the morning. There was no way they were going to get involved with known villains. Brian was to find other mugs to pass any information on to if he still wanted to continue his extra money making scheme.

Back at the shop, Benny was trying to concentrate on getting through the afternoon. He just wanted to get the meeting over.

The one thing Reg and Dick were good at was staying just ahead of trouble. They had spent most of the night trying to think of the best way to dispose of the goods.

As daylight broke the rain laden sky, they were both exhausted. What sleep they had was disturbed when the rain tapping on the window of the flat sounded as though it was a knock on the door. This was no way to live. They had to cut their losses and decided they would toss the silver into the river. The Lea was not far away.

With the stuff in a bag together with a brick, they made their way along the local canal towpath and, with no one around, Reg took a swing and heaved the load into the middle of the river. It sank immediately.

They got into the car and made for the open road. They didn't care where it ended.

In Angel Street, things were beginning to get back to routine. Joan was still feeding Stan's cat but she was getting a bit annoyed about the state of the back garden there. The nettles were running riot and she was having to avoid getting stung as she made a pathway through the now long grass. The cat was still using the shed to live in and that was where she was leaving the food.

With the house still empty and locked up, everyone was waiting for the new tenant to move in. They knew, from Fred Talbot, that it was some relative of Stan.

As Joan walked back to the shop, Boss-eyed Ben was shuffling along, making his way to get some bread in. He was quite self sufficient as far as food was concerned. The only things he had to buy were bread, tea and sugar.

"'Ow are yer, Ben?"

He raised his head from the usual position of looking down as he walked.

"As yer've asked, I 'ave ter say that I could do with a bit more garden. If that garden at the back of Stan's is going ter waste, I could dig it all up and plant me veg in it. That would double what I've got now. I could also put some chickens or rabbits on it."

He rubbed the top of his head with a grimy hand. Just raising his arm released an odour which was pungent. Joan stood a bit further away from him.

"Why don't yer 'ave a word with Fred Talbot? 'E could 'ave a word with that solicitor firm and they can 'ave a word with the family. I only 'ope the new tenant don't want ter plant flowers in it."

Boss-eyed Ben pressed his lips together and frowned.

"Yer know, girl, that's a bloody good idea."

He bought the loaf of bread he needed and left the shop. As he walked away, she could hear him talking to himself. She was glad that he hadn't stayed long.

At No. 5, John had been brought home. He was not allowed back to school for another two weeks and then only to sit in the classroom for lessons. He could not take part in any games or P.E. for a while longer. Freda decided that as the weather was still good, he could sit at the front door with a couple of comics. That way anybody passing by could speak to him. He had been brought up to date with the goings on by Tony, who told the story with great gusto and elaboration. Especially the bit about having to go to the police station to be asked questions. The result of that was that he couldn't give them any more information about the blokes he had 'helped out'.

"Fred, Fred."

Liz had seen him from the other end of Angel Street. In the quiet of the day, her voice carried like a ship's foghorn.

Fred paused and turned.

Catching up to him, she sounded like a panther about to strike.

"What are yer doing round 'ere at this time? This is not yer day fer collecting rents."

Beads of perspiration were forming on her podgy nose.

"I've had to come round because the new tenant wants to move into Stan's as soon as possible. I thought I'd see if Bill could do a bit of work in the kitchen and put a new window in out back. He could, maybe, fix the shed up as well. The money is there to do it. The family are not hard up for a bob or two."

"'Oo is the tenant, then? Why does she want ter come 'ere? She must be able ter afford something better."

Leaning against the wall, Fred said, "She's living on her own and thinks it would be good to have neighbours nearby. I don't know anything about her. She's Stan's cousin from

168

way down the line, if that makes sense. I can tell you her name though, it's Hannah Bartholomew Baker. I've got to go now because I want to arrange for some work to be done by Bill. I need to leave a message with Ethel."

He strode away, leaving Liz more curious than ever. But, still, this much information was better than no information. She decided she would see if Churchy was in. As she pushed the front door open, she could hear voices. Going into the little kitchen, she found Christine sitting at the table. She turned and smiled.

Churchy immediately got up to get another cup from off the shelf.

"I wasn't expecting yer ter 'ave a visitor. I thought I'd pop in on the offchance."

Christine pulled out the chair next to her.

"I was just telling Churchy about the new bible class Reverend Michael wants to start up for the children. There isn't one at the moment."

"We 'ad one of them years ago, but the kids seemed ter go off it."

The conversation then continued on with Fred Talbot's news that the new tenant wanted to move into Stan's as soon as it had been cleaned up. She was bringing her own furniture. With no other information doing the rounds at the moment, the ladies finished their tea and appreciated the cake they had been offered, which had been made by Churchy's own hand.

Fred Talbot was not making much progress along the street. Boss-eyed Ben had caught a glimpse of him and wanted to ask him about that garden.

Finally reaching Bill's place, he glanced at his wrist watch and couldn't believe it had taken him nearly an hour to get down this street because of all the stops he'd had. The door was closed and so he quickly scribbled a note to Bill and shoved it through the letterbox. He needed to make his way home now.

The following days saw so much activity on the street that Madge, Vi and Joan were having trouble keeping up with it all. Stan's house was being made to look quite smart with the help of Bill. Ethel had decided that her contribution to welcome the new tenant was to make some new curtains for the kitchen and front room. Madge took it upon herself to clean the windows and could be seen with the sash window upstairs at the front pushed up and her sitting quite comfortably on the window ledge, cloth in one hand, with the other one holding onto the frame.

Even the Solicitor, Bartholomew Brewer, put in an appearance. He directed the flow of furniture into the property. P.C. Dave Taylor was watching from a distance.

Vi was on her knees, whitening her front step when Janet arrived. She hadn't been expecting a visit. Dragging herself upright, she dropped the brush she was using into the pail of water and stood back inside the front door. Her apron served as a towel to wipe her rough hands on.

"Hello, luv. What are you doing here today? I didn't know you had a day off."

She bent down and picked up the pail.

Janet wasn't her usual smiling self. She followed her mum into the house without saying a word and pushed the door to. Once in the kitchen, she put her handbag down on the table. She stood there. Vi looked at her.

"What's the matter? There's something wrong, I just know it."

Janet burst into tears. Pulling a handkerchief out of her bag, she covered her face with it.

"It's Brian. He promised me a brand new three piece suite. I chose a smashing one last weekend. It was going to be delivered tomorrow." She continued to sob her way through the story. "I got the old one taken away yesterday. This morning he told me we couldn't have the new one because the rise he was getting from his firm had been cancelled."

She collapsed onto the first available chair.

Vi stared across the kitchen and secretly wondered if that was the real truth. There was something about Brian that she couldn't understand. How did he manage to have so much money to spend when he was only an insurance agent?

"Oh, Mum. What are we going to do? Now we don't have anything in the flat to sit on."

Brian had done a good job covering up the mess they were now in. He hadn't received any back-handed payments from Benny for the stuff he had got him and so now his spending spree had dried up. Even worse, with the police still pursuing their investigations about the robbery, they were pulling all the stops out in an effort to tie anyone into it that had even the remotest association with the property. It was only a matter of time before his name as insurance agent for the property would come into the frame. His luck had held out for so long. It was inevitable it would run out some time.

Chapter 12

The community effort to get Stan's old house looking half decent had worked. Today the new tenant would be moving in. Fred Talbot was waiting for her to arrive. Knowing she was part of the firm of solicitors' family made her almost seem like royalty to Churchy and Liz. They didn't want to seem nosey and so they stood in Joan's shop doorway, from where they could see what was going on.

A car came cruising along the street and stopped at No. 15. It seemed ages before she got out. The driver opened the car door for her.

A rather large woman struggled out of it. She stood on the pavement steadying herself. Her bright red henna coloured hair seemed to have a life of its own. It was going in all directions. She certainly wasn't young. Her clothing reminded Liz of a fairground tent. What was that under her arm? It was a dog!

With their heads all grouped together around the shop doorway, it was a wonder they didn't all fall over.

"What do yer think of that, then? Stan's cat won't like that."

Joan walked back into the shop. The other two were still observing the proceedings.

Fred Talbot introduced himself and handed over the rent book very ceremoniously. Smiling at him, she put the key in the lock and they both disappeared inside.

The driver of the car then took various suitcases from the car and followed them in. With nothing more to see, Churchy and Liz ambled along the street and went their separate ways.

The next morning, the first to see it was Madge. She couldn't believe her eyes. She stood and stared at it. There was nobody about because it was only half seven. She turned away and walked a few yards up the street. This was a first and she was the one to see it. She hung around hoping to see someone. At that moment Bill came out on his way to work. He gave her a nod. She frantically beckoned to him. That was not what he wanted, one of the busybodies trying to attract his attention.

She waved at him again.

Oh! sod it, he thought. Now I'm going ter be late fer work.

He walked along the street and reached Madge.

Without saying a word, she pointed to the card in the window. The new tenant had placed it where it could best be seen.

Psychic analysis.

Tarot card readings.

Ouija board communications.

Bill's reaction was to laugh, and laugh he did.

"That's bloody marvellous, that is. I can't wait ter see what Churchy is going ter say about it."

Pausing for a few seconds, he then walked away saying, "That's made my day."

He was still laughing as he went.

Madge silently read the card once again and decided that she would go back home instead of going to get her paper. She would get it later. There was a lot to think about.

At the church house, Reverend Michael was about to start his day in the usual way with a breakfast of eggs and toast. He had several things on his mind this morning. His diary was full. There were christenings to be arranged with loving parents wanting his attention, a couple to be advised who had booked the church for their wedding and, later today, he was to pay a home visit to one of his parishioners who was worryingly frail.

Christine would not be having breakfast with him this morning because she was already out and about, assisting the district nurse who had said she could use her help and nursing knowledge with a visit to a particularly difficult old lady. The district nurse hoped that Christine's calm influence would make the visit easier.

Reverend Michael had settled into this parish quite easily. He had, so far, not been tested. This was about to change.

Liz decided her nets should come down and be washed, dried, ironed and put back up during the morning. She didn't want them down for more than a couple of hours. Her morning was going to be one long rush.

Churchy was due to clean the brass in the church this morning and that meant she'd be stuck in the dismal back room where all the cleaning sprays and liquids were stored. She hated the ever-present smells of them and was convinced that the cough she got every winter was down to the fact that breathing in all these chemicals during the year got on her chest.

Madge was hovering in her front room. She was silently willing one of her neighbours to walk along the street.

Pressing her face against the glass, she could just about see to the end of the street. Dr Harris was walking smartly along, his familiar bag banging against his legs as he strode out. He was in a hurry. If she was quick, she could catch him as he passed. Getting to her front door, she stood just outside on the pavement.

"Good morning. yer seem ter be in a rush. What's 'appening?"

Coming to an abrupt halt, he swapped his heavy medical bag to the other hand.

"I can't stop. I've got to get to a problem delivery. The district nurse is having a bad time with it."

He left Madge within seconds of having reached her.

Looking up and down the street, she went back indoors, still with the image of the card going round and round in her mind. If she didn't find someone to talk to about it, she would make herself have a bad turn. She'd heard about Ouija boards and what she had heard was not Christian. It all seemed a bit like something to do with the devil. At that moment she realized that the person she should be talking to was Reverend Michael. That, she decided, was what she would do. The Tarot cards were nothing special. She had been to a woman at the fair who did those. She told her that she would be receiving some good news soon and, sure enough, a few weeks later Fred Talbot told her about Stan's generous gift of having her home improved. She dismissed the fact that everyone else would receive the gift as well. She was the one who knew it was going to happen before anybody else did.

The knock on the front door made her jump. She looked at the clock. It was eight.

Liz was waiting impatiently for her to get to the door. As soon as it opened, she indicated she wanted to come in.

"Yer'll never guess what I've just seen. I couldn't believe me eyes."

All this was said while she was on the way to the kitchen. She was in and pulling a chair out from under the table before Madge had even shut the front door.

Madge stood in the kitchen doorway.

"I know what yer going ter say. I've seen it meself."

The dragging sound the chair legs had made on the floor made Madge frown. It was doing her lino no good at all.

Liz actually looked worried. Nothing usually bothered her. She thought she was a woman who didn't judge people too quickly. Well, that was how she saw herself.

"I don't agree with people using those weegee boards or whatever they're called. I 'eard a woman was able ter talk ter 'er dead 'usband. That can't be right. If yer a gonner, there's no way ter speak. Another thing, does it matter if yer've been buried or cremated?"

Madge listened while leaning against the cupboard. She had intended to get a couple of cups down but, listening to Liz's ravings, she didn't know whether to shut her up or let her carry on so she could have a good laugh at the end of it.

"And another thing. If yer get ter talk ter a relative and ask them a question, 'ow do yer know whether they're lying or not? If they lied ter yer when they were 'ere, why would they change now they're dead?"

Madge said nothing. She wasn't sure what to say.

Liz looked at her in anticipation of some answers.

"I'll put the kettle on fer yer. Why don't yer get the cups down?"

Liz filled the kettle seeming to talk to herself. There were so many things she was confused about.

With her hands wrapped around her cup of tea, Liz and her mental image of the devil dancing around the room if you got involved with a Ouija board had come to the surface.

"Would yer visit this woman ter see what she's about?"

Madge had been thinking about doing just that.

"I might do. Perhaps me, you and Churchy could all pay 'er a visit."

Liz finished her tea and put the cup down.

"I was going ter do me nets this morning. Now I'm all behind. I'd better go."

Seeing her to the door, Madge said she was going to see Reverend Michael if she could catch him in to ask him about all this. She would report back to Liz and Churchy when she had some answers.

Madge decided now was the time to get her paper. If she went to the church house while she was out, she might get the chance to speak to the reverend.

Crossing the street, it was obvious that the card was being noticed. There were three people standing outside No. 15 and one of them was Churchy. As she turned, she just caught sight of Madge heading for the church house. Breaking away from the others, she put on a burst of speed and managed to catch up with her. Now she was breathless and took a few seconds to gasp some air into her lungs.

"Yer not one fer visiting the church much. What are yer doing 'ere?"

Madge was a bit taken back by her personal question. She was still standing short of the path leading up to the front door of the house. A few more paces and she would have made it without being seen.

"If yer must know, I was going ter ask the reverend what 'e thinks about the woman at Stan's."

Churchy's face lit up. "I'm just about ter go in ter start me cleaning. I'll come with yer if yer want."

This was not what Madge wanted. She probably wouldn't be able to get a word in edgeways if Churchy was with her.

"No, that's all right. I'll leave yer ter get on with the cleaning and I'll let yer know what 'e says."

Taking the hint, Churchy made her way around the back of the church to start her cleaning and Madge knocked on the front door. Reverend Michael opened it.

"Hello, Madge. You're lucky you caught me in. I seem to have to be everywhere today."

Madge stepped back.

"I wondered if me, Churchy and Liz could see yer at some time ter ask some questions about Tarot cards and Ouija boards."

Reverend Michael was a bit surprised at this. He didn't know anything about the tenant of No. 15 yet.

"What a strange request. Certainly. Perhaps you could all come here at six. I should be finished with the day's appointments by then."

Madge turned and walked back down the path, leaving a bemused Reverend Michael in the doorway wondering what could have brought that request on. It wouldn't be long before he'd find out.

With the news of the new tenant at No. 15 now having spread like a wildfire in a forest, each time anyone passing the house, whether they needed to be there or not, paused to read the card.

From the shadows of her front room, Hannah had been silently observing all the excitement the card had created. She was pleased because it would mean she would have lots of people wanting to use her services. It was time she showed herself.

Opening the front door, she took the couple who were standing outside by surprise. Her large frame, enclosed in an equally large dress, was a sudden burst of colour. She stood with the dog nestled almost in her armpit. With the sudden confrontation of people, the small dog began barking, each bark becoming louder. For such a small dog, it certainly was loud.

She put her hand on its head and patted it until it stopped.

Stepping out of the doorway, her chubby face became a broad smile.

"It's nice to see you. I've only just moved in. You are more than welcome to visit for a reading."

The couple on her doorstep were from another street and had come round to see for themselves what the rumours were about. They were both elderly. The woman stood timidly next to her husband and stayed silent, but the man spoke up.

"My old mum used to do Tarot cards and I think I've got her set indoors, but I don't know how to use them."

Hannah didn't want to give him any advice about how to use them, she wanted customers who were interested in her reading of them and paying for the privilege.

"Those cards won't be any use to you because they don't belong to you. They were your mother's cards and special to her. They would have absorbed her personal energies. Can I ask your name?"

"Certainly. I'm Trevor Banks and this is my wife, Elaine."

He had a puzzled look on his face.

"I didn't realize that the cards would only have a meaning interpreted by the owner of them. Why do you think that is?"

Hannah was getting a bit put out by these questions. She wasn't here to tell the secrets of the cards to just anybody.

"I expect your mother had them in a special box or cover of some sort and might even have slept with them under her pillow. That way her energies would have been absorbed by them." Smiling, she said, "Well, Mr Banks, you are quite welcome to come along to see me for a reading. Just let me know what time suits you."

As they left, walking slowly along the street, Hannah could see they were talking as they went. She was hoping that not all her would-be customers were going to be like them.

Madge was glad that Reverend Michael had agreed to see them. If Churchy and Liz didn't get the right advice about Tarot cards and Ouija boards they would be concocting some very imaginative stories to spread about. Angel Street could end up the devil's den in the East End of London.

Madge wasn't sure how Reverend Michael would handle the situation. She had assumed he had some knowledge of these things.

Churchy was in a right old state. Liz was very quiet.

When they reached the church house they were pleased to find Christine waiting for them. Reverend Michael had been delayed and so Christine was going to give them some tea until he arrived. It had been a while since they had been in the front room of the house and Reverend Michael had puts lots of carved wooden items on the desk in the window. A pretty cover was draped over the old settee and the table in the middle of the room had an enormous silver tray with cups and saucers on it. There was a strange mixture of things in this room and it was obvious they had been collected by the reverend from places abroad he had visited. Madge was pleased about all this because, as she had hoped, the reverend was a man of the world and probably had some knowledge of all kinds of worship and beliefs whatever they were.

Churchy and Liz seemed confused by what they saw, as it was so different from how this room had been when the old Reverend Michael and his wife lived here.

One of the carved figures on the desk was a fertility icon and Churchy was trying not to look at it because of its obvious significance. Madge noticed the way Churchy was positioning herself on her chair so that the icon would not remain in her view. She had to smile.

Christine was her usual cheerful self. She poured the tea, offered cake and made casual conversation.

As they heard the back door slam shut, Reverend Michael appeared in the doorway of the front room. With his usual grin and with hands outstretched, he greeted each of them individually.

Sitting down he said, "Now, how can I help?"

Madge explained why they were there and wondered if he could advise them about the things this new woman was introducing to the people of Angel Street.

He settled into the nearby armchair.

"Well, ladies, I can imagine your concerns about these things. I have to say that during my overseas travels I have come across lots of different beliefs and customs and none of them seem to have really done any harm. It is, though, easy to be frightened by the unknown. Tarot cards have been used for hundreds of years. Think of them as looking through windows in the past and present. They are not going to be able to change anything, only give you something to think about, depending on who is reading them and explaining them for you."

The atmosphere seemed to change as Liz became more relaxed, her shoulders visibly sinking down. Churchy stopped crossing and opening her hands up and Madge stopped fidgeting with the cross and chain she was wearing.

Liz sat forward on her chair.

"The other thing this woman does is use a weegee board."

Madge interrupted her. Looking at Reverend Michael, she said, "She means a Ouija board."

He smiled.

"If yer can send messages on it, does it speak ter yer? I just can't see that. I don't think yer can plug it in like yer do the wireless."

Reverend Michael was doing his best not to smile.

"No, it's usually a wooden board with letters of the alphabet and words such as yes, no and goodbye on it. It also has numbers nought to nine on it."

They were all giving this their full attention.

"There is a pointer that you use and that is what you ask your questions with, by spelling them out."

Madge frowned.

"'Ow long do yer 'ave ter wait fer an answer? Do yer get one the same day or do yer 'ave ter come back?"

Reverend Michael didn't know how he could explain things. For once in his career he was almost lost for words. He sighed.

"Perhaps I can explain it a bit better for you. If there is an answer to be had, and with everyone's finger on the pointer, you should find it is moving to the letters of the alphabet to spell something out."

With that, Liz said, "Well, it's no good me trying ter contact me dead 'usband because 'e was no good at school."

The others all looked at her.

Churchy was puzzled as much as everyone else.

"What's that got ter do with anything?"

Liz looked up to the ceiling, her eyebrows almost disappearing.

"Yer see, 'e was no good at spelling and so 'e couldn't send me a message, could 'e?"

They all collapsed back into their chairs.

Christine appeared to ask if they wanted any more tea. Madge decided she didn't want any more or she would float. The tea was declined.

Churchy had been thinking about all this.

"Do yer remember when that bloke 'Oodini died? 'e was the one 'oo did all those tricks while 'e was tied up. I remember it said in the paper that when 'e died 'e would get a message back to us what it was like on the other side." She made the sign of the cross on her chest. "So far as I know, we're all still waiting fer 'im ter get back to us."

Reverend Michael couldn't stifle his laughter any more and he laughed out loud. It somehow broke the atmosphere and they all ended up smiling and chatting in general.

Before they got up to go, Reverend Michael assured them there was nothing to fear from either the Tarot cards or the Ouija board, only their imaginations would decide what they thought.

As they left the church house, they noticed the light was fading. It was going to be a pleasant evening and they all decided it had been a worthwhile visit. They would meet up in the morning and pay the woman a visit to test her out. Fired up with answers to a lot of their questions, they would each spend their evening deciding what they wanted to spend their money on. Tarot cards or the Ouija board. It was probably going to be a sure bet it would be the cards.

They would, however, not be the first people to visit Hannah because Fred Talbot had mentioned Boss-eyed Ben's request to be able to use the garden ground at the back of the house to grow his veg on.

As Ben made his way along the street this evening, the silent curtain twitchers were amazed to see him at the door of No. 15. Surely he wasn't in need of her services!

Opening the door, she greeted him almost like an old friend and that didn't go unnoticed.

In the passageway, which in these small houses was usually dark, Ben looked up to where a small crystal light was hanging. The movement of air when the door was opened had caused the droplets to move and cast shooting lights across the ceiling.

Hannah sensed his awkwardness and said, "Let me show you the garden and then you can make your mind up if it is worth using."

They made their way into the kitchen and stood in front of the window. The scene in front of them was that of a sad and neglected plot. It wasn't large and was, as he knew, a tunnel garden just the width of the house.

"What do you think, then, Ben? They tell me you're very clever at growing things, even on bad ground. I don't know much about gardening but if you could clear that lot and make an allotment out of it, you are more than welcome. I could also use the company."

Despite the fact that the odour emanating from every movement Ben made had reached Hannah's nostrils, she didn't seem to care. They both stood silently staring into the wreckage of what, at one time, had been an acceptable space.

The only disturbance in the foliage was a beaten path leading to the shed at the far end, which had been Joan's constant route when leaving food for the cat.

Ben turned to Hannah and, for the first time in years, pulled himself up to his full height, escaping from his usual bent position, his lined and sunburned features revealing clear blue eyes. Something had happened to him when he entered this house and he was not sure what it was. Hannah's presence made him feel it was time for a new start.

"Yes, I think I could use this land. I don't like seeing it go to waste."

Hannah turned and, smiling directly at him. said, "Let's mark the occasion with a drink. Rum, brandy or whiskey? What's your poison, Ben?"

He pointed to the brandy bottle.

There was something mystical about this woman.

Chapter 13

Churchy could clearly see the shadow. She couldn't make out if it was a man or a woman. It was in the distance and yet it seemed close. There was nobody else about. She walked as quickly as she could in an effort to get to the end of the place she was in. No matter how fast she walked, she didn't seem to cover any distance. There was a continual sound as though people were marching, almost in an effort to catch up to her. It definitely sounded like boots on the ground. It didn't occur to her to call out or see if anyone else was here. It was no good her trying to actually run because she was no good at that. She was still walking but getting nowhere. It was getting warm. When she thought she might stop to catch her breath, she found herself continuing on. It's getting a bit dark now. I can't remember why I came out. I didn't need anything.

Her body felt uncomfortably damp. I'll end up stinking like Boss-eyed Ben in a minute. Why can't I find where I'm going?

Directly ahead of her was a large wooden bench. I don't remember that being there before, she thought. Oh, well, perhaps I'll sit down for a minute.

Her thoughts were still coming fast and confused. As she went to sit down, she hit the floor with a thud. It was dark. She was sweating. The bed quilt was half on the bed and half off it. She had landed with her head only inches away from the corner of the bedside cabinet. She stayed on the floor in a tightly curled up ball of tension. Her legs ached and her nails had dug into the palm of her hand. She was exhausted.

Reaching up to the mattress, she uncurled herself and hauled her slight frame up and onto it. The effort made her collapse across the bed. She lay there for a minute or two.

Thinking to herself in the silence of the bedroom, she realized it had all been a nightmare. She'd only gone to bed an hour ago. She had the rest of the night to get through.

She suddenly felt cold. Pulling on her woollen dressing gown, she decided a strong cup of tea was called for. Throwing the quilt back onto the bed, she slowly made her way downstairs and was relieved to find the familiar kitchen exactly as she had left it. Really, there was no reason why it shouldn't be but, at this moment in time, she was still a bit shaken up.

Settling into an armchair, she sipped her tea and, despite the lateness of the hour, decided she'd have a bit of the cake she had left. It was comforting. She didn't want to go back to bed and so allowed herself to settle down for the night where she was, her dressing gown and slippers like a comfort blanket.

The sound of the milkman's bottles rattling just outside the front door woke her up. She got up and looked out of the scullery window. It was a bright morning although there were quite a few clouds about which looked like rain. She busied herself getting washed and dressed. Having cut some bread, she put some margarine and jam on the slices and settled down to her breakfast.

She'd slept well in the armchair. She made her way along the passage and unlocked the door. The girls would be there soon to talk about their intended visit to No. 15 but already she knew she would not be going with them.

Joan at the shop was pondering about how she was going to take time out of the shop to get to the market, so that she could stock up on a few things. She usually left her husband to deal with customers for the short time she would be gone.

It was now the end of October and Boss-eyed Ben wouldn't be able to supply her with much, now he wasn't planting anything out at this time of the year. The only things he could let her have at the moment were eggs from his chickens and some kindling. All the other fruit and veg she could lay her hands on would have to come from the market.

She wasn't expecting to be busy this morning and so this would be a good time to go.

With the street coming alive in its usual way, the addition of a few strangers didn't go without comment.

Hannah's card had certainly been a source of curiosity for many and discussion by the usual gossips.

Hannah decided she would pay the corner shop a visit. Hopefully, she would get the chance to chat to some of the locals and show that she was not such a mystery figure after all.

Wearing her brightest flowing frock, which covered her ample body and with her unruly hair slightly tamed by a ribbon, she tucked Oscar under her arm as usual and made her way along the street.

Once outside the shop, she was pleasantly surprised to find a notice in the window which said local eggs were available, with Boss-eyed Ben's chickens being good suppliers and, now that flour rationing had ended, the shop had a good supply of it.

Hannah thought carefully what she would use some of her precious food coupons on. With Ben hoping to start work on the jungle of a garden, she would need something which she could offer him at the end of each day.

Although all meat was still rationed, she knew she could get a newly skinned rabbit occasionally from her family because they owned a good bit of land where they lived and, while visiting her, could help out with freshly caught game. Sometimes they provided a pigeon. Ben would appreciate such things. She surprised herself that she was making plans.

Hannah entered the shop in her billowing frock like a ship under full sail. Hearing her enter, Joan's husband came out of the back room and stopped dead in his tracks. He was a background husband and now he had a larger than life woman in front of him.

Oscar started barking in a frantic fashion. Hannah stroked his head. The startled look on Joan's husband's face made him seem like a man on stage who had forgotten his lines.

"I do apologise for my dog barking. It's just that he gets frightened when he sees a stranger. He thinks he is protecting me.

After a brief look around, she purchased what she needed and left.

Strolling along the street, as she drew near home, she could see the two figures of Madge and Liz waiting outside her home. Churchy had told them about her nightmare and decided all this was playing too much on her mind and so she would give this visit a miss.

With the greetings over, they entered the house. The crystal light in the passage had the same effect on them when the flow of air hit it as it did on Ben. With a warm greeting Hannah ushered them into the front room.

The tastefully decorated room was not wasted on Madge. She had, years before, worked in one of the big houses on the outskirts of London and this room had all the trappings of that. Everything in here was quality.

"You caught me out doing some shopping. I'll just put these things in the kitchen and then we can have a chat."

The dog was still tucked under her arm. It seemed almost an extension to her breast.

Liz had been in a bit of a quandary earlier, wondering what clothes to put on. As Hannah was not your normal Angel Street tenant, Liz thought of her as almost royalty. Madge told her not to be so bloody stupid.

When Hannah returned she was minus the dog. Madge was relieved. She didn't like little dogs.

"What's yer dog's name?"

"Oscar. Sometimes I call him Oscar Wilde because he goes crazy some days."

Liz looked at Madge, leaned closer to her and whispered, "That was that, yer know, bloke, wasn't it? Perhaps 'er dog is a bit strange as well."

Pulling a couple of high backed carved wooden chairs out from the table, which was covered with a dark red velvet cloth which hung down to the carpet, Hannah said, "Please sit at the table. I like to be able to read your faces when we speak. I am so pleased you have come."

Her smile was genuine.

"Would you mind if I ask you a few questions about yourselves before we start?"

To Madge it was obvious that they were not going to be given any scares. Hannah was going to choose the lighter readings.

Madge's first reaction was that Hannah was paving the way to what she was going to reveal. How could she make sense of the cards when she didn't know anything about either of them? She felt ready to tell a few white lies.

Looking directly at Madge, Hannah said, "Perhaps I can start with you. Please tell me your name and why you decided to pay me a visit."

Madge pressed her back into the hard chair and took a deep breath.

"My name is Madge and that's all yer need ter know in that respect. I thought I'd come along ter see yer because I'm always interested in something new on the street."

Hannah looked surprised and felt a little hostility in the air.

"Well, that's an honest start."

Looking at Liz, whose frame seemed to fill the chair, she said, "Have you come for the same reason? I expect your curiosity has got the better of you as well. Perhaps you could tell me your name?"

"Liz." That was all she said.

Hannah put a black silk bag on the table.

"I keep my cards in this bag at all times. They are special to me and I am the only person who can read from them. The most important thing is that the person who is getting the reading is here to, hopefully, learn something from them. That person must put aside any preconceived notions. Let's start with you, Madge."

Removing the cards from the bag, she placed them on the table.

"Did you know that Tarot cards were used during the Crusades? I don't know what guidance all those poor knights in armour received but I bet their fate was already written."

She was trying her best to lighten the mood of apprehensive tension in the room.

"Do either of you know anything about the cards?"

There was silence for a few seconds. Liz hadn't said anything yet but suddenly found her voice.

191

"I don't believe in all this, yer know. I'm only 'ere ter see if my future 'as got anything in it worth looking forward to. I'm lucky really that me 'ealth is quite good but money is always tight. I was only saying the other day that it would be good if I could get some idea of what to expect."

Madge shot her a look and Hannah remained silent, observing the two of them. Liz continued on.

"My old mum used ter go ter a woman fer a reading every time the fair came round. She told 'er that she would come into money. She waited and waited but none came 'er way."

She slumped back on her chair.

Madge decided she was ready for Hannah to start.

"Can we get on with it?"

"I won't confuse you with too much information but I will tell you that there are two sections of Tarot cards – the Major Arcana and the Minor Arcana. The Major Arcana is made up of twenty-two cards. Those cards could show what the person having the reading is there to learn about. The Minor Arcana has fifty-six cards and can show up different everyday occurrences. Perhaps they can answer a particular question that someone is looking for."

Hannah carefully picked the cards up and began shuffling them.

"Whoever wants the first reading should tell me when to stop shuffling."

Madge immediately said, "Stop."

"I think I will keep the explanations simple for this reading and so will use the three card spread. There are lots of different spreads or patterns the cards can be laid out in, but that might be confusing for your first reading."

The room suddenly seemed very quiet. Even Liz had not uttered another word or fidgeted on her chair.

Madge was ready.

Hannah carefully laid down three cards next to each other. The first was The Empress. The second was Strength and the third one was The Tower. They all looked at them. Hannah smiled and looked up at Madge.

Pointing to The Empress card, she said, "This card shows an earth mother, caring and nurturing. The card is also associated with springtime. Do you have any children, Madge?"

"Yes, I've got three boys."

"Looking at The Empress card, I can tell you that this points to abundance and domestic comfort. You should not react too negatively to setbacks and problems. You are a coper. The one thing you should guard against is someone trying to manipulate your thoughts. I believe you don't like being alone."

Looking at the next card on the table.

"This one means Strength. This shows courage and fortitude. It is ruled by Leo. This card indicates you recover rapidly from illness or any other difficulties. You also like to stand up for what you think is right. This card shows inner strength but you have to decide how to use it. You might offer a friend advice in the hope of helping them. The one thing you must avoid is letting others undermine what you believe."

This isn't going to be too bad after all, thought Madge.

Hannah frowned and closed her eyes for a split second. Looking down she said, "The Tower has shown itself."

"Is that bad or something?" Madge's relaxed state suddenly disappeared.

Continuing with the reading, Hannah said, "No. Don't worry. The Tower is here to challenge you. Just when you think things are going well disruption comes into your life.

This will mean changes but don't worry about them. The experience will make you stronger. Be willing to learn why things have gone wrong, whether it is the loss of someone special or some material loss. Be willing to rebuild your strength."

Hannah then gathered up the cards and placed them back into the pack.

"There, that wasn't anything to be afraid of, was it? I hope you are happy with the reading. Now that I know you are willing and open to hear what the cards say, perhaps we could have another reading at some time."

Looking at Liz she started shuffling the cards again.

"Please tell me when to stop."

Liz waited a few seconds and then almost shouted, "Stop."

Hannah felt confident that the same spread would suit Liz. She peeled three cards from the stack. The first to appear was Judgement. She laid it down. The next one was The Sun and the final one was The Star. They lay on the table side by side.

Hannah smiled.

"These are all positive, Liz. I like these. This one, Judgement, means you judge all major changes you encounter. You are aware that a decision could affect the rest of your life. You face any problems that come along. You wonder if you have become a better friend. You are prepared to make any changes that are needed to make things better. Be aware of what surrounds you. It does, however, reveal a fear of death or illness."

Liz leaned forward as if she couldn't hear everything being said.

"The Sun is your next one. This really can signify the summer. This shows you have a sunny personality. Your health and vitality are a result of your sunny disposition. You are honest and usually hide nothing. You don't rush into anything. You rely on your intuition. The one thing you should avoid is over-doing things and wasting energy."

Taking a second or two to clear her throat, Hannah continued. Smiling, she looked at the final card. It was The Star.

"You've heard about wishing upon a star? Well, this card tells us that you will always keep going when the going gets tough. You are optimistic that things will get better. You are always willing to help a friend. They can always rely on you. Sometimes you feel opportunities have passed you by. The Star shows good health. It also signifies that you are willing to share your thoughts and knowledge if it will help a situation. You enjoy trying to create good for everyone. You have nothing to fear."

Sitting back, Hannah put the cards back into the black silk bag.

Madge and Liz were still silent.

"I hope what I have told you will help you understand the Tarot cards better. They are not always bad news. Please think about these readings you have had and make up your own minds about them."

Liz felt almost relieved that nothing scary had come out of all this. She would be able to reassure Churchy that there was nothing to worry about.

Madge thought it had been a bit of a waste of time. She had almost hoped something spiritual was going to happen at the readings. She felt a bit disappointed. Standing up, she told Hannah that she had helped her understand more about the suggestion that something might happen, rather than that something dreadful was going to happen. Everyone she had told about her proposed visit to Hannah had warned her not to go.

Now that the reading was over, Madge gazed around the room. She had not realized the walls were covered with a paper which looked oriental. It was beautiful. The window at the front of the house was framed by curtains which depicted birds she didn't recognize, some of the silk outlines catching the morning light. The sheer fine white curtains covering the glass window were very fine and delicate.

On the wall over the fireplace, was hanging a copper disc depicting the sun and the moon. It shone like gold.

The room felt peaceful and yet alive with thoughts.

She noticed Liz gazing at the disc over the fireplace. Pointing to it she said, "That reminds me of a shield that a warrior from the old days would have."

Hannah exchanged looks with her and said, "That has been in the family for generations and is passed down to anyone who has the gift of reading the cards."

Finally, with the agreed fee paid, they all stood up to leave the room.

Outside in the passage Oscar started barking and yapping in a frantic way. He had been silent in the kitchen during the readings. They all went out to see what he was barking at.

He was standing at the foot of the stairs, the hair on his back seeming to stand up. He was looking up the stairs and would not stop barking. Hannah attempted to pick him up but he stood as solid as a rock. She was unable to move him. He continued to gaze at the top of the staircase. They all looked up. Not even the window on the landing was open and so he couldn't be barking at something that had flown in.

Hannah decided to investigate. She began climbing the stairs and, at about midway up, the picture on the wall came crashing down. It made all of them jump.

Liz visibly shook.

"Did yer see that? What made that 'appen?"

Hannah turned and came back down the stairs. She had to side step the frame and broken glass on the stair tread.

"Do you know, that picture has been with me wherever I've lived. I can't even remember where I got it from."

Looking at the sad remains of it, Madge said, "Well, it's done for now, unless yer can get it reframed."

They had all forgotten about Oscar, but at least he'd stopped barking. Instead, he had gone over to the front door and was scratching at it. Hannah was surprised. "He's never done that before. Usually he prefers to stay in." She went over to him.

Madge and Liz were now keen to leave and moved forward. Hannah opened the front door just enough for them to get through. She didn't want Oscar getting out. He might come to harm.

Too late. He was out of the door and scampering as fast as his little legs would go. He was along the pavement in seconds. None of them had been quick enough to stop him.

"Now what am I going to do? He'll never find his way back here on his own."

Hannah's face was getting very flushed and contorted with fright. She was on the brink of crying.

Ever practical, Madge said, "Don't worry. Me and Liz will go up ter the end of the street. There's a bit of a grass verge up there. 'E may stop there fer a pee. Why don't yer get some of 'is dog biscuits or something and go after 'im? 'E might be ready ter see yer if 'e's scared."

They all parted company, hoping Madge's idea would work.

Liz was trailing a bit behind Madge during the chase. She was getting very out of breath. Panting heavily she said,

"I was going ter see Churchy ter tell 'er about the readings, but now I've got all this ter tell 'er about as well. I've gotta stop fer a minute."

They had both reached the small grass verge but there was no sign of Oscar.

"I wonder what made that picture fall down? It seemed strange that the dog was barking at something only 'e could see, and just before the thing fell off the wall. Do yer think Stan is 'aunting the 'ouse?"

Madge sighed.

"There yer go again, making more of it than is necessary. Dogs bark at anything and that picture 'adn't been put up properly."

A deflated Liz looked at the ground. "I suppose so."

With no sign of Oscar, they both turned back. Ethel had seen them rush by and was now at her front door.

"What are yer doing? The Olympics 'ave finished."

A gasping Liz said, "Yer couldn't do us a cup of tea, could yer? We both need one."

Ethel stepped back and invited them in.

"Bill told me about the card in that woman's winder. Yer 'aven't been fer a readin' yer and are now running away from the devil?" She smiled and poured the tea out. "'E came 'ome and 'ad a good old chuckle. 'E said you two would be the first ter pay 'er a visit and 'e was right."

Sitting in Ethel's homely kitchen, the two of them felt able to tell her about what cards had come out of the shuffled pack and what they had been told.

"So did yer learn anything from them? Are yer going ter win the Pools or be told that someone 'as left yer a lot of money? I 'ope the news wasn't bad and that yer in danger. Thinking about it, though, I don't think those people are allowed ter give yer any really bad news, are they?"

Finishing her tea, Madge put her cup down.

"There was one strange thing and nothing ter do with the cards. That dog of 'ers suddenly started barking at thin air. 'E was looking up the stairs all the time. There was nothing to bark about. The next thing was, a picture fell off the wall. It crashed down and broke. Shame really."

Ethel was listening with her eyes firmly on Madge.

"Don't stop there, then. What 'appened next?"

"Once the front door was opened, 'e shot out like a bat out of 'ell. We all ran after 'im but 'e was too quick. That's why we were running. 'E don't usually go out. I've never seen 'im on the ground. 'E's usually tucked under 'er arm."

Liz was the first to stand up, pushing the chair back until it hit the wall behind her.

"Sorry about that. I didn't realize the wall was so near. I've got ter find Churchy ter tell 'er about our visit. She wasn't very well this morning and so missed it."

Ethel wondered whether that was the case or whether she had simply chickened out.

"I'll tell Bill 'e was right and that you've paid yer first visit. Did she 'ave a crystal ball as well?"

As they walked back up the street, they both had a feeling that the curtain twitchers would be wondering what was going on. They would have seen the two of them going into No. 15 and then seen them rushing out and running up the street. Had something in the house scared them? The street would be buzzing with rumours.

Chapter 14

By the end of the day Oscar had been found. He had been adopted and taken home by a couple of kids. Of course, the mother of them soon found out where he had come from and, apart from the fact she told the children they couldn't keep him, she wondered if he was a devil dog and couldn't return him quick enough.

Madge had reported to Joan when she popped into the shop and bought herself a copy of *Woman's Own* so that she could have a quiet sit down and read through it.

Liz made her way to Churchy's house but the door was firmly shut. She must be at the church. She didn't want to go over there. She would lose most of her evening and she had planned to listen to the wireless. There was a mystery play on tonight and she liked them.

The morning was very gloomy. The sky was a low-hanging grey and it didn't look like it was going to lift. Boss-eyed Ben had got up this morning and decided that with an extra plot of land to tend, he would work out with Hannah what was to be done.

His usual appearance was one of a man who looked much older than his years. He had part grown a beard which was the result of him not bothering to shave every day. His hair was rarely seen because he always wore an old knitted hat. The hair it was hiding was thick and a peppered brown which was turning into an even lighter shade with the onset of grey. He never bothered to bathe much because working the land and sweating a lot with the effort, it didn't seem worth it. When he noticed people were keeping a distance from him, he knew it was time for a bath.

During the war years he had been a pilot in the R.A.F. Not only had he survived the whole terrible experience, he had flown many a sortie over enemy lines and so had seen plenty of action, witnessing towns being destroyed and friends not returning. Those memories would never leave him. He had not spoken of his war years to anyone. They wouldn't understand.

He looked across the room. His clothes lay in a heap by the wardrobe, just where he had left them last night. Something told him he should use this day as a new beginning. Hannah had inspired him.

Surprising himself, he opened up the wardrobe and rummaged through the long-forgotten clothes until he came across some old favourites he could work in.

He would go down to the public baths and have a hot bath and a shave. He could then emerge with his clean clothes on, like a butterfly from a chrysalis. Hannah had invited him along to a bit of lunch so they could talk about what he would be doing in the garden. He felt he had somehow turned a corner and found Hannah easy to talk to. They shared conversations he couldn't have with the usual residents of Angel Street.

Once his plans had been agreed by Hannah, he could bring his tools and other equipment along and have them ready to start in the morning. With daylight fading now at about half past four, he would make the most of the following days by starting early.

The next morning, Ethel was putting out the washed milk bottles to be collected. She knew there would be the usual people about; Churchy, Liz or Madge doing their shopping or simply chatting to whoever had time to stop.

Looking along the street, she could see someone pushing a large wheelbarrow along, piled high with garden tools. As he drew near, she could see it was Ben—or was it?

"'Ello, Ben. I didn't recognize yer."

He was tall instead of stooped. He'd shaved off his tatty beard. His blue eyes shone out from the familiar tanned features. He knew he wouldn't be able to get far before he was seen.

"'Ow are yer? I've taken over the garden at No. 15, which should give me some extra veg ter sell. When Stan lived there 'e never did anything with the land. One good thing about that is 'e never put up a shelter. That would 'ave been a lot of work, ter get rid of it. I've gotta go or Hannah will wonder where I am, because I told 'er I was going ter make an early start."

Grabbing the handles of the wheelbarrow, he shoved the whole thing forward onto the front wheel and began pushing it along the pavement. Ethel watched him make his way to the passageway that ran beside No. 15, where he disappeared. Pushing the front door almost closed, she smiled at the thought of Ben finding a soul mate in the new woman. It might be the making of him.

At the corner shop, Joan was rearranging the goods on the counter. The magazines there had been shuffled about by customers who were trying to decide whether to buy one or not. She looked up to see a young girl standing across from the shop. She didn't recognize her. Running the shop, she had got to know so many people, even if they were from some of the other streets. Because they stayed open until late, customers came from all over the place.

The young girl was still standing, just staring at the shop. She looked to be about fifteen or sixteen. She was wearing a brown coat and carrying a handbag. Her hair was a light colour, almost blonde. Apart from that, Joan hadn't noticed anything else about her.

The boy who delivered all the newspapers to the shop arrived. He slapped the pile of papers down on the floor. Within seconds he was back on his bike and gone.

Joan walked around the counter bumping into some of the sacks with veg in, standing lopsided near the doorway.

"Eric! Come and shift some of these sacks. I nearly broke me neck getting round 'em."

She had been married to Eric for the past ten years. He was a quiet man and very patient when Joan was in one of her organizing moods. He was slim and looked younger than his thirty-two years. His short, light brown hair clung to his scalp in ripples which curled around the back of his ears. He was a very good looking man. Joan had been the envy of many of the women in the area when she became engaged to Eric. He was book keeper and she was the one who ran the shop and did all the ordering. They were a good team and were making a fairly good living out of the shop. Sadly, they had not had any children but accepted that perhaps that was meant to be. They had not sought help or advice. They were both too embarrassed to approach the doctor about it.

Looking up, Joan noticed the girl wasn't there any more. Perhaps she had been waiting for someone.

One person she did see in the street was P.C. Dave Taylor. He was walking very briskly. She stood just outside the shop and noticed he had stopped at Vi's house. She opened the door and he went inside. With nothing else to see, Joan went back to sorting things out.

Vi had been more than surprised to see Dave at her door. She immediately sensed it was bad news. Why else would he be calling?

In her now agitated state, she stood almost motionless just inside the kitchen door. She wasn't sure what to do. She wanted to know why he was here but she didn't want it to be bad news.

P.C. Dave knew his very presence in somebody's home usually meant he was the bearer of bad news. Smiling at her, he placed his helmet on the table.

"Sit yerself down Vi so we can 'ave a chat."

He pulled a chair out.

She was more flustered than ever now.

"No, I don't want to sit down. I just want to hear what you've got to say. Out with it."

"All right then. Brian, yer son-in-law, is in hospital and in quite a bad way. 'E was taken in late last night. Yer daughter 'as been with 'im overnight."

Vi went visibly pale. She put her hand up to her mouth and made a groaning sound. She staggered. P.C. Dave grabbed her and, supporting her, got her to a nearby chair. She collapsed onto it.

Looking up to his face, she quietly said, "What's the matter with him?"

P.C. Dave was now in a very difficult position. He had been sent round to her with the news because the sergeant knew he was an old friend of hers. It seemed P.C. Dave was the best person to speak to her. He sat at the table next to her.

"I don't know the full story, but it seems 'e 'as upset some very nasty people 'e was doing business with. These people don't mess about. I understand 'e 'as been quite badly beaten up. I don't know what 'is injuries are but it would seem 'e needs emergency care."

Vi was ashen. She didn't understand any of this.

"How did he end up in hospital? What about Janet? I need to see them."

P.C. Dave decided a drink was called for.

"'Ave yer got any brandy in the 'ouse? Yer look like yer could do with a drink."

Vi remained silent. She couldn't think.

"I'll make yer a cuppa. That'll settle yer down a bit and then we can decide what yer want ter do. I'll arrange a lift fer yer to the hospital."

He got up and went over to the sink in the scullery to fill the kettle. There was a thud. Looking around, he could see Vi lying on the kitchen floor between the table and the wall. He rushed over to her. She seemed to be unconscious and her face was dripping with sweat. Her face and lips were grey. He was not sure he should move her in case she had injured herself when she fell. She was lying in an awkward position. It was now a minute since she had collapsed and she was still unconscious.

Getting to the front door, he called out, hoping someone would hear him. Of course they did.

Churchy was the first to appear, quickly followed by Ben, who had heard him shouting while working in the garden of No. 15.

P.C. Dave went back into the kitchen. Vi had not moved.

Ben rushed in. Looking at the situation, he offered to run to The Bell and phone for an ambulance. He was gone almost at once. Churchy knelt down and P.C. Dave moved the table and chairs away.

Vi's breathing could barely be heard and she had a look on her face that didn't seem normal. With her eyes closed and her body lying almost rigid, she had not moved a muscle. Churchy looked up at P.C. Dave.

"I don't like the look of this. What's been going on? Why are yer 'ere anyway? She looks as though she 'as 'ad a shock."

Ben came back into the kitchen. They both stared at him. It was a lot to take in really. His whole appearance seemed to have changed.

"The landlord is phoning fer an ambulance. It shouldn't be too long. 'Ow is she? What's 'appened?"

It wasn't long before they could hear the clanging sound of the ambulance bell as it got nearer and nearer. By this time, most of the residents of the street were congregating outside Vi's house. Little groups had formed. Liz pushed herself forward, claiming she should be in there because Vi was a close friend.

Christine came over from the church house and had a quiet word with some of the people in the now increasing crowd. The pub landlord could be seen pushing his way between as many of the neighbours as he could. He only wanted to report that the ambulance had arrived at the end of the street and they needed everyone to clear a space so that it could park.

Once the ambulance men entered the kitchen they quickly got to work on Vi. They spoke quietly to each other and then it was decided that Vi should be taken as soon as possible to the hospital. They feared she had suffered a stroke. This they whispered to P.C. Dave Taylor, not wanting anybody else to hear.

At the hospital, Janet could be found staring at Brian, who was lying motionless in a neat and tidy bed in a small side ward. In the silence, she felt totally alone.

Harry, from the street, had just arrived at the hospital in his ambulance. His shift had only begun an hour earlier. With the ambulance carrying Vi racing into the hospital car park, he stepped out of its way and was observing what was going on. To his surprise he saw Vi on the stretcher being carried into the main entrance, where a trolley and two nurses were waiting to receive her. He rushed over to it and was shocked at her appearance. She was immediately rushed further down the corridor and into a cubicle. At that point, he received a message that his ambulance was needed elsewhere and he and his partner quickly took off, with Harry wondering what had happened in Angel Street to Vi and what her injury was.

In the clinical cleanliness and sterile atmosphere of the ward Janet was sitting in, she did not know what to think or do. How had Brian ended up like this? She felt exhausted, just observing him while she was sitting at his bedside. It was night and the curtains were drawn around his bed. The dim light that shone in the ward cast shadows on the walls. With the occasional footfall of the night nurse answering the call of a patient, the only other noise was the distant click of a door along one of the never-ending corridors. In the last few hours she had gone through disbelief, confusion, floods of tears and fright that perhaps he would not recover from all his injuries. She had been told that it seemed he had been knocked down and repeatedly kicked. Two of his ribs were cracked, his back was badly bruised and he had sustained some damage to his kidneys. His right arm was also broken. His eyes were black and swollen and he was suffering from concussion. He had been unconscious when he was brought in.

A nurse had brought her endless cups of tea, but she hardly touched any of them.

It was daylight now. She hadn't noticed the morning had begun.

A nurse came through the curtains and drew them back. She was here to check on Brian. Janet decided to stretch her legs and walk out of the ward to the corridor. That was about as far as she could manage. Her cramped legs began to give way. She settled down on the first seat she came to. One of the nurses, once again, brought her a cup of tea. Someone else had left one under the bench. Perhaps they couldn't face more tea either. She put her cup on the floor next to it.

Trying to get her thoughts in some order, her next thought was to get word to her mum. She would be a comfort to her while waiting to see if Brian was going to regain consciousness. Her mum would know what to do. The police had been informed of the beating and they wanted to speak to her as soon as possible. Yes, she thought, her mum would be the one to have with her at a time like this. She would get word to her and speak to the police when she arrived.

In a cubicle on the ground floor of the hospital, doctors were working on Vi. They surrounded the bed she had been placed on, with a purpose that was well practised. They each spoke out loud, saying which procedure they had reached and these were recorded. Her heartbeat was being continually checked, her blood pressure taken. The doctor gently lifted her arms, looking for any physical movement. He carefully raised her eyelids to check for a response to the light being shone onto them. There was none. Vi seemed to be fighting against the treatment. She was strong willed but frail in body. In her unconscious state, she seemed unable to withstand the enormous effort being played out to stabilize her condition. Every effort was being made by these strangers to revive her.

One of the nurses gently took hold of Vi's hand. It was cold and lifeless. The rhythm of her breathing changed. She let out a long breath and her chest sank. Another check of her pulse and seeking a final heartbeat, the doctor stood back from the bed. Vi's body was limp. He looked at his watch and noted the time on the records before him. He sighed. He knew that no matter how many people he saved, he always remembered the ones he couldn't.

Back in Angel Street, nobody could find out what had happened.

Ethel stood in her doorway, talking to Christine.

"Perhaps we should ask that woman at No. 15 ter look into 'er crystal ball and let us know what's going on."

They both laughed.

Harry's shift was over now and so he decided that before he went home, he would see if he could visit Vi to find out how she was. Making his way up to the floor where new admissions were taken, he couldn't believe his eyes when he saw Janet sitting hunched over on one of the benches in the corridor. She looked dishevelled, her discarded jacket barely on the back of the bench with its sleeve hanging loosely on the ground. Her face was smudged with make-up, which showed she had been crying. Two cups of cold tea were under the bench, where her handbag lay open. She looked exhausted. Harry silently approached her.

"Hello, luv. I saw your mum come in by ambulance and wondered what she'd done. She looked a bit peaky."
He didn't want to say she looked awful. "What ward have they taken her to?"

Janet straightened up.

"What are you talking about? I'm here because Brian has been brought in. I've been here all night. He's in quite a bad way."

Tears started streaming down her face. She searched for her handbag to get a handkerchief out.

Harry sat down beside her.

"What's happened to Brian, then? Has he been in an accident?"

Janet told him about the beating he had taken and that the police wanted to speak to her to see if she had any idea why it had happened. She wanted to contact her mum to ask her to come to the hospital to sit with her.

Harry didn't know what to say.

Between sobs, Janet said, "Why did you say she had arrived by ambulance? I haven't been in touch with her yet. I don't understand."

Standing up, Harry said, "You wait here and I'll see what's going on. I know a few of the staff in reception."

He hurried away, thinking a desperate state of affairs was beginning to unfold. He was used to the unexpected happening because being an ambulance driver, he was mentally prepared for any situation, but at this moment in time, he really didn't want to know the outcome.

At reception the day was just coming to life. Patients had started to appear who needed minor ailments dealt with, although they had got themselves worked up about having a hospital appointment in the first place. Nurses were shepherding them into various cubicles for treatment.

As he was about to approach the receptionist, he noticed a trolley being wheeled out from a cubicle at the far end of the corridor. He quickly made his way to it. The doctor recognized him. The trolley was covered by a pure white sheet, which draped over the outline of a small body.

"Good morning, Harry."

Looking down at the trolley, he said, "This is not a good way to start any day, is it? The lady hasn't been named yet. The ambulance men who brought her in are just giving the nurse what details they have."

Harry swallowed hard.

"Would you mind if I took a look? I might know her."

The doctor stood back.

Lifting the sheet just enough to reveal the face, he took a deep breath and held it for a few seconds.

"I know this lady. Her name is Violet Brady and she lives in Angel Street, where I do."

For a moment, the routine noise of the hospital seemed to vanish.

"What happened to her? I didn't know she was ill."

"It appeared she suffered a stroke. It was enough to kill her, I'm afraid. There was nothing we could do. I'm sure she didn't know what was happening to her, which is a blessing."

Harry was still staring at Vi's face. It was then that he suddenly remembered Janet sitting upstairs.

"Christ! Her daughter is sitting by the bedside of her husband, who has been admitted as he is not too good at the moment. What am I going to tell her?"

The doctor sighed.

"At least we will be able to put a name to her. Do you feel up to letting the daughter know what's happened? Is she the only next of kin?"

Harry could feel his own heart thumping as though it was a clock, ticking away time before he would have to deliver the bad news. How could he refuse?

Making his way slowly up the hard stone stairs, he had never noticed before how bare the walls were, with no distraction of coloured prints or softened images to lessen the impact of bringing bad news.

"Harry, Harry."

Someone was calling him. He turned. It was Reverend Michael. Now, not being religious or a church going person, he looked up to the ceiling and almost said a prayer. Reverend Michael rushed over to him. His smile was as welcome as his outstretched hand.

"The people in Angel Street have asked me to find out how Vi is. They are all very upset and confused that she has had to be taken into hospital. I can't find out where she has been taken. Do you know?"

Standing in the well of the staircase, Harry pulled him to one side.

"I'm afraid she died shortly after being brought in. She had suffered a stroke."

Reverend Michael leaned heavily against the wall. They were both silent.

"The trouble is, Janet, her daughter, is upstairs sitting, at the bedside of her husband who is quite badly hurt. He was set upon by some blokes he had fallen out with. She's been here all night. She was going to get her mum to sit with her but now I've got to tell her she's passed away. It was unexpected and sudden. She won't be prepared for it."

Reverend Michael pursed his lips.

"If you feel able to tell her what has happened, I'll hold back for a while until she's over the initial shock and then I'll join you. If we both appear at the same time, she might get hysterical, but I'm here if you need me."

Harry continued up the flight of stairs on his own, glancing over his shoulder at the solemn figure of Reverend Michael.

By the end of the day, the news had reached Angel Street. Everyone here had grown used to dealing with difficult and unexpected situations over the years, but it still hit hard when one of their own had died without any warning. Everyone was having the same thoughts but nobody was voicing them. They didn't need to.

That evening, the church had provided some comfort to those who simply wanted to sit in silence for a while. It would seem that Reverend Michael's friendliness and genuine love for these rough and ready people was what they had come to appreciate. It was as surprising to them as it was to him.

Chapter 15

Over the following days the police were more than keen to speak to either Janet or Brian. They were being pressured to find out more about the sort of people Brian had been associating with. The house which had been recently burgled was the home of a so called 'business man' who was known to the police. It was also known that to encroach on his family home and remove any objects would mean feelers would be put out for information on who had been involved. Money was the route to getting this information and he had plenty of it.

Brian had made some progress and was now conscious and had not shown any problem with his memory. He was in a lot of pain but did remember what had happened, although he wasn't sure he wanted to. Janet had decided she wanted her mum cremated so that she could keep her ashes on the mantelpiece. Reverend Michael was helping her with the funeral arrangements and was secretly glad that she had decided on a cremation, because otherwise it would have meant a burial at the City of London Cemetery, as the local one was full.

As was to be expected, the women of Angel Street were planning a tea after the service and, although a lot of the foodstuffs were still rationed, they somehow would find enough to put on a good show.

They had all decided that bunches of flowers would be better than a wreath from the street, because they would make the church look full.

With the prospect of Brian not being able to work for some time, they could not afford to pay the rent on the flat and so Janet had decided they should move into her mum's now empty house, if they were allowed to.

Fred Talbot, the rent collector, had been approached and he was speaking to the bank about it. They, in turn, would contact the solicitors, Brewer, Barnett & De'Ath. Liz thought that sounded sensible and it would mean there would be someone there they already knew. When she heard that Janet was to keep Vi's ashes on the mantelpiece, she wasn't too happy about that.

Fred, in turn, was on tenterhooks. He hadn't mentioned to his wife Mavis that Vi had died; after all, she didn't know her. The problem was, though, with another property in the street changing hands, she would have wanted the chance to move in. He was hoping the current situation would be resolved and that Janet and Brian would get the place.

At the hospital, only two people were allowed around the bed during visiting times. Janet had been going every day but now the police, on hearing that Brian would be in there for some time, asked if they could have one of the visiting times to question Brian. They were being pressed to get some information out of him. There had been a whisper on the street that he had been involved in setting the burglary up. He was known to them but had always managed to avoid suspicion. Janet still had no clue as to why they wanted to speak to him about the burglary. She had assumed he had been set upon by strangers who had wanted to rob him.

On this particular day, Harry had managed, between shifts, to nip up to his ward for a quick hello. When he reached the double doors of the Ward, he peered through the small window and could see the curtains around Brian's bed were drawn. Alarmed at this, he found a nurse.

"What's happened to the chap in the bed with the curtains around it? Has he taken a turn for the worse?"

She also peered through the window in the door.

"Oh! That patient. No, he's making good progress. The police wanted to speak to him and so the curtains were pulled around the bed for privacy."

Harry stood back. He couldn't go in now. Puzzled, he wondered why the police were interested in Brian.

In the Angel, word was going around that the blokes who had taken young Tony had something to do with Brian getting beaten up. All the regulars had voiced their opinions and there seemed to be some truth in the rumours. Tony hadn't been able to give the police much help as far as names were concerned but he did give a description of them and it was the brown suit that reminded him of the one his uncle wore. That was something that rang a bell with the landlord, the day the stranger had been drinking in there. Also, the brief conversation they had was about Tony and the scrapes he usually got into.

Back in the real world, Madge could be found chatting to Liz.

"Where do yer think we should 'ave the tea we are going ter put on fer Vi? I 'ad thought of 'aving it at my place but I don't think that would work out. My furniture's too big ter shift ter make room."

Liz was pondering. She put her bag of shopping down.

216

"What about if we ask if it could be in Vi's 'ouse? That would make sense, wouldn't it?"

Raising her eyebrows, Madge seemed pleased with that idea but was a bit annoyed she hadn't thought of it.

"Well, that sounds like a good idea. We can't 'ave anywhere too big because we don't want the world and 'is mate turning up. We've only got the food we can scrape tergether between a few of us."

Liz continued on,"It don't matter 'ow much we 'ave ter make room by shifting the furniture about because there's no one ter complain. We could also 'ave the tea in the front room as well as the kitchen."

Madge drew in a long breath.

"I think yer've got a good idea there, girl."

Suddenly Liz looked worried.

"I've just 'ad a thought. I don't think I'd want ter put a tea on with Vi's ashes in the room. It wouldn't seem right."

Madge looked at her.

"Don't be bloody daft. The tea will be on the day of the funeral. Vi's ashes won't be given ter Janet fer about another two weeks."

Further up the street, the lone figure of a young girl could be seen hanging around the corner where Joan's shop was. She wasn't trying to hide from view but just didn't move on. Joan happened to notice her again.

Calling out to Eric, who was, as usual, out back, she stood to one side of the doorway where the girl wouldn't be able to see her. Eric came into the shop wiping his hands on a grubby cloth. He also smelt terrible. He'd been boiling beetroot.

"What?"

Joan pulled him to one side and pointed to the young girl.

"She's been 'ere before. She just stands there. What do yer think she wants? Do yer think she's trying ter find someone around 'ere? If she is, why don't she just ask? It's all a bit peculiar if yer ask me."

Eric looked at her.

"I don't know 'oo she is, why should I? I'm always out back. She don't look as though she's selling anything because she 'asn't got any bags or boxes with 'er."

He turned and went back to his beetroot boiling. The whole place was stinking of them.

Joan didn't have any customers in the shop and so she thought she would go over to the girl to see if she could find out who she was.

"Can I 'elp yer? You've been 'ere before and I wondered if yer needed ter speak ter anyone."

The girl seemed a bit taken by surprise. She hadn't expected anyone to speak to her.

"I'm sorry if I was staring at your shop. I didn't mean to be rude."

She was well spoken and Joan immediately wondered why she was in Angel Street of all places. There was something about her. She didn't seem to fit here.

"I'm sorry to have been a bother."

She looked almost lost, although she was too old to be lost. Joan couldn't leave it at that.

"There must be something I can 'elp yer with. I know most of the people around 'ere. If yer trying ter find someone I expect I can 'elp yer, if yer've got a name."

The girl listened intently.

"I don't want to use up your time. You must be busy, running a shop."

Joan's interest was getting stronger. The girl hadn't said she wasn't looking for someone. She was sure this was worth a bit more coaxing out of her why she should be interested in her shop.

"Why don't yer come over ter the shop? We could chat fer a while. I'm sure I can 'elp yer."

The girl hesitated.

"No. Not today. I don't feel ready yet. Perhaps I will come back tomorrow."

Smiling, she turned and walked away from a very confused Joan. Not ready yet. What did she mean by that? Anyway, she was grateful she had refused Joan's offer because the shop was still stinking of the beetroot.

At the hospital, the police had managed to get some information out of Brian. He hadn't wanted to give names up but knew he was in trouble anyway and didn't want to make things worse for himself. He had told them about Reg and Dick and the part they had played in the burglary but, apart from that, he couldn't help them. He felt safe in hospital and didn't particularly want to leave until the stolen property had been recovered and the debt had been paid.

Janet was still waiting to hear from Fred Talbot as to whether she and Brian could take over the rent book of Vi's house.

In the meantime, he had agreed to let the girls have a funeral tea there, as a mark of respect. The funeral service would be at St John's and everyone was pleased about that. They could all attend, even those taking a couple of hours off work to be there. The girls had got together and worked out who would contribute what from their meagre rations but it looked as though they could feed about twenty.

Despite the fact it was a funeral tea, everyone was pleased they were going to have a get-together where they could all mull things over. The last time they had done that was for Stan's funeral.

Hannah and Ben seemed to be getting on well. He was working in her garden three days each week and on his own plot the rest of the time. His new appearance had been maintained and although it was now into winter, he had still been labouring in shirt sleeves, his muscular arms heaving the tons of earth into workable areas.

He seemed at ease with Hannah and had even told her about his time spent as a pilot during the war. She was a good listener and genuinely interested.

Noticing how Ben had blossomed in her company, Churchy had decided that she might approach Hannah herself to find out direct from her about the Ouija board thing. She didn't want the girls to know about her visit; they might make fun of her. Now she had made her mind up, she decided she would wait until the evening to visit her because there would hopefully be no one about and also, Ben would have finished work and gone home.

Vi's funeral service was going to be in a couple of days time and she wanted to ask Hannah if she believed in life after death, among other things. If anyone would know, surely she would.

She shifted the nets in her front room and the street was empty. Now would be the time. The coast was clear. With a clean frock on, she ran a comb through her hair, picked her bag up and made her way along to No. 15. Knocking almost quietly on the door, it wasn't long before Hannah appeared. With a broad smile she said, "How nice of you to visit. What can I help you with?"

She opened the door fully and gestured that Churchy should come in. This was the first time she had been in here. Stan had never invited people in. The crystal lights in the passage once again moved with the flow of air when the door was opened. Churchy saw their reflections on the walls. To her it was the start of an imagined magical journey. They went into the kitchen. Ben was in the scullery, splashing his face with water and running his wet hands through his hair. He turned.

"'Ello, Churchy. I'm just off, but it's nice ter see yer."

Hannah smiled at Churchy.

"Have you come to tell me about the funeral?"

Churchy hesitated. She had hoped Hannah would be on her own.

She moved closer to her and, almost whispering, she said, "I'd like ter ask yer about that weegee board of yours. Can I 'ave a go of it?"

Hannah smiled. She was surprised. It must have taken a lot of courage to come here.

"You know, it is always best if two or three people are using it. It makes it more interesting. If you don't mind and Ben can stay a little longer, the three of us could use it."

Churchy looked alarmed.

"I thought it was supposed ter be personal. If Ben is 'ere, will it work? 'E's not a relative of mine."

Hannah could see Churchy had no idea of what a Ouija Board was about and admired her for asking to try it. She assured her Ben's presence wouldn't make any difference. Ben agreed to take part; as far as he was concerned, it was an innocent way of giving people news that they wanted to hear and was doing no harm.

Hannah's full figure was shrouded in a silk floral patterned frock that seemed to go on forever. It hid her ample frame and also made her look quite mystical. It was a way of dressing she had adopted years ago.

She brought the Ouija board to the table and placed it in the middle. They all sat down. Churchy was starting to wonder if she was doing the right thing. Hannah could see she was nervous.

"Try to relax, Churchy. There is nothing to worry about."

The planchette was placed on the board. Hannah directed them to lightly place two of their fingers on it.

"Churchy, ask your question."

She froze, not wanting to speak.

Hannah looked at her.

"Please ask your question clearly."

She looked at Hannah.

"Is it all right if I ask about me brother George? 'E died during the war. 'E was with 'is unit, being flown to another country. I don't know which one. It was all very secret. We were told the plane crashed."

"Ask your question and give his name."

"George, can yer tell me if yer all right? I'm always thinking about yer."

They waited with their fingers held lightly on the planchette. It slowly moved. It first pointed to the letter 'J'. It then went to the letter 'A'. The room was silent. They all remained calm. The next movement took them to 'M' and it then pointed to 'E'.

Churchy was confused. She looked at Hannah and took her fingers off the planchette. She was not sure what to do. Hannah also removed her fingers from it. She remained silent. Only Ben was still controlling the planchette. He had not removed his fingers from it. He looked across at them.

"That thing is going ter spell out the name James. I just know it. 'E was my brother, 'oo died in an air crash."

222

His expression was telling them he was nervous.

Excitedly, Churchy surprisingly said, "Ask 'im where 'e is."

Ben stared at the board. The others placed their fingers back on the planchette. There was no movement. They waited a few more seconds. The planchette began, once more, to glide over the letters of the alphabet and stopped at 'P'. They waited again. It then pointed to ''E'. They all looked at each other. Everyone was remaining calm. Only the ticking of the clock on the shelf could be heard. The planchette then glided to 'A'.

Ben seemed to be holding his breath. It then moved to 'C' and finally 'E'.

They all took their fingers off the board and sat back on their chairs. They all seemed exhausted. Hannah was the first to speak.

"Ben, I think you have just received a message from your brother, that he is at peace."

With a worried and confused look on his face, he said, "'Ow did that 'appen? This 'as got ter be a trick."

Churchy looked at him and said, "Yer've never told us yer 'ad a brother. No one knows about 'im. It wasn't a trick."

She stood up.

"I'm not sure what 'appened 'ere but I'm going now. I need a cup of tea or something."

She picked her bag up and headed for the front door. As she let herself out, she felt more confused than ever about that bloody weegee board.

The next morning and, without mentioning Churchy's visit to Hannah, the girls had a meeting to make the arrangements to rearrange the furniture in Vi's house. By midday they were happy with what they had achieved. Liz had one more question, though, which was troubling her.

"What do yer wear ter go ter a service fer a cremation? Is it different from a funeral?"

The other two just looked at her.

"Do yer still wear black? I've never been ter a cremation service before."

Madge laughed out loud.

"Vi won't care what yer put on fer the service. Me, I'm going ter wear me new blue coat with a bright brooch on it. Vi always liked a bit of glitter."

At the corner of the street, the young girl had returned. This time she came over to the shop. Joan looked up from the pile of papers she was tidying up.

"Oh, 'ello again. yer decided ter come back then. Just give me a minute."

She finished sorting out the papers from the magazines and rubbed her now grubby hands down the apron she was wearing.

"That bloody ink from the printing always comes off. Now, what can I do fer yer?"

Looking directly at Joan, she said, "My name is Audrey Cook. I have recently been given information about my family which I was not aware of. The man I have always thought of as my father has recently died. Because of that, my mother thought it was now the right time to tell me that he was, in fact, the man who fell in love with my mother and also, me. I was, I am told, only a few months old at the time. They married not long after."

Joan was leaning against the counter listening to her story. She crossed her arms.

"Well, what a nice story, but I don't see what it's got ter do with me."

The girl knew this was going to be awkward.

Just then, Liz came into the shop. Looking at the girl, she said, "Are yer waiting ter be served? I've got a list of stuff I want so I'll come back later. I need ter 'ave a word with yer anyway, Joan, about the funeral tea."

Joan ran her hands down her apron to smooth it over.

"No, don't go. The young lady is looking fer somebody but I 'aven't got a name yet. We 'aven't got that part of 'er story yet, yer know 'ow it is when yer telling a tale. I bet it's someone that yer remember."

"O.K., luv. What's the name? 'Ave yer got a name?"

"Eric." That was all she said.

Joan drew in a long breath and Liz's eyebrows shot up. The silence in the shop seemed to go on forever. Even the sounds from the street seemed muffled.

Liz looked at Joan. Putting her shopping bag down, she said, "I know a couple of blokes called Eric."

Joan shot her a look that would have melted ice on a winter's day.

"What's all this about then? Why are yer looking fer 'im? Does 'e owe yer money?"

Audrey smiled. She was very attractive when she smiled. Her complexion was flawless, her teeth were pearly white and the way her hair cradled her ears and then tumbled onto her face made her look very impish.

"No, he doesn't owe me money. I just need to speak to him about something my mother has told me. I don't want to cause trouble but I think it would be best if I could find him and speak to him myself. My mother said I would probably find him somewhere in these streets and so I thought I would ask about him in your shop."

Joan went behind the counter as though it was going to create a barrier between herself and the girl, should she need one.

Defiantly she said, "Yer must 'ave 'is surname as well. Without that, yer don't stand a chance of finding 'im."

"Mason."

Joan's breathing pattern changed. It was now rapid.

Caught up in all this, Liz decided to stay and find out what this was about.

She said, "It just so 'appens I might know someone of that name, but yer'll 'ave ter come back termorrer if yer want ter speak ter 'im."

Audrey seemed happy with that suggestion and left. Joan, in the meantime, was still standing behind the counter.

Liz looked at her. "I 'ope yer didn't mind me saying that. Yer didn't seem yerself and so I thought she should come back another time."

Joan remained silent.

Liz put her shopping list on the counter.

"Perhaps 'er mum knew 'im at school or something. She seems determined ter find 'im. The name's a bit of a coincidence though. It would be good if there's money in it. The other Eric I know lives near the market but 'is name ain't Mason."

Joan still remained silent.

"Now, can I get some of this stuff from 'ere or 'ave I got ter go further afield fer it?"

Joan emerged from her silence.

Picking the list up she said, "Let's 'ave a look, then."

Looking at the scrappy bit of paper, she read it.

"I can do most of this and what I can't get 'old of, yer can probably get in the market."

They put some of the items on the list together and Liz left. That had been an interesting visit, she thought as she walked along Angel Street.

The afternoon seemed to drag on forever. Not many people came in and Joan was still confused about the strange girl. She wouldn't mention it to Eric until tonight, once they had closed the shop. It was worrying. What could it be about? There was no one she could speak to about it. The girl said it was not about money. Perhaps she was a relative Eric hadn't told her about. It would be nice if a relative was looking him up. He was, after all, an only child and his mother and father, who had died a few years ago, hadn't mentioned any other family. Come to think of it, they hadn't wanted to talk much about the past, but then, they had produced Eric late in their lives and were very old fashioned. They had been people who didn't speak much about family matters. They preferred to keep things private.

Eric was listening to a play on the wireless in the back room and had only just noticed the time. Joan was sitting in the shop. She just couldn't settle to listen to the wireless, her thoughts were getting more and more confused as she tried to think of an answer to the fact that girl wanted to speak to someone called Eric Mason and the coincidence that she had found her way to Angel Street and the shop. She would have to confront Eric about that before she went to bed, or she would be awake all night.

Eric came into the shop.

"Isn't it about time we closed up, luv? There won't be many people about now."

Joan looked up.

"There's something I need ter speak ter yer about. I'll pull the blinds down and call it a day."

She stood up. Once the shop had been closed she went into the little back room. Eric had continued to listen to the play on the wireless.

She sat down at the table. It still had their used tea cups on it. She pushed them to one side and leaned forward.

"Do yer know anyone in yer family called Audrey Cook?"

He looked at her. Thought for a few seconds and said, "No, I don't think so. Why do yer ask?"

"Well, there's been a young girl trying ter find someone in this area with the same name as yer. She said 'er name was Audrey Cook. She's coming back termorrer. Perhaps if yer see 'er, yer may recognize 'er."

He didn't seem bothered by this news.

"I'll make yer a nice sandwich and a fresh pot of tea. We could 'ave an early night. It's been a funny old day."

Joan, still sitting at the table, was thinking the same thing. She wouldn't get much sleep tonight, that was for sure.

Chapter 16

The next day, everyone who was going to contribute to Vi's funeral tea was busy baking and getting tablecloths ironed and plates out to go onto the tables, with a variety of cups and saucers and any cake stands they could find. Even Christine, from over at the church house, was baking biscuits for the tea.

Churchy was arranging all the flowers, which had arrived in bunches, in as many places as she could around the altar and the pews. It looked very colourful already and she knew there were going to be quite a few more to come. Everyone had known Vi. It would be a good turnout.

Brian was still in hospital, but Janet, of course, would come early on the day of the funeral because she wanted to spend some time alone once the coffin had been brought into the church. The police hadn't questioned her any more because the names that Brian had reluctantly given them seemed to be keeping them busy with their enquiries. Fred Talbot would be coming to the funeral, out of respect, and he hadn't told his wife Mavis about it, but she had found out about Vi's death anyway and she would be coming. That could make things difficult if, as was possible, she could find a chance to speak to Janet during the afternoon about her mum's house now being available for rent. She still had her eye on it. Fred was worried because he had already spoken to William Slater, the bank manager, and he was arranging with the solicitors that Janet and Brian could move in next week.

Ben was still a bit confused about what had happened when Hannah had got the Ouija board out for Churchy. There had to be something Hannah had done to create the message which came through. One thing was for sure. It was true, he hadn't spoken of his brother. He had been so devastated when he died that Ben had decided his memories of him wouldn't be shared with anyone. Although he didn't believe in the afterlife, he felt some comfort that the message had said James was at peace. His mind was still wondering when, as he once more thrust the spade into the soil in Hannah's garden, he heard his name being called out. It was Liz. She knew he would be working today and got herself down the narrow passageway and into the garden.

Calling out to him once more, even though he was only a few feet away, she stood by the fence that looked as though it had seen better days.

"I'm glad I caught yer. I'm after some information. The years yer've been around 'ere, can yer remember anyone that 'ad a daughter called Audrey Cook, about sixteen or seventeen years ago?"

Ben straightened up and, pushing the spade into the freshly dug soil, put his hands into his pockets.

"Audrey Cook, yer say. Nope, I can't say that I do. Why do yer ask?"

"Oh, it's nothing really. There was a young girl that came into Joan's shop and was looking fer someone. She said 'er name was Audrey Cook, the girl that is. I just thought yer might know of anyone called Cook."

Ben reached for the spade again.

Liz said, "I'll let yer get on, but if yer do remember anything about a Cook family, let me know."

She shuffled off.

At the shop, the day was dragging on. Joan was in a bit of a state, continually watching out for the girl in between serving people. She had been over to Vi's with the fruit pies she had made and they looked good on the table with all the biscuits and cakes. Everything was being made ready by Madge. Only the sandwiches needed to be made up in the morning. The Angel had provided some beer and lemonade. The much used and chipped enamel tea urn was brought over from the church house.

Best clothes were being brought out from wardrobes and aired and hats brushed off. Everything was going well for a busy day tomorrow.

By the end of the day, the girl had not reappeared. Eric hadn't given the girl any more thought. This morning he was going to have a haircut and then go on to the market to arrange for a couple of sacks of potatoes and carrots to be delivered to the shop. Life was good. They had both survived the war and set up the business, which was doing well. They were a good partnership, himself and Joan. With all the marital troubles among men returning from the war and wives and other women finding more freedom, they didn't have any of those problems. His time spent in the army had been traumatic but he had learned to drive and had also become an engineer. He knew he would be able to get a job in civvy street with that qualification under his belt. However, once he had been demobbed, Joan decided they should become shopkeepers. They would be independent and had customers on their doorstep. They had both grown up in the area. Joan was reliable and level headed and Eric was the one who kept an eye on their budget and preferred to stay in the background. He didn't like complications or confrontations.

They had agreed they would close the shop for a couple of hours so that they could both go to the funeral and tea.

It was cold this morning and that meant the church would be freezing. With no heating in there to speak of, he hoped the service wouldn't go on for long.

As he made his way to Ron's, the barber, something made him think about what Joan had said. There had been a stranger interested in the shop. What did she say, the girl looked about sixteen. He didn't know who she could be. Anyway, the funeral was going to be at eleven o'clock and so he had better get himself in and out of Ron's as fast as he could. His mate in the market could be relied on to get the sacks of potatoes and carrots round to the shop during the morning. He could leave them outside if they weren't there.

The street seemed to have taken on a feel of celebration rather than sorrow. Everyone was somehow involved with the seeing off of Vi. People wanted to be seen to be present. Many of them had been seen going into the church already. They were either paying their silent respects or simply wanted to get a seat at the front.

Christine was helping Churchy to bring in the remains of the flowers. The church organ was being played by Beryl, who had always been the person used for these occasions. She had quite a selection of hymns she played. Her daughter, present to turn the pages of the music score, stood to attention next to her.

Outside the clouds had parted enough to let the winter's watery sun to escape and a ray of light had been caught in the colours of the stained glass window over the seats where the choir boys were sitting.

Janet had spent a few quiet moments standing next to the coffin, which rested in front of the altar. A simple wreath of ivy leaves had been created for Vi by a friend. Janet had asked her to make it for her because her mum had always said that ivy never died. Janet put her hand on the wreath and closed her eyes for a few seconds, lost in thought. When she turned, she was surprised to see the church filling up. She hadn't been aware of people coming in. She took her place in the front stall where Liz, Churchy and Madge were sitting.

Reverend Michael came over and had a quiet word with her and seemed surprised how full the church was. The service began.

Sitting near the back were Joan and Eric. They had arrived later than they had wanted to but had eventually made it.

During the course of the service, Eric looked around while everyone was standing during one of the occasions when a hymn was being sung. He knew everyone present, except for a couple of people standing near the doorway. They were in the shadow of one of the pillars. He couldn't make out who they were. Joan nudged him when she saw him looking away from the hymn sheet. She frowned at him. He got the message and carried on singing.

Once the service had finished, everyone began streaming out of the church. Many of them were speaking to Janet as they left. Reverend Michael was on hand to chat to anyone who wanted to stop. He knew quite a lot of them. Usually when the congregation were there for a funeral, they were people from other areas but on this occasion, they were known to him, which pleased him because they had started to return on a Sunday morning for a service. His sermons had been a help and guidance to a lot of them.

Those who were going to Vi's house for the tea were slowly making their way over the road. Joan was chatting to Madge and the two of them were walking ahead of Eric. He was still wondering who the mystery couple were. They were two women. They hadn't attempted to speak to anyone and had held back during the service.

"Joan, I'll be over in a minute. I just want a word with a couple of people before I join yer."

She looked at Madge and said, "I bet 'e's going ter catch up with some of the blokes. 'E don't get much chance any other time."

Eric walked along the street in the direction of the shop. He felt unsettled for some reason. His walk reduced to a slow pace, he became aware there was someone walking behind him. He stopped and turned.

There was a woman and a young girl. They also stopped.

The woman was well dressed and slim. She had her hair swept back, revealing a face which strangely seemed familiar to him. The young girl did look about sixteen, as Joan had said. She was very pretty. Neither of them wore black. He didn't know what to do. He smiled and said, "Can I 'elp yer? I think I saw yer in the church."

The woman bit her bottom lip as though she was trying to think of something to say.

"It's Eric, isn't it? I don't suppose you remember me. It was all a long time ago."

There was a silence between them.

A sudden realization hit him like a punch. He continued to look at her. In his own mind he knew who she was now.

"It's Dorothy, isn't it?"

She smiled, pleased that he had remembered her name.

"Yes, it's me. I heard about Vi dying and thought I'd pay a visit to the old street out of curiosity. Nothing changes here. I recognized a lot of the people at the service but I didn't want them to see me. That's why I stayed in the doorway with Audrey."

Eric didn't know what to say.

"I'm sorry if I am a surprise to you. This is a meeting that's been a long time coming. I'm Dorothy Cook now."

Eric's memories were now flooding back and he didn't want them to. He had blocked out the teenage experience that had nearly killed his parents with anxiety. Dorothy had been his first real girlfriend. They were convinced they were in love and nothing could part them. Those few months during that summer were played out as though they were in a film. He had left school and was working at a local bakery. With money in his pocket, he could take his girlfriend out and buy her a box of chocolates. At sixteen years old he felt ready to spread his wings.

Two months into the friendship, Dorothy told him she had missed her period and that had never happened before. They were both convinced, in their naivety, that she must be ill or something and that it would start again any day now. They had done it a few times but Eric was sure he had been careful. The places they had been to make love hadn't been very nice. They could only use hidden places in the local park when it was dark and they were sure no one was going to be about. Wherever they chose, it seemed like heaven to both of them. Dorothy also told Eric that as she was nervous about it and not very relaxed, she couldn't possibly get pregnant.

The first indication things were not going well was when he called for Dorothy one evening and was confronted by her father at the front door. His expression was like thunder, waiting to explode. He was dragged into the passage as though he was a naughty schoolboy.

Dorothy's father marched him into the front room. He knew this was serious.

Slamming the door shut, Dorothy's father pushed Eric into a chair.

"Do you realize what you have done? Do you realize that my wife has had to see the doctor?"

Eric was speechless. Why would he be telling him this? Perhaps she was seriously ill and he was trying to blame him for it.

He had only seen her a few times because him and Dorothy usually met at the corner of the street.

Eric looked up at him in this dimly lit room. He was a tall man and, on this occasion, he seemed like a giant.

Eric's memories were racing around in his head as though they were recent. His most vivid memory was the words spat out at him in that cage of a room: 'She's pregnant.'

At this moment, standing in Angel Street, all that seemed a lifetime ago. Only a few people were about, some still trailing out of the church. He was silent.

Dorothy could see he wasn't going to say anything. He was just standing, looking at her.

"I haven't come to make trouble for you. I've had a good life and have been happily married for years to a fantastic man. Sadly, he died six months ago. Audrey and me are very well provided for."

It had only been about five minutes since the start of this one-sided conversation but he still didn't know why it was happening.

Further along the street, Joan had come out of Vi's house to see what was keeping him. He should be at the tea with the others by now. Looking along the street, she could see he was with a woman and the girl she had spoken to in the shop.

Joan called out to him. Startled, he turned and waved, calling back, "I'm just coming."

Dorothy suddenly blurted out, "This is your daughter. I thought she should meet you at some time. We'll go now, but we'll have to make time for you two to meet up properly."

They both hastily walked away and were soon out of sight.

This morning had exploded into a nightmare. It was only meant to be a time for memories of Vi and friendships. It had suddenly become a situation which could put his lifestyle and marriage to Joan under pressure, as he had shut out the pregnancy. Dorothy and her parents had moved away, the situation remaining a secret between only themselves and Eric's family. He had no idea if the pregnancy had resulted in the birth of a healthy baby.

His own parents were so distraught about what had happened that they never spoke of it and, bearing the secret of it, their own health had been ruined. They were truly relieved when he had met and married Joan but they never revealed his troubled past and neither had he.

It was ironic that their childless marriage had been blamed on him. Obviously that wasn't the case. If Joan found out she would be devastated.

Walking along the street, he could see people milling about outside Vi's house. At least something seemed to be going well today.

Joan was still outside.

"What 'ave yer been doing? Was that the girl that came into the shop? Did yer find out if yer knew 'er?"

Looking past her, Eric said, "I'll tell yer about it later. Are they dishing out the drinks in there? I could do with one."

A worried look was on Joan's face.

"What do yer mean, yer could do with one?"

Just then Fred Talbot appeared in the doorway, glass of beer in hand. Fred looked at him.

"If you are thinking of going in there, you'd better be quick because the food is going fast. I must say, they've done a good job. Vi would have been pleased."

On the way through the door, Eric smiled and said, "I'm going in fer a drink. I 'ope they've got some of the 'ard stuff."

Joan looked even more worried.

Churchy and Liz were talking to Ben. Like the others, he'd known Vi for years. Janet was mixing with everyone and was giving an update on Brian's progress. Ethel and Bill were standing in the scullery and he was showing anyone who would listen all the work he'd carried out in there with the improvements that had been made, compliments of Stan's legacy. It seemed a shame now that Vi wouldn't be here to enjoy them.

The afternoon wore on and Reverend Michael decided to say a few words about the day. Everyone took that to be the finishing touch and most of the people there decided to make their way home. The place looked like a hurricane had been through it but Liz, Churchy and Madge got stuck in and made progress in clearing it. That had been another little bit of history over and done with.

Joan was keen to find out what Eric had been saying to the woman and girl. What had she said her name was? Audrey Cook. Perhaps he had known who they both were after all. It was a bit much though that they had chosen today to visit the street and also, that the meeting had taken place in the street.

Once back at the shop, they went into the back room and Joan took her hat off and carefully put it on the sideboard. Her coat was put on the hanger on the back of the door. She hadn't spoken and neither had Eric. She sat down at the table.

"What's the story about the woman and the girl then? She seemed to know yer."

Eric was dreading this showdown. He was almost staring at her.

"I 'aven't told yer before, but when I was about sixteen I got a girl into trouble. She was my girlfriend at the time and we intended to stay together and get engaged."

He was now beginning to sweat.

"'Er parents moved away with 'er before anyone else knew about it. I thought 'er dad was going ter kill me. My mum and dad never got over it. They were ill fer a long time after that."

Joan was staring at him in disbelief. She shifted on the chair.

"So, what are yer telling me? Was that the old girlfriend and was that the child?"

Eric silently nodded.

"I 'aven't seen 'er since we were parted. I 'ad no idea what 'appened after and I never knew if she 'ad the baby."

Joan looked on the point of crying.

"So yer telling me yer've got a kid."

She started sobbing as though she would never stop. Her body was heaving with every wail.

Eric went over to her. He wasn't sure what to do for the best. She pushed him away.

Between sobs, she said, "The girl don't even look like yer. Maybe it's all a big mistake. That woman lost yer then and now she wants yer back."

"No, it can't be that. She said she ended up married to a nice bloke that saw the two of them all right. She said they were well provided for when 'e died. She told the girl the story and thought she ought ter meet me. I don't even know where they live. Once we've 'ad a chat, we probably won't see them again."

Joan dabbed at her eyes with a crumpled up handkerchief.

"Why did she choose ter come today? She certainly knows the way ter get yer attention. Was she always like that?"

Eric didn't know how to deal with all this. He hated any upset to his day and also hated anything that upset Joan.

"She used to know Vi and read the notice in the paper about 'er death that Janet had done. She came ter pay 'er respects and that was all, really. She knew I still lived somewhere around 'ere but didn't expect ter see me today. She was going ter ask the girl ter find out if I was still about, that's why she 'ad been 'ere the other day."

Joan was now regaining control of herself. Looking at him through still watery eyes, she said, "What are yer going ter do, then? She'll be back, yer know she will. Everyone in the street will find out about what 'appened all those years ago."

Eric drew in a long breath.

"The best way ter deal with this would be fer me to meet the two of them somewhere else and get the meeting over. I don't know what I'm supposed ter do about things."

With the shop open again, the two of them worked in an uneasy calm. Not much was said and they were both caught up in their own thoughts. Joan was thinking perhaps it would be best if Eric met the woman and the girl to talk things over. It would all be history now and, once the girl was given a chance to speak to him, any questions she might have could be dealt with then. She had her own life to get on with now.

Joan was also thinking there was no way the woman could prove the girl was Eric's child. Had someone else got her in trouble and Eric was an easy target, the way he felt about her at the time? If he could father a child then, why couldn't they have children?

It suddenly began to dawn on her that it was her fault she couldn't get pregnant.

Eric had to admit to himself that Dorothy had taken good care of herself. She was slim, elegant and very attractive. Marriage to a man older than herself had obviously given her the confidence to allow her daughter to find her real father, now that the time was right.

In the back room of the shop, Eric replaced the tins of food on the almost empty shelves, ready for when Joan would want them to be transferred out front.

He stopped and looked down at himself. What had Dorothy thought of him when she saw him after all this time? He looked older than his thirty-two years. His colourless face was the result of being in the shop every day and him not seeing much sunlight. The suit he had worn to Vi's funeral was years old and back on its hanger in the wardrobe. He probably wouldn't need to get that out again soon. He was beginning to feel life for him had stopped when they bought the shop business. Their social life was non-existent. They rarely ventured out to The Angel for a drink. Joan had decided they should keep the shop open until late. He felt he had turned into an old man.

Now, he realized, he had a chance to break away and arrange to meet Dorothy and Audrey on their own turf. The next time he saw them, he would arrange a meeting way from Angel Street.

He was feeling more positive and found the surprise that he had fathered such a pretty daughter had raised his spirits and boosted his confidence. To meet with Dorothy again was something to look forward to. He would smarten himself up and hopefully surprise her that he was more than just a shopkeeper. He actually harboured ambitions for the business but could not say anything to Joan about them, because he feared Joan wouldn't want change. At this moment in time, in the tiny back room, he couldn't explain it but he felt he was ready for change. Any change. His mood was giving him thoughts away from the shop and the thought of Dorothy's interest in him made the future more promising.

Chapter 17

Over the following days, Angel Street returned to its usual busybody self. Brian had been discharged from hospital and he and Janet had moved into Vi's house. What possessions they had in the flat had been brought round on a van by a friend. Needless to say, people were watching. P.C. Dave Taylor had paid them a visit to update them on the search for the people who had beaten Brian up. Liz had also put in an appearance, her habit of trying to see beyond the frosted glass in people's front doors being something that Janet would put a stop to at theirs.

Ben was still clearing Hannah's garden and was making some progress. The ground was now, in the winter months, setting like concrete in the frosty mornings. They had struck up quite a friendship and he was a regular at her home most Sundays for lunch. Hannah was still receiving callers who wanted Tarot card readings but not many requested the services of the Ouija board.

Christine, over at the church house, had started up a sort of women's group which was proving very popular. Most of the people who attended were really only there to catch up on gossip. One of the women mentioned the young girl and the woman who were seen in the shadows of the church on the morning of Vi's funeral. No one had any information about them.

At the shop, Joan was trying to act normally but she felt her safe world had been invaded. Eric was somehow more distant and lost in his own thoughts. She wouldn't stand in his way if he wanted a meeting with the woman and girl. How could she? If the girl really was his daughter she would probably want to see him every now and again.

Dorothy had decided she would make the first move and wrote a friendly letter to Eric, suggesting he visit her and Audrey at their home. They lived in Chigwell, which was easy to get to on the train now that their station had opened. A date and time was written into the letter and it was going to be up to him if he chose to see them. When Joan saw the letter arrive with the handwritten envelope, she knew who it was from.

"Are yer going, then? She might keep pestering if yer don't."

Trying to hide his enthusiasm, he said, "I'll think about it. It'll be a chance ter catch up, if nothing else."

Who was he kidding? Certainly not himself. He thought Dorothy very attractive and it made him realize just how much Joan had let her looks and figure go.

Reading the letter again, he decided that as the date suggested for his visit was only a couple of days away, he would go.

After the shop had been closed for the night, they sat down to their evening meal. The wireless was on and playing a selection of Victor Silvester music. It lightened the present mood.

"I think I will go to visit Dorothy and Audrey. She gave me a date and time they would be home."

Joan put her knife and fork down.

"So it's Dorothy and Audrey now is it? Before, it was that woman and girl."

He looked up. "Don't be like that, luv. I'm only curious."

Two days later, standing outside Chigwell Station, he felt apprehensive. Had he done the right thing? He smiled. This was the second time the suit had been out of the wardrobe in a week. He reached into the pocket. The letter had been folded and unfolded so many times that it now took on the look of an old manuscript.

Dorothy had written precise instructions of how to find them. It would be about a fifteen minute walk. He wasn't familiar with this area. The houses seemed large, standing within quite big gardens. They seemed imposing. He could now understand why Dorothy had said they had been well provided for.

Finding the property, he stood at the front gate and looked at it. It was a red brick property with large windows. It had a brick and wooden porch with a black wrought iron lamp hanging in the centre of it.

Walking up the path to the front door, he noticed the red and black tiles which reminded him of the pathway leading up to the church house. That made him feel guilty to start with, because this was a visit to an old girlfriend, even though he was married. The thought of the church was still in his mind as he struck the iron knocker on the door. It was almost immediately opened by Dorothy. She must have been looking out for him. Framed in the doorway, her appearance was as smart as he remembered when they spoke in Angel Street. She certainly didn't look like any widow he knew.

Stepping aside, she gestured for him to come in.

"I'm glad you decided to come. I wasn't sure if you would."

They went into a large room at the front of the house. There was a welcoming roaring fire which crackled with logs, the sparks flying upwards into the chimney each time one of them slipped into another position. Two large leather settees were either side of the fireplace, with a low table separating them.

Dorothy sat down on one of them and invited him to also sit down. He wanted to look around the room but instead, concentrated on facing Dorothy.

"Audrey is making some tea for us. It's a bit too early for a stronger drink. She is very excited about having the chance to speak to you. You won't say anything to upset her, will you?"

Eric looked surprised at this.

"Why would I want ter upset 'er? Yer know me better than that."

In the warmth of the room, he was aware of the earthy smell of the leather. Dorothy stood up.

"I'll go and see how Audrey is getting on with the tea. I'll be back in a minute."

Eric felt himself relaxing, which surprised him. He had thought this was going to be a very tense meeting. He glanced around the room. He was only used to possessions that were either useful and necessary or utility and basic. The way this room had been furnished showed taste and style, or what he thought must be style. It was all so grand, in his view.

A portrait hanging over a carved wooden sideboard was obviously of Dorothy and her husband, with a very young Audrey sitting between them. His eyes were also drawn to the collection of silver items spread along the top of the piece of furniture.

Dorothy and Audrey came back into the room. As she placed the tray on the table, Dorothy still had a way of sighing as she came close to him that he remembered from the past. He didn't want to be reminded of that. Audrey sat down opposite him.

It was all he could do to hide his surprise. She smiled at him. It was as though the last sixteen years had not existed. She even tugged at the chain of her necklace in a nervous way, as Dorothy had done when he gave her such a present.

With the tea poured, the conversation also began to flow. Audrey had lots of questions for him. She lost her shyness and wanted to hear about how he had met her mother. She wanted to hear about what part he played during the war. She was also surprised to find out that he could drive and said that she wanted to do that. They had found a subject close to both of them and he said he would be willing to teach her if she would like that. Her beaming smile told him she would.

While all this conversation was flowing, Dorothy had not interrupted it. She was loving the unexpected bond they seemed to be creating.

Audrey continued on with the questions without any prompting.

"I am learning to use a typewriter and also learning how to do shorthand. I want to be a reporter on a newspaper."

Dorothy looked at Eric, knowing he probably didn't have any idea what shorthand was.

"If Audrey becomes good at typing and learns how to take notes when speaking to people, she could get a job as a junior reporter, perhaps on a local newspaper. That is a good career for a girl now."

This was all too much for Eric to take in. He had an ambitious, lovely daughter in front of him, who wanted to take on this newly freed world with thoughts only for the future. It was wonderful. He almost felt born again with her excitement and ambition.

He looked across the small table at Dorothy. She was sitting back on the settee observing the two of them. She was smiling. It was the smile he remembered. They had hardly spoken. There had been so much he had wanted to ask, but none of it seemed important now. The fading afternoon light was the only indication that Eric's visit had been longer than intended. The questions he had memorised to ask Dorothy that had kept him awake at night now seemed answered without being asked. He knew this was his daughter. He felt so relaxed with her.

It was time to go. He became aware that he had not once thought of Joan, waiting at home to hear about the meeting. She was hoping he would say it had all been a mistake.

Showing him to the door, Audrey gave him a hug. He noticed the necklace she was wearing was the one he had given her mother on their last meeting.

As Dorothy said her goodbye, her movement triggered the perfume she was wearing. It would be yet another memory he would go home with. Dorothy suggested he return again soon. He should let her know when.

Standing on the platform at Chigwell Station, he knew his train would arrive very soon. He didn't want it to. He wanted to stay in the new place his thoughts were trapped in. Everything he didn't want to happen at the meeting had forced itself into the visit. He didn't want his adolescent memories of the excitement he had felt when he was with Dorothy to silently find their way back into his thoughts, but they had. He didn't want to feel the love for a daughter he had just discovered to overwhelm him, but it did. How could he carry on with his life the way it was at the moment? He slumped onto the bench nearest him.

It was dusk now and it was becoming cold, but he felt he was glowing. He needed time to think. He wasn't used to being unsure of himself and his emotions. It had been a long time since emotion had played a part in his life. His marriage to Joan had initially been loving but with a business to run, other things had taken priority. They seemed to find no time now to become intimate. The routine they had both adopted for each day had not changed in a long time. He began to realize how his life seemed to have been mapped out for him once Joan had decided they should become shopkeepers. What would he be doing now if they had not married? Perhaps he would be using his skills as an engineer. Perhaps he would now be the proud owner of a car. Having learned to drive in the army, that experience seemed to be going to waste because the purchase of a car was not something Joan deemed necessary.

The light of the train as it neared the station jolted him out of his thoughts. He got up from the bench and boarded it as though sleep walking.

Within the space of half an hour he would have stepped out of what could have been, and into a stark reality which showed no hope of him realizing the ambitions he had harboured for some time. They would not be on Joan's agenda for the future. What was he to do?

The lights of the shop shone out as he made his way along the street. He knew instinctively that Joan would have been in and out of the shop doorway, watching for him.

"Eric, yer seemed ter be gone fer ages. Did yer miss yer train or something?"

He immediately realized that was another of Joan's habits. She liked to know exactly where he was at all times.

"No, luv. I stayed longer than I intended at Dorothy's place. There was a lot ter talk about. Audrey wanted ter tell me about 'er ambitions ter become a reporter fer a newspaper. She's learning about what skills she will need. She's a bright girl."

Joan fussed unnecessarily about rearranging the jars on the shelf behind her, as though she was trying not to listen.

"Yer told 'er yer probably wouldn't get much chance ter visit, I 'ope. What with the shop and the books ter keep up ter date."

He looked directly at her.

"No, I didn't. The girl wants ter learn ter drive and I said I would teach 'er. That will mean a visit each week until she gets through it all."

The expression on Joan's face said it all.

"Oh, yer did. What's that going ter mean? I'll tell yer what it will mean. It'll be me staying in the shop on me own. What am I going ter tell everyone? They'll want ter know where yer are."

Eric didn't want all this fuss. His new found anger was rising.

"It's nothing ter do with the bloody neighbours or customers what I do with me time."

Suddenly there was nothing but silence. They both stood in the shop only feet apart and yet it could have been miles apart.

Over the next few days, the uneasy alliance between them seemed to be opening up a chasm that hadn't been there before.

Eric decided he would do his best to make each day as normal as possible. Joan had decided to keep the conversation to a minimum. He thought he would pay some extra visits to the market to pick things up that they really didn't need at the moment. He also wanted to avoid the atmosphere in the shop, which the customers were picking up on. Churchy was first to mention it.

"Ave yer 'ad a row or something, Joan? If yer don't mind me saying it, the two of yer seem ter be at odds. When I saw Eric at the market the other day 'e 'ad a face like thunder."

Joan was not going to tell her anything. You didn't need to buy a paper for news. Just tell Churchy anything and it would be out there quicker than a rat could run up a drainpipe.

Later that day, Reverend Michael came in, which was very unusual. Christine did all the shopping for them. He had, in fact, come in thank her for all the help she had given for the tea at Vi's funeral. He was visiting everyone who had contributed.

"It's nice to be in a parish where families pull together. Everyone in Angel Street seem to be so open and honest. That is a trait you don't find everywhere."

Where has he been? thought Joan. There was more sniping going on in this street than there was in the trenches.

After he had left, Joan looked around the shop with its cluttered shelves. The sacks of vegetables were always propped up against the wall. They never looked very inviting. Even the calendar over the counter showed a dismal winter scene. The floor was grubby and marked by the passage of customers. The whole place needed a coat of paint. Even the dim light, which hung forlornly from a grubby shade, seemed to be struggling into a glow. She hadn't noticed before how the place had slid into a timely standstill. Perhaps it was now that they ought to brighten it all up. She also guiltily thought that would keep Eric busy for a while, which would mean he would not have time to visit the woman and girl. She didn't want to even think of their names.

Over at the market, Eric was chatting to a couple of the stall holders. These were people he had been at school with. No one in these streets seemed to have ventured very far.

He brought the name of Dorothy into the conversation. Of course they remembered her. One of them said, "I 'eard she married some bloke a bit older than she was and that 'e 'ad a business that was doing well. I think they 'ad a daughter."

Eric took a deep breath and hoped no one noticed.
One of the others added, "Didn't I 'ear they were living over Chigwell way, in one of them nice 'ouses?" He frowned. "'Ow did we get onto talking about 'er?"

Eric said, "I saw 'er the other day. She's a widow now and lives with the daughter in a very nice 'ouse."

"'Ow do yer know that? 'Ave yer been there? Yer used to see a lot of 'er, didn't yer?"

Eric had started something here he hadn't intended to.

"Yer'd better not let Joan know about yer seeing 'er after all this time or she'll 'ave yer guts fer garters."

They were all laughing now.
"She's a widow, yer say. Yer could do all right there delivering some things fer 'er." He winked. "Be careful 'ow yer tread. Yer know what they say. A second bite of the cherry tastes sweeter."

They all roared with laughter, including Eric.

Over the course of the next few days, Joan had gradually hinted that the shop needed brightening up. Eric thought he ought to agree. It was decided that they would close up one of the Sundays coming and clear all the muddle so that he could paint everything a fresh cream colour. The door would be given a couple of coats of green paint because Joan had said the *Woman's Own* magazine, which was like her bible, showed pictures of cream and green kitchens and they all looked nice.

All the time Eric was working on the improvements, his mind had been made up that he would contact Dorothy to agree a next meeting. Joan would just have to be reasonable about it, as he had done all the painting she had wanted.

The reply to his letter came a few days later. Joan was furious that the woman had written to him again. She didn't know it was in answer to his own.

"I told yer she'd keep pestering yer, didn't I? The woman's a bloody menace."

Without even opening it, Eric said, "She needs ter know when I can start teaching Audrey ter drive, that's all."

With her face contorted with rage, Joan shouted, "If she's been so well cared for now she's a widow, she can afford ter pay someone else ter teach the girl."

Eric turned and walked out of the shop. This was not going to work. He knew it wasn't only Audrey he wanted to see, it was Dorothy as well. His feelings for Joan had, somehow, changed. He felt trapped.

The next day, he made it quite clear that he would be gone for a while because he would be with Audrey. There was a lot to sort out if she was going to learn to drive. A car would have to be purchased for her.

Joan's reaction to all this was worse than he could ever have imagined. She screamed at him. She punched him in the chest.

"I'm telling yer now that if yer go over there again, don't come back." She spat the words at him. "I can run this place on me own. If yer go, don't expect ter get any money out of it. See 'ow yer get on without money."

He didn't know what to say or do. She must be having some kind of a breakdown. He'd heard about women taking on like this. Should he call a doctor to come and see her?

"Calm down, luv."

He tried to grab hold of her but she escaped from him. He tried again and this time he got her in a bear hug, locking her against him until finally she seemed to collapse. He managed to walk her into the back room. Releasing his grip on her, she sank down onto a chair. The room was horribly quiet. He still didn't know what to do. He couldn't get her a drink because she wasn't a drinker. Anyway, they didn't stock alcohol. Tea didn't seem the right thing on this occasion. He wracked his brain to think if they had anything in the shop which calmed people down but, of course, they didn't. If he asked someone to go for the doctor they'd want to know what it was all about. He was getting himself in a state now. This was crazy. All he wanted to do was visit his daughter who was, in his eyes, an unexpected gift. Surely, no one would deny him that, not even Joan.

He decided he would wait until the morning, when perhaps Joan had recovered and then he would stick to his plan to visit Dorothy and Audrey and tell Joan she would have to be reasonable about it.

Chapter 18

To his amazement, the next morning Joan was her usual calm self. She hoped his visit to see the girl would go well and that it would be a good idea if he helped her in any way he could. She would see him later that day. She was going to busy herself with what she called shop business. He was really taken by surprise at this turn of events. He wanted to question her new attitude but knew he should wait to see what sort of welcome he received on his return.

His visit to Dorothy and Audrey was as good as he had hoped it would be. He was greeted by both of them as if he was a family member. He immediately relaxed as they all sat around the table in the huge kitchen with their cups of Camp coffee.

The room was at the back of the house and opened onto a beautiful garden. The winter sky was full of racing clouds but the kitchen captured all the brightness they offered.

Over the next couple of hours, they all discussed what would be the best way to help Audrey to achieve her ambition. The lessons in typing and shorthand would continue while Eric, with a sum in mind for the purchase of a car for her, would visit some dealers to carry out the negotiating. By the end of the day he had agreed a purchase.

He felt he had done all he could during this visit. As he said his goodbyes 'til the next time, Dorothy's lingering look and the familiar way she was twisting the chain of her necklace prompted his feelings for her to soar. He didn't want to admit to himself that, although their romance was in the distant past, his feelings for her had not changed.

He was, once again, sitting on the platform of Chigwell Station. There were a lot of people standing around. As the station had only opened up a few weeks ago, most of them were probably there to say they had used it. It was good that things were moving on. There needed to be a new beginning. He was ready to welcome any changes to his life. He was starting to feel he had more to offer than just book keeping and shoving goods around in the shop. He was restless. This was 1948 and he wanted to feel a part of it. Everything seemed to be improving now the war was over and the whole country was keen to bring about change. He felt he was in a new world sitting here, a world that was completely separate from the one he occupied in Angel Street. The people there remained the same as always. They seemed happy to be locked into a false sense of security. Things were changing for the better and he knew a lot of them didn't want their usual way of life to be altered by all the new things that were being offered. They blamed the Americans for a lot of the so-called improvements to their everyday lives.

He began wondering what greeting awaited him from Joan. She seemed to have reconsidered the situation and come to her senses. She must have been awake most of the night considering her options. Each time his sleep was disturbed, Joan seemed to be lying silently beside him, as though she was sleeping.

As he sauntered slowly along the street, he felt in no hurry to reach the shop.

He found the door closed with a note taped on it that read, 'Closing early today. Sorry for any inconvenience.'

He pushed on the door. It was obviously locked. He nervously tapped on the glass panel. Joan emerged from the back room. She looked very smart. She was wearing a dress she had bought during the summer, which she said was for any special occasion. Her hair, which was usually tied back, had been brushed in a very nice way. She smiled at him as she silently unlocked the door.

The woman he had left at the shop this morning seemed to have a look and a manner about her that he did not recognize. Most of their married years had, on his part, been acted out in a compromise situation. He had initially been happy and settled into the life they had created for themselves. Being in business, they had been looked upon as a cut above the rest of the street. He felt very uneasy at having been locked out of the shop for no apparent reason.

"What's going on, luv? 'As something 'appened?"

Closing the door behind him and, once more, putting the lock on again, she swept past him and into the back room. He sheepishly followed her in.

The table had some typed up papers on it. There was also a business card which, although small, seemed to dominate the whole scene.

She walked around the table and sat down. He couldn't imagine what all this meant.

She leaned back on the chair and said, "I've put the property and shop up fer sale as a going concern."

That was all she said. She was waiting for a response.

"What do yer mean? This is our 'ome."

He wasn't sure what else to say. She must be joking. This shop was her life. Yes, she must be joking.

Her voice showed no emotion whatsoever as she told him about her day and what she had done.

"As this 'ome, as yer call it, was bought in my name with the money me dad left me, I went ter see a solicitor first thing this morning to ask 'im if there would be any problems if I sold it. I told 'im it was a 'ouse on the corner of the street with the front room turned into a nice little earner of a shop. 'E said there wouldn't be. I then went ter see the bloke 'oo sells property, in the high street, yer know, the one by the butcher's, and 'e said 'e would be pleased ter sell the 'ouse and business fer me."

Eric just stared at her. He couldn't believe what he was hearing.

"Well, are yer going ter say something then?"

Joan folded her arms across her chest in a defiant mood.

"I've already given the solicitors all the paperwork fer the place. They need ter see the books fer the shop as well but I told them they would 'ave ter wait a few days fer them because I want ter see the bank manager first, ter show 'im 'ow well the shop is doing. Also, I need ter see exactly what is in the account."

She paused for breath.

"I will start putting stuff aside ter pack from upstairs. The property bloke told me 'e didn't think I'd 'ave much trouble selling up."

She finally stopped talking.

Eric was motionless. Finally, he found his voice.

"Where are we going, then?"

She pursed her lips.

"We are going nowhere. I'm going ter make a new life fer meself and what the future 'olds, fer yer I don't know. There's always the chance yer can shack up with that woman."

Now the penny dropped. That's what all this was about.

With panic in his voice he said, "Yer don't understand, luv. She's only a friend. It's Audrey I want ter 'elp."

Joan stood up.

"Too late! There's a couple of weeks before yer need ter move out. I'll 'and the place over when the time comes."

He needed a drink. He didn't want to use The Angel or questions would be asked. Drinking at this time of the day for him was not normal. No. He'd go to The Bell.

"I can't believe yer done that and not even talking ter me first."

He let himself out of the shop and, in a daze, walked along to The Bell. Luckily, there were quite a lot of blokes in there and so he wasn't noticed. The barmaid was new and didn't know him so he could merge into the background. He asked for a whisky and added some water to it from the jug on the bar. He went over to a corner table and sat down.

She means it, he thought. He was staring out of the window just occasionally taking a sip of his drink. That was the only movement he was making. His mind, though, was racing in all directions. He was just beginning to realize that this unexpected chance had come at a time when he was starting to feel he should be doing more with his life. He was still young. He was fit and he had a trade he could use. Companies were advertising for engineers. The country was being rebuilt. He could hardly help that cause if he was stuck in the back room of a small shop doing the books. He also had Audrey to think about. She was going to be the next generation, who would have unheard-of opportunities to create a better life for herself.

He knew he would not be free to marry again for some time but, with Dorothy's friendship, he felt fate had brought them back together again and she had shown a willingness to rekindle this friendship. His thinking was going in all directions. He no longer felt lost and confused. He was almost relieved.

The dull drone of conversation in the pub seemed to calm him. He was looking around and thought, possibly most of the men standing at the bar were in marriages almost of convenience. Their meals were cooked and ready, their clothes were washed and ironed and the homes they shared with their wives were probably well kept. That situation wouldn't change and they would spend the rest of their lives acting out the same routine. The opportunity he now had to begin anew began to dawn on him. He felt elated.

While negotiations were going on regarding the sale of the property, Eric had quietly and discreetly moved out and into a couple of rooms over a shop in the high street.

He would continue to work in the shop each day while Joan kept up the pretence that nothing had happened.

It didn't take long, however, before Ethel and Bill knew the place was up for sale. As a local builder, word soon got out when a property changed hands. What they couldn't understand was that neither Joan nor Eric had announced that they were leaving the street. It was only when Liz observed strangers wearing suits visiting the place that the street's grapevine began to flourish.

Within days, the carefully orchestrated future changeover had blown into a full noteworthy piece of news. With the combined brains of Churchy, Liz and Madge, they had worked out that the mystery woman and girl had been Eric's downfall when he was a teenager and that the whole saga had come back to haunt him.

Liz couldn't resist mentioning, while having a cuppa with Churchy, that these things always come home to roost at some time or another.

"I bet Joan is feeling a bit awkward now. She always said it was Eric's fault they didn't 'ave kiddies. That's proved 'er wrong."

Churchy was pleased to add her bit of gossip.

"I 'ear once the shop 'as gone, Eric is going ter move in with 'is fancy woman. Madge told me the other day that Joan is going ter 'ave a bit of a 'oliday down Devon way, where no one knows 'er. It's the name of the only place she knows that's far away. Because it's on the coast, it's almost abroad. It seems this little set to 'as done a lot of folk some good. We even get a new shopkeeper to train up out of it."

They all laughed.

"We are told there's a lot of change going on and there certainly is, down our way."

Chapter 19

By the time the New Year arrived, so had the new people taking over the corner shop. Things were being altered in a hive of activity like never before. Whoever the new people were, they hadn't shown themselves and still no one knew anything about them. Workmen were employed and the buzz was that two blokes had bought the place. Liz was worried even before the new owners had been seen. How would she be able to nip along there for a chat and gather gossip? Everyone knew that place was an information centre. If anything was happening, that was the place to get the lowdown on it.

Bill's firm had been employed for the job of refitting the place. He had seen the plans and knew exactly what they had to do. This was going to be an eye opener for a lot of people. The old ways were changing and new ideas were coming in and they wouldn't suit everyone. Nevertheless, improvements and modernization was inevitable. This was, after all, 1949.

He was trying to avoid Churchy and Madge because he knew they would quiz him about what was going on. It wasn't a secret but he didn't want to be the one to reveal all. Ethel was also scared someone might knock on their door, pretending to borrow something, when all the time they would be wanting to know more about the works going on as Bill was bound to have told her. Why, she thought, did life have to be so complicated?

The first person to notice that the interior of the shop was rapidly changing from the cluttered space of a food store to a more open area was Hannah. She kept her thoughts to herself for the time being.

Liz was annoyed at the upheaval because her legs were playing her up and with the shop closed, it meant she had to go to the high street shops for her groceries. The sooner the shop was up and running again the better. How long does it take, she thought, to tart the place up a bit and get the goods in so that the shop could be opened again?

Ethel looked at the clock on the shelf. It was half twelve. Bill would be in soon for a sandwich and a cuppa. The kettle on the stove was already sending plumes of steam up towards the discoloured ceiling in the scullery. It was a wonder the ceiling stayed up, it had been bombarded with hot moisture for years. Thank God, even Hitler hadn't managed to shift it.

It was cold out and all the doors were closed and so she didn't hear Bill come in until he reached the kitchen.

"It's bloody cold out there this morning. It's a good thing the job is an inside one."

He took his boots off and sat heavily on the chair by the table.

"Yer'll never guess what the shop's gonna be. Never in a 'undred years."

Ethel stopped making a sandwich for him and frowned.

"Don't tell me it's going ter be a shoe menders or something."

"Nope."

"A pawnbrokers?"

"Nope."

"An ironmongers? We could all do with one of them. Especially if they sold paraffin."

"Nope."

"All right. I give up."

With a smile on his face he said, "A bloody 'airdresser's fer women. Not even a barber's."

Ethel looked surprised.

"What! Why do we need one of them?"

With a deep sigh he said, "It beats me that anyone can make money out of that. I've only ever known yer ter 'ave yer 'air done once and that was fer a wedding and we don't go ter many of them."

Ethel couldn't believe what she was hearing.

"Are yer sure yer 'eard it right?"

Tapping his fingers on the table, he was getting impatient, waiting for his sandwich.

"Well, are yer doing that sandwich or not?"

Ethel's thoughts were ranging from where was she going to shop now and how was everyone going to meet up while queuing with strangers.

Between bites of sandwich and slurps of tea, Bill continued on.

"We've completely gutted the shop and back room. Yer wouldn't recognise it now.

We've got two sinks ter put in and two seats with them dryer things that look like bombs on poles in the back room. There's mirrors ter 'ang as well."

He paused for another bite of his sandwich.

"The front room is going ter need a lot of shelves put up and a small counter will be in the corner. Two blokes that have got the place are going ter need a bench put in fer customers ter sit on while they wait their turn."

"Two blokes!" Ethel spluttered.

"Yep. I've only met 'em the once and they're probably a couple of nancy boys." He smiled and waited for a response.

"Yer 'aving me on. They won't last five minutes around 'ere."

Bill sat chuckling to himself.

"We should 'ave got more friendly with that woman that moved into Stan's old place. She might 'ave been able ter warn us about it. 'Er cards might 'ave given us a clue."

Ethel sat down.

"Don't be daft. They don't work like that. Does anyone else know what's coming?"

"I saw Churchy going by the place, walking very slow like. I think she 'ad been sent on a scouting mission but she didn't stop and ask any questions."

Having finished his sandwich and drunk the last of the tea, he put his boots back on and stood up.

"Don't worry if anyone asks yer what's 'appening ter the shop. Yer can tell them what's going on. It won't be a secret fer long."

With that said, he went out, closing the door behind him.

No sooner had he left when there was a knock on the front door. Oh, now what? I've got things ter do.

She went along the small passage and saw the outline of Madge through the glass door panels. She reluctantly opened up.

"I 'ope yer not busy, Ethel, but I 'ad ter pop along ter see yer. I waited until Bill 'ad gone."

They both walked down to the kitchen, Ethel thinking Madge must have been on the lookout all the time. Nothing escaped these people. Perhaps if she sneezed indoors, someone would knock to ask if she had a cold.

"I was wondering if yer knew 'ow the new shop was getting on. There seems ter be a lot of stuff going on in there. I noticed Bill was one of the workmen."

She paused, waiting for Ethel to say something.

Reluctantly, Ethel decided to tell her the news Bill had come home with.

"It's going ter be a ladies 'airdresser's."

There was complete silence. The only sound to be heard was someone going upstairs in the house next door. With the walls of these places being so thin, you could almost hear a pin dropped by a neighbour.

"What! Yer must be kidding. That can't be right. What do we want wiv one of them?"

Ethel started to clear the table, leaving an amazed Madge standing like a statue, not moving. She didn't want to get into a conversation about it all.

"That's all I know, apart from the fact a couple of blokes are setting up business there. I don't know anything about them or where they're from."

She walked into the scullery. She was not going to tell Madge what sort of blokes they might be. She didn't know Madge's views on what Bill had called 'nancy boys' and didn't particularly want to know.

Breaking the silence Madge said, "I can see yer busy, Ethel, and so I'll leave yer ter yer jobs."

She turned and left the kitchen, letting herself out.

Ethel was glad she had gone but knew fully well that her speedy exit wasn't so that she could get on with her jobs but to make tracks to Churchy or Liz to give them the startling news she had just heard. Even better for her was the fact that she had found out about the place before they had.

If they could all get together, this would take more than one pot of tea to mull over the facts.

As luck would have it, who should be shuffling along the street, but Liz. Gathering speed, Madge shouted and waved at her. That was enough for Liz to wait for Madge to catch up.

"Yer'll never guess what I've just 'eard."

Liz reacted with the required look of wonder. She loved anyone who started any conversation with something like that.

Madge wanted to spread her news to the people who would use it best.

"It's going ter be a 'airdresser's on the corner. What a waste of time that'll be. We could all use a decent shop there like the one we 'ad before. It only needed a bit of paint used on it. I don't understand it."

Liz's expression said it all.

"Come round mine this afternoon. I'll get Churchy there and we can talk about it properly."

It wasn't long before the new shop was the talk of the street. No one could understand it.

As the work progressed, it almost became a place to visit on the way to the high street shops. Churchy was the most put out, because her legs were not too good this winter and the extra distance she had to go to get her groceries was becoming a problem. Naturally she had mentioned it to Reverend Michael.

"Can yer see what yer can find out fer us? If them two what are opening up there are nancy boys, because they're 'airdressers, yer ought ter find out a bit about them fer us."

Reverend Michael couldn't help but smile. These people didn't like change and to have a mystery and people they were not sure of coming into their lives was all a bit much to take in.

Looking at Churchy, he wondered if it was too late for her to accept what she called 'different people' coming into Angel Street.

"Leave it with me. I'll introduce myself to them and find out where they are from."

He walked away from Churchy with a smile on his face. If only she knew what the world was like beyond Angel Street.

Over the following days, Bill was beginning to be impressed with the quality of work the two blokes were asking for. The best materials were being purchased and the place was shaping up into a very nice salon, as they called it. A sign writer had arrived and very artistically created a board above the front window printed up with, 'Lewis & Guy – Ladies' Hair Fashions.'

Bill hadn't had much chance to speak to them, but finally made time. He didn't want to ask them if they wanted to go for a pint and so he waited until he saw them making coffee. That, for a start, was different because they only drank tea in their house.

Approaching them while some of the workmen were working on the front door and window, he wasn't sure what to say. He needn't have worried, because one of them turned and saw him.

"The men are all doing a good job for us. We weren't sure how it would turn out but it's all coming together nicely."

"They're good blokes," said Bill. "We've worked tergether fer years." Seizing the moment, he continued on, "Where are yer from? I don't think I've seen yer around."

"No, you wouldn't have. We've been learning our trade by working in a hairdressing salon up west for the last three years. It was well paid and so we decided to set up shop here. We got the premises for a price we could afford. With all the new styles coming over from the States, we decided it was time to offer them to the ladies around here. They can come in and have a chat and a coffee while they have their hair done. It's all the rage now."

Bill didn't know what to say. He was surprised he liked them.

"Will yer be living upstairs? It's quite a nice little flat up there."

"Yeh. We'll muddle through up there until we get sorted out. Me and my brother are used to sharing. I'm George and he's Lenny."

Bill was rather confused.

Scratching his head, he said, "Where does Lewis & Guy come in then?"

He laughed.

"Well, George and Lenny doesn't sound too cool for a hairdresser's, does it?"

That evening, after Bill had told Ethel all about the blokes, he thought, I could 'ave asked them ter go fer a pint after all.

Ethel was tickled pink that they weren't nancy boys after all and almost felt cheated out of a good laugh once Churchy, Liz and Madge had been told the real story.

Winter had now set in, with some days beginning with a slight covering of snow along the street. This didn't last long though, because the continual passage of people more or less all day long soon dispersed it. There wasn't much going on after the Christmas festivities had faded away and everyone needed a lift.

No one had heard any more from Eric and it was assumed he was living with his fancy woman. Also, no one had had as much as a card from Joan, wherever she ended

269

up. Hannah was doing nicely, with regular customers hoping she could tell them they were in for a New Year windfall.

One thing in the area which had been noticed by Liz was the amount of 'coloured people' as she called them appearing in the high street. There had been quite a bit on the wireless about a ship called *Empire Windrush* which was coming in from the West Indies, wherever that was.

"Surely they're not going to unload that lot on us. I know they've got ter go somewhere, but our blokes need the work, not them."

She had got herself quite worked up about it. If what she had heard on the wireless was true, it sounded as though they were going to be invaded again. If they said it on the wireless, it must be true.

Reverend Michael had been readily accepted by Churchy and Liz even though he was from 'over there', as they called it. He had been very approachable from day one and they found he was a good sounding board when they had something on their minds.

He had found out about George and Lenny for them and had added a bit more information than Bill had contributed.

The street was renewing itself. Janet and Brian had settled well into her mum's house and Brian had recovered from his injuries and was working again. Hannah was popular giving out her readings. Even Boss-eyed Ben had maintained his new look. Word was out that clothing was coming off rationing in March and that was only a few weeks away.

Reverend Michael had noticed, though, that his congregation was thinning out. People were busy. Even gossip had dried up. He decided it was time for a party. He would offer the church hall and leave Churchy to suggest it to the others. After all, with all these new people around it would be a good way to get the street back to its busybody ways. It worked.

Churchy, Liz and Madge spread the word and soon it was decided that a Saturday night would be good. They had soon found themselves organizing the food and even the publican from The Angel offered to help out with the drink. The 'boys from the hairdresser's', as they were called, were invited and they accepted.

Christine decided she would have her hair done and even Ethel was talked into having a perm for this special occasion. There was also a rumour going around that Lenny had asked Christine out to the pictures. There was a new film out called *Whisky Galore,* with Basil Radford in it.

Angel Street was up and running again and there would be a lot more stories to be told in the coming year. There would never be a dull moment in this street.